THE FLAME OF THE WHITE HORSEMAN

TALES OF THE FOUR HORSEMEN
BOOK ONE

JESS K. CHAVEZ

For the seekers,
May you discover that you are loved far more than you could
ever imagine or hope for.

CONTENTS

GLOSSARY/PRONUNCIATION

Elohim {El-oh-heem} - God the Creator

Elohim Shomri {El-oh-heem Shaw-om-ree} - God my Protector

Feminea Potentia {Fem-in-Eah Poh-TEN-C-ah} - Female Power/Strength

Malkhut Shamayim {Mahl-KOOT Shah-MY-eem} - Kingdom of Heaven

Ohr Ein Sof {Or Ine Sawf} - Infinite Light

Atik Yomin {Ah-tick Yo-mean} - Ancient of Days

Ruach {Roo-ahhk} - Breath or Spirit of God, the source of life

Elohe Tishuathi {El-Oh-Hee Tish-ew-wath-I} - God of my Salvation, or
  God who Saves

Lavo Veshuv {La-Voh Ve-Shoe-ve} - Come forth

Baim Lyy {Bay-Mm Lie} - Return to me

PROLOGUE

Hell is empty and all the devils are here.
William Shakespeare

Sidora hated the city.

The evil that seemed to permeate everything slid over her umber skin like a heavy coat, giving her the creeps and agitating her mood even further. Any cities still standing had decayed into skeletons, barren husks that only housed the specters of broken lives and shattered dreams. A veritable utopia for the parasitic and the malicious.

She just needed to do the recon that Elias had requested and get out of here. But as the hooded figure she followed glanced sideways at her, she knew she'd be doing more than recon tonight. He headed into the dark alley.

Like the steady beat of a drum, her heartbeat urged her to secure the missing piece of the prophecy. Time was running out. The Prophets had been looking everywhere for years without so much as a whisper, until a few weeks ago.

The sole purpose for fighting for this world was finally coming to a head, with a unique weapon that had been foretold hundreds of years ago, back when the world was not so lost and the scales had not tipped so gravely into darkness.

But in order to have any hope of victory, she first had to find the missing piece of the prophecy. So here she was, stuck in this cesspool following this pestilence through the grime-covered alleyway, the pungent scent of urine and rot saturating the air.

This guy clearly knew Sidora was following him, which meant her assumption that he was an Upper Amilign was most likely correct. But the Prophets had worked hard to keep her identity a secret. Most assumed that the Prophets of The Way were just a group of wise old men who studied ancient history and scriptural texts. The Prophets preferred that ignorance, because women like Sidora were one of the most powerful tools in their arsenal.

Trained by the Horsemen themselves and educated by the scholars, Sidora liked to think of herself as a secret weapon. She always kept looking forward because nothing good came from the past. She didn't know a single person not marred by the scars of darkness. So she did what she always did: focus on the present and her role in helping bring about change.

She headed down the dingy alley, for all appearances looking just like any other woman after a long day of work, weary from grinding out a life in this dark and desperate place, eager for the sanctity of home. Her white spiraling hair was tightly braided and piled high on her head, away from her face. Easily hidden in her hood and out of the way if she needed to fight.

Heading further into the depths of the alley, the darkness reached for her. Grateful for a cloudless sky, and the moon casting a faint, pale glow, Sidora saw the outline of the man standing still, waiting for her.

He turned slowly. Most of his face was shadowed by his hood, except for his pale chin and thin lips, both barely visible in the dim moonlight.

"Why are you following me, woman?" he demanded. "What do you want?"

Might as well be direct in return. Sidora had never been one for beating around the bush anyway. She pulled her hood back and smiled at the man.

"Oh, nothing much...just the destruction of the Amilign and the eviction of all you scum from my world. But I'll settle for the papers you carry." A sly smile lit her face.

A slight tic at the corner of his mouth was his only reaction. She'd been following a lead about a meeting happening in one of the clubs the Amilign frequented and, in a total stroke of luck, she had gotten eyes on a scroll being passed to this guy. With a prayer to Elohim that it was what she needed, she'd followed him.

"A follower of The Way," the hooded man sneered. "Interesting. And to think I thought this night would be boring. They say knowledge is power, but in this case, it won't matter. The scales of balance are tipped in our favor. The Horsemen are as good as lost. Take a look around you: our influence in this world saturates everything. You are wasting your time, woman. You know it as well as I do."

Sidora had never been one for useless, feather-fluffing prattle, and wasn't about to start wasting her time arguing with this puffed-up waste of space now. Plus, the less this Amilign knew about the knowledge the Prophets have, the better.

"The end is near," the man practically spat. "The Horsemen will be leashed to darkness, whether out of choice or not. The Prophecy of the Four Cores is simply old folklore meant to give hope to those unwilling to submit to the inevitable."

She could play this one of two ways. Fight him for it, or talk him out of it. As much as she was itching for a fight to shut this guy up, Elias's voice resounded in her head: *"There's power in subtlety; you need to be less eager to jump into a fight."*

Ever so slowly, she sauntered closer to the man, exuding a calm confidence. "I don't know what the future holds. But if you're so sure, then you'll have no problem with letting us have those papers. I mean, we're just a bunch of dusty and desperate scriptural historians, right? But I'd understand if you wanted to hang on to it because some part of you thinks we're a threat."

Her subtlety needed work, but it rubbed her the wrong way to not just take it from him like she knew she could. She still had a long way to go to learn the kind of patience Elias wanted her to have.

"What threat?" he snapped. "There is no threat in this world compared to the power of the Amilign. We serve true power and, as a reward, have been given true power. And we are not in the habit of freely giving anything that is in our possession, as you well know. Your words are wasted breath, woman."

Sidora smiled as she realized this night would end her way after all. Dropping to the ground, she swept a leg out, knocking the man off his feet. He twisted in the air to land on his hands and feet in a low plank. She anticipated the kick that he sent back in her direction, watching as he lifted off the ground. The Upper Amilign moved in unnatural ways, a sign of the demonic presence deep within. Clearly, this was no low-ranking member. And if Sidora was anyone else, she'd probably be freaked out and distracted by the otherness in him, a tool they often used to their advantage.

But having been trained by Horsemen since she was young, Sidora knew that the Amilign were still basically men. Catching his leg, she twisted it, flipping him onto his back. Momentarily surprised, he left an opening for her to strike a foot between his legs. Still one of the easiest ways to incapacitate a man, demon or not. As he lay there, stunned and groaning, whimpering like a wounded animal, she took the opportunity to snatch the scroll out of the inner pocket of his coat.

For all his Upper Amilign status, this guy was clearly no warrior; he must be one of their so-called archivists.

"Well, that was disappointing, but thanks for the work-out, it helps me shed the slimy feel of this place." She smirked at his fetal-like position. Walking out of the alley, she headed swiftly down the street back to the safe house. She weaved in and out of the abandoned cars that littered the streets, relics of an old world. There were still some working vehicles, but with the fuel as limited as it was, only the exceptionally wealthy or connected had access. And that typically meant a connection to the Amilign in some way.

The urgency to read the old parchment pressed on her. Picking up the pace, she ran the last mile.

The safe house was nothing more than an old shed in an alley next to an abandoned brownstone, but it was unassuming, so it was easily overlooked. It was the formerly plush and flashy places that tended to attract unwanted attention. This part of the city had been fairly abandoned long ago, as were most places that catered to families at one time. Most of the history of this part of the world had been long forgotten, as if a veil had been dropped over the past.

The Prophets believed it was, at least in part, the active presence of the demonic that now clouded minds from the truth. But when you added in a history of endless wars that altered the landscape and horrifying atrocities against innocents, it was understandable why that history had been easy to suppress. Personally, Sidora hated thinking about her own past, so she could relate.

As the darkness had grown and spread, it drove those with a desire to protect their young away from the remaining few cities still habitable. Any who remained were killed, and cities had become hubs of darkness. Sidora thought it had something to do with the old saying "Misery loves company." Cities were now places where dark things flourished and like called to like. The vulnerable were preyed upon, the desperate came hoping for something to fill the void, and often they got it, just not in the way they were expecting. Safety was a rare commodity.

Itching to look at the parchment, Sidora entered the pitch-black shed, the musty scent of dust and cedar welcoming her. The sooner she could find the answers, the sooner she could leave this hellhole. The shed had been reinforced to make it livable for small amounts of time, but she couldn't wait to get back to the mountain fortress of The Way. Built over time into a cliff face, surrounded by forests, it was safe and hidden, and unless you knew the trail in, it would be almost impossible to stumble upon. It had been her home for as long as she could remember.

She quickly closed the door to the shed and secured the latch. Perching on the cot, she pulled out a flashlight to read the parchment. It was tattered and a bit faded, but mostly legible. It spoke of the Prophecy of the Four Cores. Most of which, Sidora already knew, but the Prophets had been searching for the piece that would help them pinpoint the timeline and help them find the Four Cores. These Cores were the key to this weapon of Heaven.

She bent her head and read:

"When the tipping point has been reached and darkness is unrestrained, four riders will be drawn forth out of necessity to lay waste to the world. Their destruction will be absolute. The only hope for mankind is in the gift of four living personifications of Elohim's heart, the essential Cores of his Pure Love. Each Core is created to bond with her Horseman, forever breaking the hold of darkness on them with the power of Elohim's love. The Horseman will then ride for Malkhut Shamayim, bringing about the destruction of all evil in the world. But if the heart of the Core is rejected or fails, the Riders will be leashed by hell, and all will be lost to darkness."

Sidora had read and studied this before, and could almost recite it from memory. Malkhut Shamayim was the Kingdom of Heaven. And the riders being leashed by hell was what the Amilign man had been referring to in the alley. The Riders, or Horsemen as they were also known in some translations, were a final judgment and appeared when darkness had grown beyond control. And they were well past that point in this world.

The Horsemen were the final roll of the dice. They would either be fully leashed by hell to bring about the destruction of the entire world, or they would be freed from their leash by the Four Cores and instead bring about the destruction of all darkness. But it was a path they would have to choose. And if they failed to connect with their Core, their light and balance, then all would be lost. After all, it had always been light that drove out the darkness.

But Sidora didn't fear because she knew something that the Amilign didn't: that when Elohim created a way forward through the darkness, He gave power to His faithful to guide them.

She kept reading.

"The Cores have been given a gift of Malkhut Shamayim, but this gift of Heaven will be unknown to them until activated. But just as they are touched by Heaven, they will also be pursued by evil. Evil must be overcome, dreams will guide, and love covers in multitudes."

The Prophets had been unable to uncover what the gift of Heaven was referring to, but Sidora believed it would be revealed in time. The "pursued by evil" part was why the Prophets of The Way worked so hard to uncover the whole prophecy, so they could find the Cores and protect them. The clock was winding down, the situation reaching a level that made everyone desperate.

They had to find the answer soon.

As she read, she skimmed over parts that had been committed to memory, eager to find the answers to questions that had plagued the Prophets for decades. The text became more faint and worn, making it harder to determine the words. But the last line, she'd never seen before, and Sidora just knew this was the text for which they had been searching for years.

"Born orphaned, alone, and unnamed, they will be brought to the world on a day made holy by its twin of seven. You will find them with three of sevens; a unique mark of Heaven they will bear."

She froze. This was it. Some of the prophets guessed at the Cores being tied to Elohim's holy number somehow, but this confirmed it. But today was July 7; it couldn't be a coincidence that today's date was a twin of sevens. Only three more would pinpoint the location of the Cores.

But this left her no time. This was why that Amilign

trash in the alley had been so smug. He knew they were out of time.

She wanted to throw something or hit someone. She should've taken her time with that dirtbag in the alley. But anger and despair would get her nowhere. Sidora knew something big was coming, because she had felt the yearning in her spirit. She had to trust that this journey was not for nothing.

She calmed her mind and asked Elohim for guidance. As she did, she felt the pull to head to the hospital. Gathering the papers into her bag, she ran out of the shed, not even bothering to close the door. The nearest functioning hospital was a few blocks away, and just so happened to be on 7th Street. One more seven; this had to be it.

Sidora was good at blending into shadows and sneaking in. As she made her way to the birthing wing, she snuck into a closet near the nurse's station. Cracking the door, she could overhear two nurses talking.

"Just another day of tragedies around here," a voice muttered. "And you're certain there's no next of kin?"

"They are running the mother's prints through the system again," a second nurse chimed in, "but the first search came up empty. Definitely an orphan. I'll call the youth house tomorrow and see if they can take her."

Sidora had found her. Quietly sneaking away from the voices, down the hall to the nursery, her heart pounded in her chest at the culmination of years of searching. There, lying in the #7 bassinet, was a beautiful, dark-haired baby girl, born at 7:00pm according to her tag. The last two sevens.

An orphan, nameless and alone, and with striking golden eyes that almost glowed. This was her, one of the Cores. But just one? Sidora had hoped she would find all four here, but this was the only baby in the nursery. That would make sense with the whole "alone" portion of the prophecy. Why couldn't things ever be easy? She wasn't sure what the last piece claiming a mark of Heaven meant, but there was no time to waste; she would have to figure that out later. Sidora felt deep in her spirit that this sweet baby was the answer to so many questions, and she knew for certain that Elohim was guiding her.

She snuck into a supply room and quickly dressed in a pair of doctor's scrubs. With electricity being spotty at best and insanely expensive if it worked, it was typically saved for emergencies and life-threatening situations, so she didn't need to worry about fancy security systems. There was just one middle-aged guard making the rounds. She waited until he slowly meandered by, then headed around the corner and snuck into the nursery.

Quickly tying a few baby blankets together, she wrapped them around her body, creating a makeshift baby carrier. She gently picked up the now sleeping newborn and secured her to her chest. Putting on the doctor's overcoat, the baby was neatly hidden underneath. Sidora grabbed a few containers of formula and threw them into a hospital bag before calmly walking out of the nursery and down the hall. She quietly slipped into the stairwell, grateful maternity wards in the remaining cities were almost always empty, most families having fled long ago.

City hospitals were typically filled with only the most desperate. So while emergency rooms were full, staff were always in low supply and often pulled from other parts of the hospital to help. As it was, there were few hospitals even still active, and those that were functional often had entire wings that were no longer operational. Locked up due to lack of resources.

As she exited the first floor and headed for the main doors, Elias's instructions, *"Hide in plain sight"* filled her mind. Sidora was good at making herself appear small and meek. Her dark skin and white, corkscrew curls were striking, but she could easily put on the "sweet, safe, older lady" vibe like a well-worn pair of gloves—one of the benefits of her unique hair.

The hospital doors opened, and he felt an urgency in her spirit. The Amilign were near. Making her way to the lobby, she walked right out the front doors, shoulders slumped like an overworked doctor finished with a too-long shift.

She would not be going back to the safe house again. As Sidora looked down at the sweet, sleeping baby, she felt a shift in her purpose and knew that this little one was her life's mission. Something inside her leapt at the thought. She'd make the long journey to the Refuge of the Prophets' and dedicate her life to keeping this baby safe.

They had one of the Cores. All was not lost.

CHAPTER 1

ALMOST 19 YEARS LATER

LUCIA

Darkness surrounds me like a thick blanket and my breath comes out in visible puffs as I ready myself for the attack.

The moon is a luminescent sliver, casting an insignificant glow that does nothing to help me see in the dark stone courtyard, the lights having been extinguished hours ago, at curfew. I try to steady my breathing, but the pounding of my heart, like a stampede of wild animals, makes it an impossible task.

Out of the dim night, a fist comes at my face, which I miraculously block out of sheer panic. Then another, which I clumsily push aside, still managing to take a hit to my shoulder. I am giving up ground, being pushed back. A huge mistake in a battle.

When I see a leg flying toward my head, I know it's over. I brace, waiting for the impact. But none comes. Blinking, I see the leg frozen in midair, inches from my temple, hovering as if suspended by a rope. I sigh and watch it return to its fiery, red-headed owner, who is now glowering at me with those sharp green eyes.

"Nope, nope, definitely no," Ansel huffs, rubbing her temples. "You cannot show any hesitation, Lulu. You have to fully commit to these moves, otherwise don't even bother trying."

I know she is concerned for me. We have become fast friends in the six weeks since she's been visiting the ashram with the Feminea Potentia, or FP, a group of all-female warriors. Connected by some unknown thing that's drawn us together from the beginning, we've been meeting secretly ever since. Honestly, it feels like we've been friends forever.

I'm not sure what led the FP to make such an obscure visit to the mountain ashram of the Amilign, but I am glad they came. Their arrival marks pretty much the first time in my almost nine years living here that I have been surrounded by other women.

And I finally have a friend.

Well, a friend I can spend time with and talk with, at any rate. There has always been Dee in the kitchen, but she is mute, and an extreme wallflower who desperately clings to the status quo and prefers the fringes. In a way, we both wear masks here, but for me, it is my biggest pretend. Whereas, for Dee, she craves to live within the lines the monks have drawn for her. It's also rare that I can get down to see her, and she almost never leaves the kitchen.

I can understand wanting to blend into the background in this place—I often operate that way too—but I wish she wouldn't try to do that with me. So each day that goes by with the FP here, I count as a blessing, dreading the day they leave and take Ansel with them and everything returns to the dull routine of before.

Ansel hates that I live here, not that I have a choice in the matter. It didn't take long for her to develop a distrust of the monks in the weeks she's been visiting, and it has only grown, which is what led to us being out here in the middle of the freezing night. This whole self-defense thing is uncharted territory for me.

If I'm being honest with myself, I have always struggled with my place among the monks. But when you have no other options, it is sometimes easier to overlook things, rather than having to deal with the uncomfortable truths. I have spent the past almost nine years avoiding conflict and attention, so the idea of putting myself in its path is a hard concept to wrap my head around.

"I am sorry, Ansel," I say, realizing I haven't answered her. "I really am trying. This just feels so foreign to me."

Her lithe form wraps me in a bear hug as she speaks softly in my ear. "No, I should be apologizing. I shouldn't be so hard on you. I mean you can't even wear proper training attire." She lets out a frustrated sigh as she pulls back, her hand moving restlessly through the copper hair.

"I mean, I'll never understand why they force you into those stupid brown dresses. Look at you, you look like a sack of potatoes, for crying out loud." She gestures with a hand, the other firmly planted on her hip.

"Uh, thanks?" My brows lift as I try to hide a smirk at her comparison. I've always thought the same thing.

"You know what I mean, it's not an insult to you. I mean, is this thing even made of burlap? It's like they put you in the most cheap, shapeless garbage they could find."

"I think it's homespun cotton, but that's all supposed to change once I become Bolster Sage."

A weighted silence falls, heavy with all the unspoken questions and doubts that plague us both.

"I am just scared for you, Lulu. I want to take you with me when we leave, but I know that's not possible. Seeing as they don't allow us much, if any, contact during the day, like we're going to corrupt you or something. Your creepy monks wouldn't stand for it. It kills me to leave you here without giving you something to protect you." She sighs, but the tension doesn't leave her shoulders and she chews on her lip again.

"What is it? I know that look," I chide. "Something's eating at you. I mean, something other than your usual scorn toward this place."

"It's just, I don't really understand why the FP is here. The longer we stay, the more confused I become. Especially given that some of our leaders seem different. And any time I ask questions, I'm ignored. I mean, they've never been very forthcoming with information before, but now it's like they're hiding something. It's setting alarm bells off in me like crazy and it boils my blood to sit here and just wait."

"So you've never been called into their meetings while I am in my lessons?"

"Never. I just train in the courtyard, day in and day out. At first, we had an audience, like we were here to teach the monks a thing or two. But we've had no one watching in well over a week, and I can't help but think that was an act." Concern etches her features.

In typical Ansel fashion, she can't stand still, pacing back and forth across the stone courtyard, her silent movements betraying the stealth of a trained-from-birth warrior. "I mean, have you seen the black door at the end of the north corridor? There's something down there. I only know that much because I caught a glimpse when someone opened it, of a staircase that heads downward. Otherwise, it's always locked and the monks pause when you walk by, as if they're waiting until you are out of earshot. I mean, if they have such pure motives, why would they need to hide something? What do you know about that door, Lulu?"

I know what she's talking about, but I don't have the answers she wants. Ansel and I have grown up in completely different worlds. She is empowered and trained. A fierce, confident, and bold warrior. In the weeks since she's been here, I've learned that the name Feminea Potentia is Latin for female strength, and they are worthy of that name. Brave, fierce, inspiring, and honestly, everything I dream about being but am not. I envy them most of all for their sense of purpose. Even their Latin motto, "Non ducor, duco," which means "I am not led, I lead." Ansel embodies this sentiment.

I, on the other hand, have been told I was chosen to become the first Bolster Sage, because of the unique marking of a star on the back of my neck. According to the monks, it was a foretelling of my place of honor among them. But the sugary words stand in direct opposition to my everyday experiences in the ashram. I am expected to fit their mold, not express any opinions or really verbalize anything not in line with their ways. When I do, I am forced to spend time in the Den of Consciousness, a room filled with smoke that leaves me feeling hazy and pliable.

They tell me it is to open my mind and empower my thinking, but really, I think it is to clear my mind and try to make me a blank slate. So my life to date has revolved around avoiding that room at all costs. There's nothing worse than being forced into such a drugged state that your mind is no longer your own. I have to fight extra hard to remember myself after time in that hellhole.

I have learned to suppress who I am, to wear a mask and do my best to blend into the background. Unfortunately, after years of living like that, I have become nothing more than a decoration around the ashram. I never push boundaries because I know it will mean time in the Den. I avoid when I can and blend in when I need to. And I hate myself for it.

My true self has been buried so deep, sometimes I wonder if I will ever see her again. But Ansel has slowly been bringing me back to life again.

Ansel must see the spiral of my thoughts on my face, because she suddenly speaks, pulling me from my pensive mood.

"It's okay, Lulu, you don't have to be ashamed with me. I know I can't begin to understand what nine years here would do to a person. I've only been here six weeks, and I feel like if it weren't for you, I'd be going mad. And I am not even under their thumb."

Ansel knows about the Den, which only increases her disdain of the monks. Especially when I confessed that I have missing pieces in my memory from my early childhood. Major gaps that feel like a pivotal piece of who I am have been removed, and what is left behind is a ragged torn hole that can't be mended.

I smile and nod at her acceptance. "I wish I could tell you what was behind the black door, but it's off-limits to me. I was told it was a place for upper-level Amilign."

By now, it must be past midnight, and the night temperatures in the courtyard make it impossible to be outside if you aren't exerting yourself. We've been standing still far too long in this frigid mountain air. I rub my arms to try to bring some warmth back to my limbs.

"Come on," Ansel smirks. "I know what you need. Time for a little greenhouse therapy."

Grateful for her change of subject, I smile. Ansel knows

the only place that feels remotely like home to me in the sprawling grounds of the ashram is the greenhouse. It's also the first place we officially met. Maybe she was drawn to it, too.

As we walk through the courtyard, heading to the stone path that will lead us outside the ashram's main walls to the greenhouse, I remember the first time I saw Ansel. I had snuck out of my room so I could see the Feminea Potentia train in the courtyard. It was their first day at the ashram, and my lessons were canceled. I was expected to stay in my room and study in private, but something deep within me urged me to go see them.

It was the first time I felt that the reward outweighed the risk. All the monks were preoccupied with their new guests, and I took a chance that no one would be looking for me. I pulled my hood low over my brow and snuck quietly to the library where I could watch unimpeded from one of the window alcoves.

These women blew me away. The way they trained and fought, they held nothing back. Their passion inspired me. And then I spotted Ansel. She seemed to be one of the younger ones out there—around my age if I had to guess—and her fiery red hair was like a beacon. She was slender but strong, focused and driven. At one point, she looked up at the window I sat in. Her green eyes locked with mine, and in that moment, I felt an invisible cord link us together. Sisters of something far deeper than blood. I knew it was no chance meeting.

She found me later that evening in my favorite place, my greenhouse, and we became fast friends. We have snuck out every night in the weeks the FP have been here. Oftentimes just talking, but recently, now that the weather has warmed up, Ansel insisted on teaching me how to fight.

"We are some kind of pair, you know it?" Ansel smiles, drawing me back to the present again.

"What do you mean?"

"Well, you live with a bunch of creepy old dudes, and I live with a bunch of uptight, secretive women. Neither one of us has any real freedom."

"Yeah, well, at least you get to learn how to be useful and powerful," I retort. "You have purpose and skills. You're bold and fearless. I have nothing but my greenhouse."

She reaches over, grabbing my hand and pulling it through her bent arm as we walk along the stone path. It's lined with patches of almost melted snow, mixed with the new growth of grasses and flower buds that become more prominent the closer we get to the greenhouse.

"You do not have nothing, Lulu, you have me. And you may not know your purpose yet, but I know you are made for big things. You're just incognito right now." She smiles warmly, a twinkle in her green eyes.

CHAPTER 2

As I walk through the silent marble halls of the mountain ashram, even my slippered feet make barely a sound. A bitterly cold air is my only company, adding to the stagnant, lifeless feel of the halls. White stone floors, walls, and ceiling; even the scattered windows have ice crystals spidering outward on the panes, appearing like fissures in the otherwise pristine glass. Adding to the frigidity of the atmosphere, and ready to burn at the softest touch.

I would know. When I was younger, I would see how long I could handle the burn on my finger, in a vain attempt to melt the crystals before I had to pull away. In a way, they add to the outward beauty of this place. But it is a hollow beauty I've become numb to over the years.

I pull my brown robe tighter around me, a fruitless endeavor to ease the chill burrowed deep in my bones. Not even my long, dark hair aids in warming me; it must always be pulled back in a coiffed bun, showcasing the star on the back of my neck. The mark is my only claim to significance in this place.

But it's not like I can hide without it; my gold eyes set me apart enough, as does being a woman in an ashram full of men. Grateful for the break in the monotony of that role, I realize I've yet to see Ansel training in the courtyard today. In fact, I've yet to see any FP around. After Ansel's revelation last night, I fear the time is fast approaching when my friend heads home and life goes back to the tedium of the past.

Afternoon lessons are canceled today for some unknown reason, but you won't hear me complaining. I take it as the rare gift it is and make my way to the refuge of my greenhouse. My steps are hurried, eager to feel a sense of purpose after long hours spent in my morning lessons.

Lost in my thoughts, I almost run right into Cain, one of the head monks, and second to Tavarious, my lessons teacher, on my list of loathing. Thickset and stocky, he's like an immovable blockade everywhere he goes, and his favorite tool to wield is the power of intimidation. His skin is more like hide and his hair is thinning on his head. He keeps it short in a military-style cut; I guess he thinks it makes him look tough.

Tough he is not, but cruel he can definitely be. I first learned of his penchant for beating the rebellion out of someone in my early days here when he took a wooden rod to me. He beat me so hard and repeatedly that he broke the rod over my back. I was twelve at the time. Lucky for me, the higher-ups determined they didn't want me damaged, so that was the only time.

Even with the pain I endured after, I much preferred the beating to Tavarious' favorite form of punishment, the Den of Consciousness. Unfortunately, I wasn't subtle in my disdain for the Den back then. I was still young and hadn't yet learned that the only power I wielded was in the emotions and thoughts I masked. So they figured out pretty easily that they didn't even need to hit me to punish me; they could use the Den.

Almost as bad as the forced time in the Den was the loss of freedom. I realized then that if I wanted to move about as I wished and to a certain extent be trusted, it required me to fit the mold they wanted. So I wore the mask, learned what I was supposed to, behaved how I was expected to behave, and bided my time. All on the off chance that things would get better. That things would one day be different. I don't remember the turning point when my dreams started shifting toward finding a different path for my life. And it has only compounded since Ansel's arrival.

"In a hurry, girl?" Sarcasm drips from Cain's words. "Eager to spend some time in your lessons?" He emphasizes *lessons* with a raised eyebrow and wink. He obviously didn't get the memo about my lessons today. All the head monks know what happens in these lessons, but Cain in particular has a special hatred for me and takes the opportunity to poke and prod me as often as possible. It's as if he resents me for the place I have with the Amilign.

"How can I help you, Teacher?" I try to dampen the unintentional bite in 'teacher' that always seems to force its way out of me when dealing with Cain. Calling this sack of meat a teacher is a joke; he's all brawn and absolutely zero brains.

His meaty hand is suddenly at my throat, lifting me to the tips of my toes. But I won't be intimidated by him. He can't actually hurt me; he's not allowed to. We both know it. Even though he loves to pretend he can. He's like a wounded animal that feels threatened, blustering about making a big ruckus, but his fangs have been removed. If I don't make any sudden movements, he'll go away.

"Watch your attitude, girl. You may think you're important around here, but you are merely a tool for our use." He releases me with a shove so that I stumble back.

Little does he know that I've never truly believed I was important at the ashram. My ability to trust in anything grew cold fairly quickly after arriving and has become nonexistent over the years. Lately, the seed of doubt I've carried with me from the beginning seems to be sprouting and growing roots, filling every open space of my thoughts. All his comment does is add fuel to what's already circling constantly in my mind.

Gah, I can't wait to get away from his odious presence.

"Be on your way, girl. Only a few more weeks of work until you experience the glory of being a Bolster Sage." His tone is mocking. Not waiting for a response, he pushes me aside and practically stomps away. As per usual after my encounters with Cain, he leaves me with an eerie feeling of apprehension that's lately been shifting to dread. And with Ansel's concerns, that feeling is only snowballing.

Opening the rear door of the ashram that leads to the greenhouse path, I am hit with a crisp mountain breeze that charges me with a wild sort of energy, blowing off any of the residual muck that tries to cling to me after spending time in the ashram. I tilt my face to the sky, eagerly soaking up the warmth of the sun's rays, ready to put winter to bed permanently.

As I trudge through the slushy snow toward the stone path, I'm grateful it's almost summer, when I can spend more of my free time tending to the greenhouse. As a child, I found snow beautiful, but here, it's become another barrier to freedom, often keeping me sequestered due to the sheer volume of snow blocking pathways and doors. Located just above the base of the mountain in a small valley surrounded by peaks, the snowdrifts around the ashram frequently pile so high that the only option is to wait it out. The area is only fully melted for a few months in summer and early fall before the snow begins to fill in again.

As I open the door to my greenhouse, the warm air surrounds me. I inhale deep notes of rich, damp dirt, laced with a sweet floral undertone. I love this place. It's a riot of color in a world of dreary and drab. The greenhouse is huge, almost as big as the ashram itself—I suppose because it's meant to grow much of the food for the ashram. Although not technically "my" greenhouse, it's the one place I've felt I belonged in the years I've been here. A sanctuary that reminds me of my childhood home. Over the years, I've carved out my own space here, where I grow and nurture the plants, even planting a few rebellious things like my fruitless crabapple tree. Such a random and useless thing to grow in a greenhouse, the small, white crabapple tree in a forgotten corner, struggling to survive and not be snuffed out.

Just like me.

When I first arrived at the ashram as a young ten-year-old girl, the monks were more apt to make a good impression on me, and after a tour of the place, they offered me one request to be fulfilled—a "gift of friendship," they called it. I've never regretted my choice. I requested a space in the greenhouse to grow what I liked, along with the seeds and supplies necessary.

Even as a child, I knew my heart, my roots.

One of the first things I planted was my crabapple tree. I often think that *crabapple* is a wretched name for a tree capable of producing such exquisite blossoms, with petals as soft as satin and as numerous as the stars. No apples or crabs in sight, just white petals perfuming the air with the scent of spring. As I spread my blanket under the small tree, I can't help but feel a little sad at how fleeting these moments of peace and beauty are. Even the blossoms of the tree will only last a few weeks before they fade until next year, and what remains is dull in comparison.

I wonder if that is the nature of beautiful things, that they can only last in this desolate world for mere moments before fading to something dull and more fitting for their surroundings. As I look up and see the light trickle through the petals of the tree, I wonder if I too have begun to fade.

Hours fly by like minutes when I am out here. All too soon, the chiming of the evening bell steals what little peace I received from the greenhouse. It's time for meditation and the evening meal. If I'm lucky, I can slip away to my room until I can meet up with Ansel after curfew.

Heaving a sigh, I brush the dirt from my hands and hang my smock by the door. I take one last, deep inhale of the only source of warmth for me in this cold place. My soul feels the most whole and complete when I am here. Here, among the works of the Creator, these things living and growing in a place where nothing should be able to do so. It gives me hope to see such vulnerable things defy the odds and overcome like that.

I reach for the door, but it flies open, slamming into the greenhouse wall. A maelstrom of red hair and green eyes stands in the doorway. Hand on my chest to try and slow the pounding of my heart, I glare at her.

"Seriously, Ansel, are you trying to kill me?"

But when I see the colorless look on her face, my hand drops, and my blood runs cold as I notice her trembling hands. She stares at me, frozen.

"What is it?"

She blinks a few times, like she's trying to organize her thoughts. Then, more calmly, she enters and closes the door behind her. She grabs my hand and leads me to a back corner of the greenhouse where she pulls me down to my knees, so we're hidden behind the raised garden beds. The rich aroma of the dirt is heavier down here, almost as if you could taste it. But it does little to ease my tension.

"I picked the lock on the black door late last night, after we parted. I had to know."

Icy fear skates across my skin at Ansel's revelation. Fear of the consequences for her if she is found out.

"There are dungeons down there, Lulu. And past the dungeons is a whole underground facility. I almost got caught, so I wasn't able to fully explore it, but I hid in a broom closet and was able to overhear a brief conversation." She inhales shakily.

"The monks spoke of something called the Silent. I think it's some kind of secret weapon that they've been creating. They were just walking by, so that's all I got. But the dungeons and the occasional screams I heard were enough."

My head spins, alternating between trying to justify what Ansel just shared to a worst-case scenario view of the situation.

"I don't know what to do with this information, Ansel," I blurt out, panic rising in my chest. "What do you expect me to do? You know I have no real freedom here. I don't even know where *here* is! The only family I have let me go with these people. And you know I can't go with you. I am trapped." My frenzied words jumble together.

Ansel grabs my shoulder, but I shrug her off.

"I mean, none of that means anything, right?" I attempt

to reason the whole thing away. "A lot of places need to have prisons or security measures in place for bad guys. And the Silent could be anything, doesn't necessarily mean it's something bad. What if it's a tool to help people?" The words feel like ash in my mouth.

The bland look on Ansel's face speaks volumes about her thoughts on my desperately optimistic theory. "The words I heard as he walked by were that the years of experimenting and research were finally culminating, and the Silent were almost ready. And Lulu, I saw through a crack in the door...he was cleaning what looked like blood off his hands."

I tip my head back against the wall of the greenhouse, closing my eyes and breathing through the storm of my thoughts. Ansel's sigh breaks the silence. I feel her hand on my arm and I open my eyes to look at her without moving my head away from the wall.

She pulls a beautiful wooden bracelet from her pocket. "Here, promise me, at the very least, you will take this and wear it always. All FP wear them—it's a tracker bracelet. It means that no matter where you are, I will be able to find you. So, if something happens and you leave this place, I will know. And nothing will prevent me from coming to you, okay?"

I have no words, so I simply nod, slipping the bracelet onto my wrist and hiding it under the long sleeve of my dress.

"I'm sorry to drop this bomb on you and leave, but I'm supposed to be meeting everyone in the courtyard. I told them I needed to use the bathroom first." She stands and looks down at me sitting in the dirt, my arms wrapped around my knees. "I know this is a lot to take in, but this is one situation where ignorance is not bliss, Lulu. I don't know why the FP came here, but I feel in my soul that I was meant to meet you, that there is something more guiding us. I'll meet you in the courtyard later tonight, okay? We can do something productive with that storm brewing inside you."

She turns on her heels to leave. I sit there awhile after she goes, breathing in the scent of the greenhouse, willing it to calm and center me. Something brushes at my mind, a memory that's trying to push through the fog, but it's been weakened over years of sessions in the Den. I get the sense it has everything to do with what Ansel said about something guiding us. Something that was told to me long ago. But like trying to grasp water, it spills through the fingers of my mind, leaving only faint wisps behind, which quickly evaporate.

Making my way back along the path from the greenhouse, my thoughts drift yet again to the beautiful white horse that's been meeting me in my dreams the past few weeks. I can't pinpoint when I started imagining this coping mechanism, but the horse has become the symbol of my deepest, most impossible dreams. The old, familiar pull that always accompanies thoughts of the ethereal animal, to choose a different path for my life. And it's with that thought I realize these dreams have stopped feeling impossible to me. They have a life and urgency to them instead.

CHAPTER 3

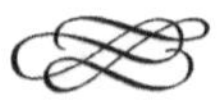

LUCIA

I wake extra early after Ansel didn't appear last night. I waited an hour before finally returning to my room. How dare she drop such an insane revelation on me and then not meet up like she promised? And as much as I wanted to go check the wing I knew the FP were staying in, I had no idea which room she was in. Not to mention, even if I did, she was bunking with others, so knocking on doors in the middle of the night was out of the question.

So instead, I lay in bed, my worried mind running away with itself as I tossed and turned all night, sleep evading me. Hoping Ansel just fell asleep from an extra late night of snooping the night before, I head to the courtyard to catch her before her training starts this morning.

But as I enter the courtyard, the deafening silence tells me all I need to know. My heart sinks. I've gotten so used to the FP training early in the morning that the silence feels extra heavy, even eerie. A thought occurs to me. The FP rode in on horses that would be kept in the barn, and sometimes Ansel likes to visit them.

I run across the courtyard, passing beneath the archway that leads to the barn and paddocks. There is an unnatural stillness in the air, and the paddock houses only five horses. I ignore the tingling in my spine. Maybe they were put out to pasture already, though it's still early.

My feet pound across the dirt of the barn floor, raising a cloud in my wake as I run to the back door. With a deep breath of the hay- and manure-scented air, I pull aside the heavy sliding door that allows the horses to roam the mountainside pasture and freeze as I take in the sight. A mist covers the field and a few birds call to each other in the distance as the sun begins to lighten up the sky. Other than that, it is completely empty.

It has finally happened. She is really gone.

The morning chill of the air only adds to the ice coating my skin as I make my way back, purposeless. I amble into the main courtyard of the ashram. The place looks different to me now. Ansel has brought color back into my world and reminded me of what I am missing in life. I love and hate her for it.

Now that she is gone, this place is an unbearable shade of grey. Not that it wasn't always dim and dark, but I feel like a blind man being given sight, only to have it taken away again. I wander aimlessly, with no real destination in mind, the hopelessness threatening to drown me. The only thing that keeps me afloat is the tracker bracelet she gave me. I rub my fingers over the smooth wood, reminding myself that someone in the world knows where I am, that I exist. This knowledge will keep me going, keep me focused.

My thoughts drift back to our last few days together. Ansel's increasing concern, or paranoia. I wonder why they left so abruptly. Or was this always the plan, and neither of us knew? My mind tries and fails to comprehend all the possible scenarios. In the end, my tired thoughts begin to sift through the memories of my early years here.

When I first arrived here as a child, taken from my home with my beloved Aunt Sid, I was confused and heartbroken, but the beauty and luxury distracted me for a bit. How could a place with so much beauty be bad? The sheets were of the softest silks, blankets so warm and fluffy you felt as though you could sink into them and forever be content to lie in their comforting warmth. Even the running water, warm at the touch of your hands, was a luxury I'd only heard about. But I've learned over the years that such things are great deceivers. Beauty often masks decay underneath. And no amount of beauty can hide the rot that is hidden under the veneer of this place. I've lived here long enough to see it clearly now.

Even the silence of this place grates on me now. It's not a soothing quiet, but an oppressively cold shroud. No music or singing, no sound above a whisper, only the bell chimes for meals and meditation time breaking the endless silence. In my rebellious imaginings, I see myself screaming at the top of my lungs, shattering the silence. I wonder if the restlessness I feel is only because of the cracked façade I can now see through, compounded by Ansel's discovery, or if there's something more out there pulling at me.

Long ago, Aunt Sid told me that I was a part of a prophecy that would save mankind. All these years later, I don't remember all the details, only vague parts, but I suppose at the time, I also didn't care to know. It only mattered to me that I was important. As a child, I loved the idea that I was more than just an orphan. That there was a special plan and purpose for me. But then I was taken away from Aunt Sid. The lofty ideals of my youth slowly dimmed and faded into tattered, hazy hopes. And any memory attempting to linger was easily suppressed by time in the Den, though I would fight to get it back.

Even the promise of a role of significance with the Amilign has started to feel like a counterfeit hope. Now, after almost nine years here, all that remains is doubt and a whisper of a dream too dangerous to expose to the light, so it remains buried in a trunk in the attic of my mind.

As I wander the cold halls, my thoughts drift to Aunt Sid and how I still miss her after all this time. I wonder if she's okay and if she still lives in the little farmhouse among the foothills, where the winds are strong, the sun intense, but the whole world feels open to you. I see it now for the slice of Heaven it was.

As a child, I hated the constant work needed to make things grow in the garden, keep things alive in the barn, and keep things functioning and clean in the house. But now, after living in luxury, I miss the work. I miss the meals made from the garden we tended, and the satisfaction of knowing my efforts contributed to such marvelous creations of culinary delight. It was...empowering.

It's ironic that I live in a place where I'm supposed to "empower self," yet I've never felt empowered here. Forced to wear the same boring, shapeless, dirt-brown dresses daily, always topped with the thick, weighty, brown robe, my long, dark hair always to be in a tight knot at my neck. Not to speak unless spoken to. Fed the illusion of freedom, knowing full well the harsh mountain landscape and extreme weather will never permit an escape. It's plain to see I am only ornamental. A useless bauble; pointless and stagnant.

The bell chime pulls me from my thoughts and lets me

know I missed morning meal and meditation, which is fine with me. I don't have an appetite right now anyway. Dee will be less busy with the morning meal now over. She'll be doing cleanup for a while yet, and I need a friendly face to keep the despair from swallowing me whole.

As I walk into the kitchen, the mounds of dishes look ready to swallow her mousy figure whole. Her sandy brown hair is cut short to her scalp; it makes her gorgeous brown eyes stand out even more.

She is entranced in her work as I approach. "Hey Dee," I say through a wide smile.

She gasps and jumps, then turns to glare at me.

"Sorry, didn't mean to startle you. Just wanted to see a friendly face."

Her eyes soften a bit at my confession and a barely-there smile lights her face.

"Let me help?" I reach to grab a towel to help dry, but as usual, she vehemently shakes her head *no*. She insists on doing things by the book, rule follower that she is, and that means that someone of my place among the Amilign should not be in the kitchen working. I technically shouldn't even be friends with Dee.

But that all went out the window when my first monthly cycle came and I needed someone to help explain. Being the only other woman besides me, she was the logical choice. Even though Dee can't talk, she showed me what I would need, and wrote explanations for me. I had been so scared, but even though Dee was only five years older than me, she'd calmed me and helped me feel less alone in this place.

Even so, I imagine if she could have it her way, she would keep me away from the kitchen and things would remain as they were. I know this feels safer to Dee, but I'm not having it. Dee needs a friend as much as I do, which is why she tolerates me turning up on occasion.

She points at the clock on the wall and gives me a withering expression.

"Yeah, yeah, I know, I'm going. I'll see you later, Dee."

Dee knows the monks run a tight ship, and my lessons follow the morning meal. She waves me off over her shoulder as she continues to chip away at her duties.

I make my way swiftly to the room where I have my lessons, hoping to beat Tavarious there, knowing full well that any supposed eagerness on my part will only make things easier today. As I walk, I feel as though I am heading into the lion's den. Ansel has planted a seed in me in more ways than one. I think back on the various conversations we had in the weeks she ingrained herself in my life.

We discussed so many things together. She told me what it was like in the outside world. How most people and families choose to live far from the remaining cities that are left. Scattered to the winds, like rare birds approaching extinction. Bikes or horses are the main mode of transportation, but a select few of the "filthy rich," as Ansel called them, have access to the luxuries of fuel, running water, and electricity. Even so, those are exceedingly rare.

Having been sheltered at the ashram for so long, I've forgotten how I lived without all these luxuries when I was on the farm with Aunt Sid. I didn't tell Ansel how I would give it all up in a heartbeat to be back there again.

The Range, the mountains where the ashram is located, is one of the few healthy areas left. To the far west is a vast wasteland simply referred to as The Wastes. The product of past wars and bombings, it is an uninhabitable and unnatural desert land. Only the very brave or very stupid dare to venture into it. To the southeast of The Range are the swamplands and the coast.

The northeast is a land of extremes. Ice storms in the winter; scorching, oppressive heat in the summer. It is home to various, scattered peoples and communities trying to eke out an existence, but Ansel was yet to travel that far. I remember seeing the eagerness in her eyes and knew she would go there one day. I envied her.

Ansel was the first one to validate my unspoken fears. She, too, had sensed the rot beneath the façade and wanted me to be able to protect myself. Even though we only got a handful of lessons in and I was a hopeless pupil, I learned that stomping on the instep of an attacker's heel will distract him long enough to get away. I suppose it's better than no defense at all. Now that I am alone in this place again, I'll just have to hope I never have to use it.

CHAPTER 4

LUCIA

That night, lying in bed, I expect sleep to evade me again, but my eyes get heavy. My thoughts start to drift to open blue skies, a cute farmhouse with a garden on one side, and the smell of crisp air laced with a hint of wildflowers. Home. Oh, how my heart yearns to be back there again.

Aunt Sid was the closest thing I had to a mother. I remember her gorgeous brown skin, lightly wrinkled around the eyes and mouth. Her white, curly hair stood in sharp contrast to the dark beauty of her skin. She always tied a bandana tightly around her head, attempting to keep the mass of wild curls under control, but only mildly succeeding. In my dream, she looks up from the garden and smiles at me, as she so often did. I always thought she looked like an angel; lovely and ageless.

"Do you know why I picked the name Lucia for you, my dumpling?" Her voice in my memory is a balm.

"Why, Aunt Sid?" I call her by the nickname I used as a child.

"Because it means Light, and you, my girl, are the most bright and beautiful light that will one day cast out the darkness in this dreary world. You are such an incredible gift from Elohim, darling."

"Why is there evil if Elohim loves us, Aunt Sid?"

"Well, my little dumpling, our Elohim gave us free will to choose, because of His love for us. In order for love to be real, it must be freely given. It cannot be demanded or forced, otherwise it would not be love. And this world we live in is a battleground. We have the choice to usher in the *Ohr Ein Sof* or invite in the darkness. Many people have chosen poorly and selfishly, and thereby given darkness a strong foothold in this world. As darkness grows in power, so does its influence."

Aunt Sid sighs, deep in thought. "But thank goodness our Elohim is Love, because love always protects, always trusts, always hopes, and always perseveres. Right, my dumpling? You'll see, He has made a way through the darkness for us."

In the unnatural vividness of the dream, I hug Aunt Sid and return to the garden, pulling weeds with a carefree air. I had many similar conversations with Aunt Sid during my childhood. I always loved how she would explain things to me. She always spoke of the world with hope and joy, and light that seemingly poured from her. I somehow remember that the *Ohr Ein Sof* to which she referred means Infinite Light.

Later that evening, Aunt Sid told me about the Prophecy of the Four Cores. Aunt Sid always firmly believed I was a part of this prophecy, based on some random numbers related to my birthday, being an orphan, and the star-shaped birthmark on the back of my neck.

I definitely don't feel like ancient prophecy material. Physically weak, untrained, isolated, and without real skills or purpose, I cannot muster the belief that it could ever be me. As much as I love Aunt Sid, her words seem like the ramblings of someone desperately clinging to hope for a better world.

The dream shifts again. I hear the sound of men's voices outside the house. Heading out front, I freeze on the porch at the sight of four men in dark brown, hooded robes standing just beyond the white picket fence. It takes a moment for the shock of what I am seeing to wear off and register that they are speaking.

"We are here for the girl," they say to Aunt Sid. "She has been chosen to train at the ashram and be elevated upon her nineteenth birthday to a role of great honor among the Amilign. Our seers have proclaimed it to be so."

I am confused. Not just because they know I am a girl, when Aunt Sid has disguised me as a boy all these years. But they want to take me away?

I look to Aunt Sid for clarity and for her to deny them. Instead, Aunt Sid walks toward me and gives me a tight-lipped smile as she says a fake, "Congratulations, my darling." I freeze as she reaches out to pull me into a hug, trembling.

She whispers in my ear, "Even though I hoped to spare you, the time has come, my brave Lucia. I know none of this makes any sense and probably won't for some time, but remember all that I've taught you. Evil is a deceiver above all, and destruction is always hidden behind a desirable package. Trust no one, and when the time comes to run, be swift, and may your feet guide you where Elohim directs."

Aunt Sid turns to the monks and says, "May we have a

moment to gather a few of her things inside?" I notice her hand behind her back is balled in a fist and trembling. So at odds with the sugary sweet and calm words she's speaking.

"You have five minutes," the monk responds, standing with the others like unyielding statues.

She takes me inside to gather my things. Her movements are brusque, her eyes distant and sad as she wipes away a stray tear. I watch as she grabs my favorite teddy bear that she made for me and puts him in my bag. Giving me one last embrace, she whispers, "Be observant and remain guarded always. And remember, my love and Elohim Shomri goes with you."

I remember Shomri means *protector*.

But there's no time to ask any of the multitudes of questions I have. With one last hug at the door, I am ushered to the gate, forced to walk between the four monks, as if I might try to bolt. I look back at Aunt Sid, desperate for more of her to lock away in my heart. Any pretense is gone from her expression and the tears cut dark paths in earnest down her rich umber cheeks.

All too soon, her silhouette can no longer be seen standing on the porch, and the place that was a safe haven for me looks like nothing more than a hazy painting of a distant memory. In no time at all, we reach a giant machine with a whirling blade sitting on top. It's making a monstrous sound and creating a whirlwind of dust and debris. It's completely fantastical and like nothing I've ever seen before. I try to shield my eyes but can't stop taking it in.

"Magnificent isn't it?" yells one of the monks over the noise. "It's called a helicopter. There are a rare few left working in the world, and only those living in abundance have the means to own one and make it fly. One of the many benefits of being part of the Amilign." They walk me to the giant metal beast and help me climb into its belly, strapping me in as it starts to lift off the ground.

A mass of emotions builds inside me as we fly through the sky into the unknown future. At the forefront are grief and confusion. Why did Aunt Sid let me leave with these strange men and how did they even find us in the first place? And why did her parting words seem to imply she knew this would happen? If that was the case, why had she never prepared me, especially considering how she was constantly warning me of the dangers of the world and shielding me from them? Even to the point of living in an isolated area far from town, calling me Lu, and cutting my hair super short to hide my feminine gender.

I recall my first view of the ashram, home of the Amilign. At first glance, it looks like an old castle from one of my childhood fairytale books. A stone wall exterior complete with parapets and corner turrets hides a large compound, a courtyard complete with white sculptures, a large, open space that looks like a landing spot for this helicopter thing, and even a pathway that leads to a large glass structure that resembles a greenhouse, but is far larger than anything I've read about in the gardening books with Aunt Sid.

The sense of awe I feel numbs the confusion and pain rolling around inside me. But that night, when I lie in my new bed alone, ten years old, missing my Aunt Sid and everything I've ever known, and facing an uncertain future, it is the tears of loss and grief that keep me company and lulled me into a fitful sleep.

The morning bell of the ashram chimes, waking me and jerking me back to the present. I stare at the ceiling stunned, blinking back tears. My unconscious mind has seemingly plucked this memory of my childhood from the forgotten recesses of my mind; a memory suppressed by too many sessions in the Den, I imagine. But the dream was so real and more vivid and detailed than I could ever have imagined.

I think back to Ansel saying something is guiding us, and I sense this memory is part of that. And Elohim—a name my Aunt Sid frequently talked about and one I have long since forgotten. What if this Elohim is guiding me now? Reaching for the comfort of that old, familiar teddy bear, I hold him tight to my chest as my fingers stroke the tattered fur.

I feel an unfamiliar texture sticking out from the seam in one of its legs. It appears to be the corner of a piece of paper, busting through a torn seam. I hate to further dismantle him, but after that dream, I suspect this is no accident. I carefully unravel the broken thread and pull the rest of the paper from the small hole. Recognition of the delicate, flowing handwriting hits me like an arrow to the heart, causing my vision to blur and my hands to shake. It's a small, folded note, purposefully sown into the leg of my childhood teddy bear. Like a bucket of ice-cold water poured over my head, the discovery soaks into me.

This action would have taken planning.

As I lie in bed, the ache of my heart feels like I've taken a physical blow to the chest. How could my Aunt Sid know what would happen? She knew enough to plan a hidden note in the leg of my teddy bear. She even had to have known what I would face in the years to come, warning me to trust no one, remain guarded, and be prepared to run. And if she did know all of this, how could she let me go so easily?

I realize the aching in my heart is not only because of the discovery of the note, but the shock of the relived memory against the stark comparison of just how alone I feel in this place. All these years later, I still don't understand why she would let me go. I grieve the not knowing as much as I grieve the understanding that the answers I seek could break my heart further. The deep-seated fear that the one relationship in my life that made me feel loved and cared for could quite possibly have been a lie. And it's that potential truth that threatens to swallow me whole, leaving nothing but a hollow husk in its wake.

I hold the note in my shaky hands, afraid to read what Aunt Sid wrote. As I stare at the tattered edges of a hastily torn page, weathered and wrinkled from the passage of time, I carefully unfold it to see a simple message.

> I made the impossible choice, of which there
> never really was one.
> But do not fear, you have never been alone and
> you are more powerful than you know.
> If there was one thing I would have you
> know above all else, it's that you are more loved
> than life itself.
> Aunt Sid

I fall back in bed, letting the note drift to the floor. Tears fall in earnest, soaking my pillow. I am desperate to bury the memories and fears that plague my mind. A vision of the white horse comes to my mind again. It seems that whenever I feel too much loneliness or despair, my mind wanders to this lovely, ethereal horse, and the storm inside me somehow calms. Along with the timing of that eye-opening dream, it's just another thing I can't explain.

I sense in my spirit I am being guided to something significant, something that may be coming to fruition soon. But above all that, I am grateful for the strange sense that I am not now, and never will be alone.

CHAPTER 5

As I head to the room of my tedious daily lessons, my mind wars with deep-seated doubt. I am to receive lessons until my nineteenth birthday, a number marked for success and abundance according to the monks. This is when I officially become the Bolster Sage, a position of honor among the Amilign.

When I was younger, I used to believe that I would begin to feel a sense of purpose the closer I came to being Bolster Sage. But then I turned eighteen, and my lessons took an uncomfortable turn, which only made the small doubts I was entertaining increase tenfold.

The monks claim that the star on my neck is proof that I was chosen for this role. A role of honor I am being groomed for, but never given any details on, only told that all will become clear when I become the Bolster Sage. In my early days here, I had lessons to further my understanding of this world. Lessons on nature and plants, the biology of the body, nutrition, and world history, despite not much being known about our world's history, the knowledge being either lost to time or suppressed.

I also had extensive lessons in self-discovery, meditating on thoughts that lead to inner strength and power in the Den. They say the purpose of the Den is to expand the mind, but I know better after all these years. It makes me feel as though none of the thoughts in my head are my own.

Tavarious, in particular, loves to teach me what he calls "mastery over the mind" during my time in the Den, but he always puts me in there after I've asked too many questions. I think he believes it will help me conform to their expectations, but I have always been strong-willed, despite having to hide this at the ashram.

I've grown to prefer the fringes. There is safety in going unnoticed. But I will always fight to remain true to myself in the one place that's still mine: my thoughts.

These days, my lessons focus more on my power as a woman, and more specifically on the power my feminine form holds and how to yield it for my gratification and fulfillment, as well as for those "under my care" as Bolster Sage. Whatever that means. Along with these obscure lessons, being in the presence of the creepy Tavarious daily sets my teeth on edge. When I was younger, different monks gave my lessons. Amon seemed bored in my lessons, like the monotony of the material was almost too much for him to bear. His indifference and boredom were far preferable to what I endure now.

When I turned eighteen, Tavarious took over my lessons and, unlike Amon, he seemed to enjoy them. Specifically, being around me. Tall and gangly, with an angular face and stringy, thin hair that hangs limply to his shoulders, he often appears as if he's being swallowed whole by the thick, brown hooded robes all the monks wear. As if it's wearing him instead of him wearing it.

Lately, he's taken to slicking his mouse-brown hair down the back of his head. I'm not sure what he's trying to achieve with this new look, but it only adds to my discomfort. I frequently catch him staring at me in ways that make me want to cover myself or hide, and "accidentally" brushing me with his arm or hand. I swear one time I even caught him smelling my hair.

Particularly these past few months, my lessons have taken on a new focus. Tavarious seems too eager, almost hungry for something I can't quite put my finger on, but a nagging fear in the back of my mind says it has everything to do with me becoming Bolster Sage. He says these lessons are about "coming into the power of my body," but he prattles on graphically about a woman's body, the purpose for my "sensual essence,"—whatever that means—and how the power I wield as a woman is different to that of a man. Or, in his words, "an intensely raw and euphoric conduit."

All I know is that Tavarious makes my skin crawl.

I have no clue how I am going to get through one more day, let alone make it to my nineteenth birthday. And lately, this seed of doubt has me questioning if I even want to. My thoughts drift to what Aunt Sid told me as a child. Her words combine with Ansel's discovery and my own fantasies of leaving this place and building a life I choose for myself. Every day that goes by, the desire only grows within me. Creating a restlessness that will not be settled.

I swallow my angst and school my features as I open the door to the room where my lessons have been for the past five years. A soft, rhythmic tapping of fingers on wood pulls my attention to Tavarious, who sits on the desk waiting for me. His face shows an eagerness he doesn't pretend to hide.

"There you are, my sweet Lucia," he says, pronouncing my name Lu-Chia instead of Lu-See-Ah. He knows I hate it. "I am excited to get started today. There's so much delicious information to share with you."

I inwardly cringe. He's trying to make me uncomfortable. I may have been raised isolated, making me naive, but I do know what I feel and he makes me want to run. I can not do this with him today.

"I am afraid I'm not feeling well today, Teacher, my stomach is not quite right," I lie. I don't have it in me to deal with him today and I know just what to say that will make him want me gone from his presence.

"Well, this is important work whether you are well or not. You want to be up to the tasks of a Bolster Sage, do you not?"

"Oh I certainly do, Teacher, but I just want you to know that I've spent the morning on the toilet and I may need to take frequent breaks to do so again throughout our lesson today." I try to look at the floor as meekly as I am able and feign embarrassment to ensure my charade is believed. I know he hates whenever I speak too vividly of anything related to bodily functions.

His face twists in disgust, a flash of annoyance in his eyes. "Well, I suppose I can give you material to study from the confines of your room while you recover, but I expect you to be committed to this work in the days to come. You cannot avoid these lessons if you are to become Bolster Sage, Lucia."

"Yes, Teacher, thank you," I speak to the floor. I know he likes me simpering before him and it grates me to do so, but I am eager to get away from him and this behavior is my fastest exit.

He turns his back to me, searching his bookshelves.

Pausing, he turns to face me. The fiendish smile on his face sends a bolt of unease through me.

"You are to wait here. I am going to retrieve a special resource just for your studies." He tosses me a cloying smirk.

As he closes the door behind him, I feel a sudden pull to search his desk. It's risky to disobey him; he takes great pleasure in punishing me when he can. But this pull is so insistent, it's impossible to ignore. I need to be quick.

Rushing around to the drawers, I start carefully sifting through things. I don't know what, exactly, I'm looking for, but I have a feeling I will know when I get to it. It's the bottom drawer that seems to be drawing my focus. Closing the one I am currently searching, my hands swiftly move to open the bottom drawer. I sift through a few things before the words "Bolster Sage" catch my attention. My stomach sinks as I notice the words written underneath in parentheses: "AKA Breeding Servant."

Pulling the document out, I see an outline of my education. I turn the page over and there's a timeline for physical training. Which I am apparently fast approaching. It includes more frequent and longer times in the Den to ensure "submission and willing compliance to the breeding schedule," along with some other things I don't quite understand. According to this, I am to begin tracking my monthly cycle to ensure the "ovulation timeline"—whatever that is. There is even a written list of monks called the "non-ovulation rotation," with Tavarious' name at the top.

There is more, but I can barely read it. I am shaking badly, the paper rustling in my hands. They may have kept me ignorant about a lot of things, including what ovulation is, but there is no hiding the meaning of "breeding servant" or "breeding schedule."

Suddenly, the urgency is back, burning through my veins. I am running out of time before Tavarious returns. I carefully place the document back exactly where it was, closing the drawer and swiftly returning to my spot by the door. Taking a few deep breaths to steady my pounding heart and calm my erratic nerves, I school my face into a mask of subservience as the door opens and Tavarious stands in front of me.

He holds a large, hardback book with intricate, swirling details on the cover. I expected far more than one book, but with the sneer on his face, I can only imagine what this book contains.

"Being the compassionate teacher that I am," he croons, "I've decided to give you three days confined to your room for your recovery. In that time, I expect you to have read this entire book, manifesting its knowledge in your sensuous nature. We will be going over this physical manifestation to your person upon your return."

Sensuous nature? *Ugh, who talks like that? Such a creep!* And what could possibly be in this book? I see this for the punishment it is—maybe I shouldn't have tried to skip out on lessons today. If I am confined to my room, I will be unable to visit my only sanctuary in this wretched prison, my greenhouse. With nothing else to do, I leave Tavarious and return to my room.

As I open the door, I chuck the book into the corner, having zero interest in anything that excites Tavarious. A sense of dread fills me, not only at the prospect of three days locked in this windowless coffin because windows are "distractions from my focus," or some nonsense, but because I know without a doubt that I cannot stay here any longer. The unknowns that have plagued me for so long have solidified, like weights pressing down on me, threatening to immobilize me like one of the statues frozen in the court-yard. Flashes of past conversations run through my head as if on a reel. All the doubt I have felt bubbles over into icy fear and resolve.

The unwanted, supposedly accidental touches, the creepy comments or looks, the fact that I am the only woman in a compound full of men. Finding that document is the final piece to the puzzle, making it disgustingly clear what they have planned for me. This must be part of the restlessness I have been feeling. And with the timeliness of the dream, I sense I am being guided. Whatever it is, it's pulling me far away from this place.

But I will not be immobilized by this discovery. Instead, I choose to be galvanized. I will see these three days as the gift they are. Being confined to my room to study means no lessons and lots of free time. So I will spend these days planning my escape. It thrills me and terrifies me; I feel as though a beast has come to life inside me and is fortifying my resolve, giving me the strength to do what needs to be done.

I finally have a purpose; no more will I be a useless bauble. I am done with restless days and nights feeling alone, with no control over my life and what I am to become.

CHAPTER 6

NICANOR

The first crack of the axe splitting the wood fills the quiet forest, causing birds to take flight. It's become a sort of therapy over the past few days. The repetitive motion of bringing the axe up, over, and down. One hit to split the wood all the way to the base.

But today is day thirty out here in the woods, and I am going a bit stir-crazy with anticipation. Elias chose me for this mission. He told me to build a shelter and wait, that I was not to make any movement toward the ashram. That last command chafed, and Elias probably knew it, but I love and respect Elias and he never makes decisions without reason.

So here I am, splitting wood I don't really need.

I took Elias's instructions a little further and built a one-room cabin, complete with an old iron, wood-burning stove. I was even able to salvage some old windows from a dilapidated building in one of the abandoned mountain towns. I finished the cabin a few days ago, and the restlessness I feel now threatens to destroy me. Even Adira is agitated, and she's always a source of calm. She prances around the property, pawing at the ground and snorting every so often, throwing her head in frustration.

I'm glad to know I am not the only one.

The drip of sweat trailing a path between my shoulder blades as I continue to split log after log is a welcome distraction as my muscles work under the repetitive motion. Work is the only thing that keeps me from jumping out of my skin right now. And with the cabin finished, all that's left to do is split firewood.

If only I could shut my mind off. Elias told me the girl is reaching the end of her time with the monks. Knowing what I know about them, I struggle to just wait and see what happens. Hope for the best and trust that it will all work out. That's not in my nature. The itch to conquer this situation and bring about the result that we desire is burning in my blood.

Elias has always been so blindly faithful to Atik Yomin, the Ancient of Days, and it's something I have never been able to muster. Don't get me wrong; this very mission I am on is proof that the ancient prophecy is real and that Elohim's heart for humanity is always good and redemptive.

I just don't think I am wired for faith or trust. I can see the overarching plan, but these smaller details where I have the ability to take control, to interject my will and achieve results...it's like nails on a chalkboard to not act. To sit back and wait. This girl is important, and as of right now, she's our only link to the Cores of Elohim. And who knows what could be happening to her in that ashram, what she's being subjected to. Nothing good can exist in that place.

To think of an innocent trapped there. I am crawling out of my skin.

I lift the axe over my head and throw it with all of my strength. Flipping end over end, it slams into the trunk of a nearby aspen tree with a loud *thud*, the force causing the tree to shudder and bend, leaves reluctantly shaking loose and falling all around like an explosion of confetti. Adira rears up onto her hind legs, feeding off my frustration and anger.

I grab my bow and quiver, and head toward her. She prances up to me and I swing onto her back before she can even come to a stop. We weave our way through the dense forest before coming to an open field. We are not even out of the shade of the forest when she breaks into a full gallop. She's always been much faster than other horses.

Gripping her with my legs, a hand on her withers, I focus on the feel of the wind drying the sweat on my skin as the sun beats down on us. My eyes water at the speed and I welcome the distraction the sensation offers. Nothing feels as free as when I am riding Adira. It feels like any moment, we are going to take flight and head up to the heavens.

Time ceases to exist as we ride and I let Adira lead. It's such a foreign feeling for me to not be in control, and I wouldn't welcome the feeling with just anyone. But I trust Adira—we have a special connection. She's intuitive and seems to know what I need as she takes us to the small lake a few miles from the cabin.

"Thanks, girl," I slide from her back, patting her neck.

I'll catch some fish and maybe take a swim before heading back to the cabin. Adira meanders up to the water's edge for a drink while I prepare my bow, tying a small string to the end of an arrow. I wade out into the water until I am about thigh-deep and then I wait. These mountain lakes are so clear, it doesn't take long until I see fish. I nock my bow, and with an exhale, I let the arrow fly. It pierces the water with barely a ripple, and suddenly the string thrashes. Child's play for me, but I don't have time to hunt actual game.

I head back to the bank, pulling the string as I go, lifting a nice-sized trout from the water. Adira has wandered off to graze, so I sit on a ledge at the water's edge, letting my feet dangle in the icy mountain water.

Starring up at the cloudless, azure sky, my mind is adrift again. I can't seem to shake the restlessness.

As the days go on, it only seems to get worse. It's been such a long wait, and many have begun to doubt the prophecy. There are many more who never lived to see it come to fruition. It's hard to believe that we could finally be at the point where the things written long ago are coming to pass, but this feeling burning in my blood tells me I need to prepare myself. Things are getting ready to change in ways I can't begin to imagine.

But somehow I sense that no amount of preparation will help me be ready for what's to come.

CHAPTER 7

LUCIA

Today's the day I leave this place, the first day of my freedom. First things first, I need food for this journey. I grabbed some of the vegetables from the greenhouse yesterday, but those won't last long, I need something with a shelf life.

I wait until the breakfast rush has passed, thinking it's late enough in the morning that the kitchen should be fairly deserted. Tiptoeing through the kitchen to the pantry shelves in the back, I scan the shelves for jerky, maybe a jar of some preserves—something small and long-lasting.

The hair on the back of my neck stands upright in warning right before a bony hand slides around my waist, the waxy skin of an arm straining, yanking me into a bony chest.

Tavarious. I can feel him all along my back as his fetid breath whispers in my ear, "What are you doing down here at this time, Lucia, and when you've been commanded to stay in your room?"

I fight nausea as I reply. "I...I'm hungry Teacher, I thought it best not to inconvenience anyone during meditation." I hate the stammer in my words, unsettled by the pressure of his skeletal body against mine.

My anger starts to simmer beneath the surface. A small form in the corner draws my eye, despite desperately trying to go unnoticed. Dee's eyes are squeezed tightly shut; she sits with her knees pulled tightly to her chest so she's below the counter height. Her whole body trembles like a leaf clinging to a branch in a storm.

I finally see that there's so much more to Dee's wallflower nature than I originally assumed. And I am kicking myself for not seeing it before.

Tavarious' nasally voice draws my focus. "Hmm, you received your breakfast like everyone else, and with your stomach ailment, I would think food would not be so appealing to you." With his other hand, he grabs the jerky from my hand. Lucky for me, I have already slipped a jar of strawberry jam into my dress pocket. I pray he didn't notice.

"Jerky? Not really a morning food, nor a food suitable for someone recovering from digestive illness." His hot, wet breath against my neck makes me feel like a rabbit caught in a snare.

He spins me and shoves me up against the shelves, his forearm holding me in place across my chest and shoulders. "I am going to walk you back to your room, Lucia, and then you are going to be fitted and dressed for your ceremony. Then you will spend a week in the Den of Consciousness preparing for the ceremony."

Confusion, fear, and rage fight for a place in my mind while I struggle to keep my expression blank and rationalize why this is happening now. The longest I've ever spent in the Den is a day; a week will destroy who I am. My eyes meet Dee's briefly, pleading, before she closes hers again and somehow shrinks in on herself further.

I am well and truly alone.

"Don't look so shocked, my lovely Lu-Chia-Ahhh," he overpronounces, easing up off me. His jaw is clenched so tight it looks as though it might crack. "You've progressed in your lessons so well that we've decided to bump up the ceremony. You are to become Bolster Sage at the end of the week. Congratulations." He says this mockingly, still playing with pretense.

This is all a ruse; everyone knows I barely tolerate my lessons. Clearly, Tavarious suspects something. He analyzes every inch of my face.

I cannot be in the Den of Consciousness for a week; that will leave me without a will of my own. A sinking feeling hits my stomach as I realize that is precisely what they want. There will be no escaping at that point, because I won't be fighting anything.

But if he's still playing the game, so will I. I school my features and don my mask.

I meekly shift my gaze to the floor, nod, and say, "Thank you, Teacher. I am truly honored." I can feel his stare as if it's burning me. He's weighing me, considering. I keep my eyes on the floor.

He seems to make a decision, because he grabs me roughly by the arm and hauls me out of the kitchen and back to my room. Yanking open the door, he shoves me inside.

"The clothier will be here momentarily," he snaps, but doesn't leave.

Tavarious wants me to fight with him. He'd like nothing more than to push me past the breaking point. Finally see me snap. Too bad for him, I've had far too much experience with controlling my emotions and masking my reactions. I will never let him have that part of me. The truth of what I feel is mine alone.

Having had enough of me for now, he slams and locks the door. I am not ready to give up yet. And thankfully, I still have the jar of strawberry jam: it'll have to be enough. I gather my few minuscule possessions: my teddy bear with the note, some ribbon, a set of silverware, a comb, a box of matches, a bottle of water, the carrots and zucchini I took from the garden, and my jar of strawberry jam. I put them into my pillowcase, tying the open end into a knot. It's not much, but it's better than nothing.

I push it under my bed, alongside my robe, and sit down to wait. This is my last chance at escape. I will need to be ready.

I take a deep breath and say a silent prayer for courage.

Mere moments later, a knock at the door startles me from my thoughts. I take a breath, steeling myself for what lies ahead. As I feared, the clothier is accompanied by another monk, and as he walks through the door, my heart sinks to see Cain grinning at me.

This just got a lot harder.

The clothier moves quickly around me with his measuring tape, writing as he goes. I grasp for a way out, and an idea appears like the dawn on the horizon. I purposely start to waver while I stand, praying this works. The clothier is still writing, but as he turns to look back at me, I flutter my eyelashes and roll my eyes into the back of my head. He stands quickly, as if to steady me, but I crumple to the ground like a sack of bricks.

Cain leaves his place from the door and I hear the unfamiliar voice of the clothier. "Get her some water. It's so stifling in this windowless room, she's fainted."

"Eh, she'll be fine. Just give her a few minutes." A typical Cain response.

"Sir, I have other appointments this afternoon, and I can't in good conscience leave her like this. I will head to the kitchen for water if you will just wait here and keep watch over her."

Cain grunts in response as I hear the clothier's footsteps start to fade. I flutter my eyelashes and moan as I pretend to wake up. I tremble, pretending to be weak and unsteady as I struggle to stand. Apparently, it works because, despite himself, Cain extends a hand to grab my arm and steady me.

"Sit down, girl, before you fall down...again. We need to get these measurements taken so I can tend to my other responsibilities. I can't have you taking up the whole day with your weak constitution."

Remembering what Ansel taught me, I lean into Cain as if I need support. Surprise flashes across his face, and he's caught off guard for a moment. I lift my foot and slam it down with as much force as I can muster on the instep of his foot. He releases an inhuman growl as he stumbles, leaning over and grabbing his foot. I reach behind me, grab my lamp off my nightstand, and smash the metal base into his head, watching him fall to the ground where he lies still. He's out, but probably not for long, given his thick skull.

My heart is pounding out of my chest. I've never hurt another person before. But as I remember the pleasure on Cain's face all those years ago when he beat me with a rod, any guilt I feel evaporates. I grab my robe, throw it on, and pull the hood over my head. After snatching the keys off of Cain's limp form, I retrieve my pillowcase of supplies and quickly head out the door, closing it behind me and locking it.

Having lived here so long, I know all the mostly abandoned paths and halls, and I stick to the shadows, walking calmly and unhurried. I see monks in the distance, but no one passes me directly. One of the perks of playing the part I have so well for so long is that I have begun to fade into the background of this place. No one expects anything like this from me, except maybe Tavarious.

There's one thing I must do before I go. I swiftly make my way down to the kitchen. The stillness unsettles me as I quietly enter the sleeping quarters adjacent to the kitchen, knowing Dee will be hiding out in there. Her cot is in the very back, and she stands in shock when she sees the urgency in my approach. I reach toward her, but she pulls back, vehemently shaking her head *no*. I step closer, but she quickly sits on the cot and scrambles back so she's pressed against the wall.

"Dee, you need to come with me," I whisper. "I am leaving, and we need to hurry. We can get out of here together." I hold out my hand to her, willing her to take it.

But all she does is shake her head repeatedly *no* and gestures with her hand for me to go. A frenzied look in her eyes.

"I know the unknown is scary, but we can't stay here. You don't have to be afraid—we can leave together. But we must go now."

She keeps shaking her head. Her eyes are almost unseeing now, as though she's been lost to a memory that keeps her chained. My heart sinks as I realize she would rather stay here, living in the familiarity of fear, than to grasp for the freedom I am offering her. Surely anything would be better than staying here. If I had time, I would try to persuade her and insist she come with me, but I am already wasting too much time being here now.

"Okay, okay, I won't push, but I won't forget you're here either. Someday, Dee, I'll see you again." I take one last look at her, her body pressed into the wall, her eyes closed, and the glimmer of what looks like a tear sliding down her cheek. With that image and promise to her in my heart, I flee.

Using the keys I stole from Cain, I unlock the padlock on one of the rear exits that faces the steep mountain incline and bolt to the tree line. There are no guards or real security other than the lock. Part of the strategy for the ashram being way up here is the natural protection offered. This mountain has been known to chew people up and spit them out—the altitude, terrain, and weather exist only in extremes. You'd have to be desperate or crazy to tackle the mountain without equipment or training.

Right now, I am both of those things. I need to get as far away as possible, as quickly as I can before Cain wakes up. I originally planned on sneaking out without notice, so I would have hours before I was missed. Now, I'll be lucky if they don't already know I am gone.

But they will expect me to take the safe road down the mountain, as the weak, naive girl they believe me to be. So I will go up the harsh terrain and around instead, keeping above the tree line, but not high enough to be seen. Then I can make my way down the other side.

Remembering the note from Aunt Sid, strength rises in me and I stamp down the fear. The restlessness I've been living with for years is finally gone, which is how I know I am on the right path.

Striding forward, I start the long journey to freedom. And for the first time in a very long time, I have hope that the future I envision for myself is not just a dream.

CHAPTER 8

LUCIA

I make my way quickly, breathing heavily in the high altitude, my lungs burning from a lack of this type of exertion. My heart has not stopped pounding for the last hour. The thundering in my blood makes my hands shake. It's a miracle I've made it this long.

On the other side of the ridge, the dense forest gives way to thin, white aspen trees. Their small, round leaves are a gentle wind chime, welcoming me to the other side of the mountain.

My legs feel like rubber, but I keep pushing forward. Pockets of snow add an element of challenge to this already difficult trek. I am determined not to stop until I am a good distance from this mountain. But it's already late afternoon, and the rapidly cooling air indicates night is just around the corner.

Reaching a big boulder with some good cover, I decide to sit behind it for just a moment, catching my breath and drinking some water. In the distance, the whinny of a horse and the faint sound of horse hooves pulls me from any rest. My heart falters. Still hiding behind the boulder, I contemplate staying put or trying to run. If I stay here, they will probably find me—this is not exactly a stealthy spot. But if I run in the opposite direction of the horses, I might be able to stay ahead of them, especially if I keep off the trail.

Mustering myself, I stand and move as swiftly and as quietly as I can away from the noise. Up ahead a clearing appears—there's no shrubbery to hide behind. Only tall grass and, in the distance, another tree line. But I can't go around; it's as if the forest abruptly stopped growing and was replaced with hay-like, golden grass.

I look around to ensure I am still alone and mentally prepare myself for the nakedness of being out in the open; then I bolt. Halfway across the field, I glance back to see the horses just making their way around the tree line from my right side. The telltale dark brown robes have my stomach plummeting. This is the perfect terrain for them to reach a full gallop. They'll be on me in no time. But I can't go back; I won't. I have only one option before me.

With single-minded determination, I run as if my life depends on it.

They're gaining on me, but I am almost to the tree line. Just a little bit further and they will no longer be able to follow on horseback. My lungs burn as if a living flame is in my chest and my legs threaten to give out, but I keep pushing my body. The safety of the tree line beckons like the arms of a long-lost love. Just as I feel the shade start to envelop me, the wind is knocked from my lungs as something launches into my back, knocking me to the ground.

We roll a few feet, miraculously missing the trees before we come to halt. The monk that tackled me flips me onto my back, pinning me beneath him. I recognize his face as one of the monks that idolizes Cain, following him around like a puppy seeking attention. His eyes hungrily rove over me as I struggle beneath him. He slaps me so hard across my face that my teeth rattle.

"Enough!" he screams in my face, spittle spraying my cheek. "Apparently the cat's well out of the bag now, so looks like I get to be the first one to break you in."

His words are like ice water poured over me. I renew my struggle with vigor. Grabbing my dress at the neckline, he tears it, exposing some of my chest to the chilled air while simultaneously trying to pull the hem up around my waist. He's all arms and clammy fingers ripping and pulling at me, as eager and feral delight pour from him, saturating the air. His filthy anticipation threatens to choke me.

This can't be happening. I scream, though I know there's no one around to help me. I kick and punch and fight his hands, desperate to stop him. Tears escape out of the corners of my eyes as desperation paves the way to despair.

Then, all of a sudden, he is thrown off me, as if plucked into the air by an invisible force.

Grabbing the torn pieces of my dress and holding them over my chest, I sit up to see the monk's prone form on the ground, an ax protruding from his chest. As if in slow motion, I turn to see a huge, muscular man, cast in shadows, his figure backlit by the setting sun. He emerges from the dense forest like an avenging dark angel. His thick, dark, windblown hair curls at the nape of his neck, falling slightly forward, brushing against dark brows and strong cheek-bones. Piercing, crystal-blue eyes that seem to glow focus on the scene in front of him.

He's shirtless for some reason; his body is smooth and strikingly chiseled, as if he's been perfectly sculpted by the hand of Elohim Himself. His pants gloved strong, thick legs, highlighting his muscular structure. He is built like a warrior and cuts a striking figure that steals the breath from my lungs.

My gaze travels back up to his eyes, by far his most captivating feature.

He strides confidently forward, menace seemingly bleeding from his pores. The broad shoulders, strong expanse of his muscular chest, and piercing eyes seem almost otherworldly. But the scowl on his face and the realization that this man just killed a monk with an ax jars me from my frozen state. My heart thunders in my chest as I stumble to my unsteady feet, holding my ravaged dress in place. I take a step back, away from him, and pause as a wave of dizziness washes over me. Looking down, I notice a dark, wet stain covers the side of my dress.

Swaying on my feet, I reach a hand out, as if to steady myself. I lift my gaze to the stranger, whose eyes are like the sharp gaze of a predator. The piercing blue grabs hold of me right before everything goes dark.

CHAPTER 9

NICANOR

I barely make it to the girl before she hits the ground, catching her up in my arms. The strange smell of strawberries surrounds her. Thankfully, the other monk saw me throw the ax at his partner and fled like the coward he is. Starting the walk back to the cabin, her soft form in my arms, my mind goes back to the rage that filled me at the scene I stumbled upon. It was fortunate I was out cutting firewood and overheard the struggle. Never in my life has such a murderous desire consumed me. My reaction has me unsettled, and even more so because I can still feel the anger simmering below the surface of my calm.

There's something about this girl that calls to me. When she stood there, her hair disheveled, dress torn and gaping, a hand reaching out for me, a protective rage filled me, the likes of which I never before experienced. Her eyes, a stunning golden hue like the afternoon sun, locked on mine, and I saw the sad acceptance of death. But layered underneath was the indignant fury and determination of someone who would not go down without a fight. Someone who had probably been fighting in some manner for a long time.

Something in her spirit connected deep within me, in a way I didn't think was possible. If I'm being honest, it scares me. Scares me because of who she is and what she means to this world. Despite where she came from, here is a girl that refuses to be conquered. Any doubt I had that this was the girl that Elias sent me to retrieve slips away. I'm amazed that somehow she found her way to me first.

I try not to jostle her as I make my way around dense shrubbery and over felled trees, her long, dark chocolate hair, like silk against my arm, swaying as I walk. She must have hit her head hard when the monk tackled her, and the fear and adrenaline got the best of her when she stood so quickly. Thankfully, the stain is not blood as I first feared, but some sort of strawberry-flavored goo. I smirk at the random discovery. I will probably forever associate the smell of strawberries with this sun-kissed, dark-haired beauty in my arms.

My smirk fades, quickly replaced by dismay at the thought.

A soft sigh escapes her pink lips as she reaches a hand up to my bare chest, resting her palm over my heart, her eyes remain closed. The innocent action burns away any defense I had in place and sends a shudder racking through me. An internal battle wages within me, and I fight to regain my sense of control. What is happening to me? There is something about her. It has to be because of what she is. Yes, that's the reason I am reacting to her this way. She's a symbol of hope, touched by Elohim. Anyone would respond this way to her.

Finally reaching the cabin, I kick open the door and gently lay her down on the bed. Though I am loath to let her leave my arms, she'll probably wake feeling safer and less confused on the bed. And I definitely need to distance myself from her. I carefully lay a blanket over her, covering the torn dress and exposed skin.

Running a hand through my hair, my mind runs through the day's events again. I quickly conclude that we can't stay here. I can easily deal with the normal monks, but the warrior monks known as the Silent might be pushing it, especially with my focus pulled to keeping this girl safe. Somehow, I need to wake her and convince her to come with me. Elias warned me about handling her with care, or she'll want to run from me. Trust will be a hard thing to earn, given where she's lived the past few years. Handling things gently is not one of my skills. But maybe Adira can do what I can't and give this girl enough of a feeling of peace to come with me.

I head outside to call Adira, and to clear my head while the girl is still out. With her formidable size, she's an imposing horse, but with her snow-white coat and mane that almost glistens, she's absolutely magnificent. I've always cherished the connection I have with her, and caring for her has been my great joy these past years. She senses what I am thinking; no words need to be spoken. I place my forehead against Adira's, stroking her jaw. She whinnies gently.

I try to calm the whirlwind of tumultuous thoughts. This is the girl that Elias has spoken of nonstop for years. One of four vital Cores that will save the Horsemen from being leashed by Hell, thus preventing the destruction of the world. Elias said she might know of the prophecy, but she was taken young, so there's no way to know how much she remembers. What's certain is that she is destined to love a Horseman.

I was chosen to get her back to The Refuge safely and quickly because of my familiarity with these mountains, and probably the restlessness that's always seemed to burn in my blood. I'll do my duty as I always do, and then wash my hands of this whole thing and focus on my job and the tasks ahead of me. After all, I am the only one who can.

I give Adira one last pat and head back to the cabin, troubled by the eagerness I feel. I tell myself it's just because I want to make sure the girl is okay, not because I want to see those golden eyes stare up at me again.

CHAPTER 10

My head aches. I slowly open my eyes to the dancing of glitter-like dust in the golden sunlight streaming through the hazy windows. The scent of fresh-cut pine fills the air.

Where am I? I clearly didn't die as I thought I would. Taking in my surroundings, I doubt Heaven would resemble a dusty wood cabin. Someone laid me on a bed and covered me with a blanket. I sit up slowly, and the blanket pools around my waist, cool air brushing across the skin of my chest. I gasp and pull the blanket up; I almost forgot about the torn dress. What almost happened to me before Mr. Tall, Dark, and Devastatingly Handsome came to my rescue.

As if my thoughts summoned him, the front door opens and he walks in. I am caught off guard by the small thrill that shoots through me at seeing him again. His very presence commands and consumes the space.

He pauses when he sees me sitting up. He looks a bit surprised as he says, "How are you feeling?"

"Um, okay I guess. Where am I?"

Moving further into the cabin, he heads to a dresser with his back to me. "You're in my cabin. You passed out and I carried you here. I was worried you were injured. Thankfully, that's not actually blood on your dress." He turns to look at me, a half-grin on his face that makes my heart skip. "The strawberry smell gave it away pretty quick."

"Oh, uh, yeah, I had a jar of strawberry jam in my dress pocket. It must have broken when that creep tackled me." Trying to shove down the memory of what happened and suddenly feeling vulnerable, I sweep my legs off the bed and stand, wanting to get my bearings.

"Whoa, take it easy." His hand reaches out to steady me. "You were out for a while. And as much as I like playing the hero and catching fainting maidens in my arms, we need to get out of here before the monks come back."

I glance down at his hand on my arm, the warmth soothing me and confusing me all at once. He must notice my glance because he lets go.

We? His words register in my foggy mind. "Wait, I...I don't know you." I stumble over my words. "I can't go with you. I've already inconvenienced you enough. If you could just spare a shirt maybe, I'll be on my way and out of your hair."

One eyebrow lifts as he looks at me. "So you're just going to wander through the woods in nothing but one of my T-shirts, smelling of strawberries, attracting all manner of creatures that will see you as a delicious snack, and hope the monks don't stumble upon you again?"

A flash of annoyance at his mocking tone heats my blood. "I am not an idiot. I have a friend that will be able to find me, and she can help me make my way home."

He throws his hands up in mock surrender. "And this home you're going to is nearby? Hidden from the monks? And where is this friend? How long until she reaches you?"

Ugh, all valid points. Not that I'll tell him that and give him more ammunition to treat me like a child. I blame the knock on the head and unconscious spell for my inability to think logically. Truth is, I didn't actually plan much past getting away from the ashram; my focus was completely on escaping.

But I don't know if I can trust this man. And it's disconcerting how easily he seems to be able to elicit such strong emotions from me when I lived the last almost nine years becoming a master of masking my reactions. What if I just traded one enemy for another?

"Look," I begin, "I appreciate your concern and your help earlier, but it's really not your problem. If you could please just provide me a change of clothes and some water, I promise to return them after I reach my destination."

Considering me for a moment, he tilts his head and those blue eyes hone in on me further. "I doubt I have anything that fits you appropriately, but I am willing to help you however I can."

"Great, I think—"

"If you allow me to get you to your destination safely," he interrupts, that sly smirk on his face again. "I have a horse and can get you there much faster. And I can ensure you arrive safely as well. Then you won't need to make your way back to my cabin to return the clothes either. It's the most logical solution."

I weigh his words. I've never had a habit of fiddling with things before, but notice myself doing it more and more as I talk with this man. Maybe it's a product of finally being able to make my own decisions, and the uncertainty and unfamiliarity associated with that freedom. But a small voice whispers to me that it's more about the man in front of me. It's as if my fingers are grasping for something to hold, something to steady me. But it is to no avail, I'm like a sparrow caught in a wind storm, plummeting from the sky.

His face takes on a more serious expression. He drops to one knee before me, placing a hand over his heart. His head bows as he says, "I vow no harm will come to you. I vow to protect you with my life and get you safely to your destination."

Rendered speechless, I just stare at his bowed head with wide eyes, my jaw hanging open.

He peeks up at me from under dark hair and lashes. "This is where you say 'I accept.'" He winks.

"Uh, okay?" I say hesitantly, still shocked. Who *is* this guy?

"I'll take it." He jumps to his feet. "I'll get Adira ready for the journey. Here's a T-shirt and some sweatpants you might be able to make work for you. I'll be outside if you need me." He turns to leave.

I wait until his footsteps fade before eagerly tearing off the only clothing item I've known for almost nine years. I wish we had time to burn it. Watching it turn to ash would be so cathartic, but the smoke would probably act as a beacon to the monks. As I put on the soft, oversized T-shirt and cozy sweatpants, I am overcome with emotions.

I actually did it. I am free. This isn't a dream.

I take a deep, shuddering breath to calm my erratic heart as unsolicited tears pour down my face in a desperate attempt to wash the last nine years away.

Standing here, holding the too-big pants in place with tears rolling down my face, I hear a quick knock and the door opens before I can respond. He stands there, a muscle ticking in his jaw as his eyes take me in. For the first time, he seems unsure of himself. I sense this is unchartered territory for him.

"I'm fine," I mutter through the tears, attempting to erase his hesitant expression. "The reality of everything just hit me suddenly."

His face softens in understanding. Then he walks up to me slowly, like I'm a wild horse about to spook. He has a small rope in his hand and he gestures to my hands tightly gripping the sweatpants.

"I figured you'd be fighting gravity with my pants, so I brought a solution." He gives me a soft smile.

He holds the rope out to me, so I take it. But unsure what he wants me to do with it, and my mind still a muddled mess from everything that's happened, I just stand there rooted to the spot like an ancient oak tree. He must see the confusion on my face because he decides to take mercy on me.

"May I help?"

I nod. Before I even have a moment to think, he is almost chest-to-chest with me. His hands at my waist with the rope. My heart begins racing as his arms wind around me, pulling the rope tight and tying a knot at my back. He is everywhere, consuming all of my senses as his lips brush past my ear, his breath on my neck. He pulls the rope into place, his nimble hands working to wrap the band of the pants over it, his fingers grazing my skin, sending shivers everywhere.

Heat floods my face and a different kind of heat that doesn't just flush my skin begins to burn its way through my blood. As he moves, my nose and lips brush the base of his neck and I feel his body stiffen. All the sensations make me light-headed as he finally steps back.

"All done." His voice is husky and uneven, and his eyes seem brighter. My thoughts are oddly slow, as if coming out of a dream. My skin feels hyper-sensitive. I watch him turn to the door.

"Wait!" I blurt, realizing I don't even know his name. "Thank you for your help..."

"Nic Cascus," he says, his voice rough.

"Thank you for your help, Nic. My name is Lu." I use the nickname Aunt Sid gave me as a child.

"Nice to meet you, Lu." He quickly leaves. And I get the strange sense that something momentous has just occurred. That this day will not be a day easily lost to the recesses of my memory.

CHAPTER 11

LUCIA

Gathering my meager supplies in the now dirty pillowcase, I head outside. I stop abruptly, stunned by the imposing and majestic creature before me. Calling this animal a horse is an understatement. By far the biggest animal I've ever seen, with hair so white it almost appears to glow. Its mane is long and similar feathery hair coats its lower legs. Its eyes are a breathtaking kaleidoscope of blue. I am struck by the sight of it and its otherness, but more than that, it reminds me of the horse from my dreams.

"Lu meet Adira, first lady in my life," Nic says with pride from beside her. Hidden by her massive frame, I only see his head peek under her neck.

"She's incredible!" I say honestly. "Can I touch her?"

I've always loved animals. They're more honest than people. Incapable of deceit, and pure of heart.

"Yes, she would love that. This girl loves to be pampered."

I bring my hand up slowly as she lowers her muzzle. I

gently rub her soft, velvety nose. She nickers as she gently pushes her head into my chest.

I bring my hand around to her neck. "Aren't you just the most beautiful thing this world has ever known?" Lost in the feel of her thick, soft mane and coat, something in me calms, instantly soothed by the contact with her.

"All ready?" Nic asks.

I nod in response.

"If it's okay, I'll lift you up so you can get your leg over Adira. She's a big girl."

I nod again.

His warm hands gently grasp my waist, easily lifting me into the air as I throw my leg over the massive animal. With no saddle to grab onto, I drop my supplies as I put both hands on either side of her, laying on my stomach against her back for stability. I was a child the last time I was on a horse, and never one as big as Adira.

"You okay?" Nic asks, humor in his eyes. "Once I get up there, you'll have something to hang onto. I promise not to let you fall off."

Somehow the thought of my arms intimately wrapped around Nic, my chest pressed against his back, does little to comfort me. A shiver of nerves coils its way down my spine as my stomach dips with hesitancy and a touch of excitement that surprises me.

I nod again. Apparently, I am incapable of speech around him. Annoyed with myself and unwilling to be some simpering damsel, I croak out, "I'm good."

This time he nods, with a knowing smile on his face. Nic secures our meager supplies, including my pathetic and dirty pillowcase, to some sort of leather harness he expertly secures over Adira. Then he pulls himself onto her back with the practiced ease of someone who's done it a thousand times, and settles in front of me. He pushes Adira forward at a slow walk. Not wanting to seem too desperate, I reach up slowly and grab the sides of his shirt, trying to keep a healthy distance between us. But I am intimately aware of every point of contact our bodies share.

After some time, Nic breaks the silence. "So, this friend of yours, you said she would find you. Do you have an agreed-upon meeting place?"

"No, she gifted me this bracelet that has a tracker in it," I say, sliding my arm through his arm to show him. "I wasn't able to contact her before I left, but she checks it periodically. She'll find me, I know it."

"And who is this resourceful friend of yours who has tracking technology?"

"It's not really her technology. She's a member of the Feminea Potentia and—"

Before I even finish my sentence, he grabs the hand-carved wooden bracelet given to me by my only friend and crushes it in his fist. I bite down on an exclamation.

"I am sorry Lu, but it's too dangerous to have someone capable of tracking you right now. Especially someone affiliated with the FP."

Ice chills my blood as I loosen my hold on his shirt. There's not much I can do from the back of a horse. But I know this; someone who doesn't want me tracked by a friend is not someone I can trust. I can only imagine all the nefarious reasons why he would want me untraceable to a friend. Weighing my options and knowing the best one is probably going to hurt from this high up, I shift my weight and swing my leg over as quickly as I can. I slide off Adira, absorbing the painful shock with my knees. I take off running through the woods, praying Nic can't follow the narrow, wooded path with Adira.

Branches whip at my face and arms, leaving stinging cuts in their wake. What feels like skeletal hands tear at the oversized sweatpants, but I keep going, pushing myself harder. Seeing an old log up ahead, I easily jump over it, crashing through a giant bush on the other side. But instead of my feet hitting solid ground, there is nothing but open air beneath me.

Fear turns my blood cold as I start to drop into what will surely be my death. But then a big hand grabs hold of my wrist, plucking me right out of thin air and slamming me up against a wall of muscle, before we fall back onto solid ground.

I lie there for a minute with my eyes closed, stunned and trying to get my rapid breathing under control after yet another near-death experience. The roar of adrenaline rages through me. Slowly calming, I feel warmth radiating from the solid ground beneath me, a soothing motion gently drawing soft circles against my low back.

Wait, warm ground? Soothing circles? I lift my head to get my bearings and my eyes lock onto crystal blue ones. A smirk spreads across a too-handsome face.

"Best fall on hard ground I've ever had." Nic winks at me.

Realizing he took the brunt of the fall, is the source of the warmth under me and soft circles being traced on my back, and not sure how to feel about the butterflies that are flittering about in my stomach, I try to push off him. But he holds fast to me, his expression turning serious, his eyes burning into mine.

"You are safe with me, Lu, despite what you may think. I know you don't trust me yet, but please give me a chance before you decide I am untrustworthy. I made a vow not to harm you and to protect you with my life, and I will do what it takes to stand by that. I am not saying your friend isn't safe, but there are things you don't know about the FP. It was a safer bet to destroy the bracelet, and for that, I'm sorry."

I sense his contrition. What he says makes some sense, but I also know Ansel. It's times like these that I wonder if I'm simply incapable of trust. Too much has happened in my life. Maybe the ability to trust is too lofty a goal for me. But still, I don't have many options and I suppose, for now, Nic is still my best bet. I could let him help me while still keeping my distance, right? I just need to keep my guard up, which really isn't hard for me. If anything, letting it down is the struggle.

"Plus, I did save your life twice." The intensity is once again gone, replaced with that easy, boyish grin.

My gaze dips to where my hands rest on his hard chest and heat floods my face. I've never been this close to a man before, and Tavarious manhandling me back at the ashram or the monk in the forest attacking me doesn't count. There is not an inch of space between Nic and me. And I am suddenly aware of all the places our bodies touch as I lie across him, our legs tangled, his hands like a brand firmly gripping my sides.

Impossibly, he must realize where my thoughts are because his eyes suddenly become hooded, a brightness to the blue that wasn't there before.

Feeling overwhelmed, I roll off him, instead of pushing off his chest, which feels far too intimate—if not rude. This time, he lets me go, his hands sliding along my hip as I move away from him.

Taking deep breaths, I stand and walk a few steps away as Nic gets up. I'm a little freaked out by how unsettled he makes me. I mean, I spent the last nine years as the lone woman among a bunch of male monks. But any contact with Nic feels wholly different, as if he pierces the deepest parts of me with a simple word or a look, busting through my protective defenses like a bull through a gate.

And the most disconcerting part is I don't even think he's trying. It's unintentional, like a natural chemical reaction, and that scares me more than anything.

CHAPTER 12

I feel supercharged. Like I was struck by lightning and instead of it destroying me, I absorbed its power and it now flows through my veins. This close contact with her, the smell of her surrounding me as those golden eyes stare at me —it awakens something in me. It's as if a power was dormant inside me and now it's alive and all-encompassing, filling my once hollow chest.

But when I look in her eyes, all I see is distrust and my heart aches with the knowledge. I don't know what her life has been like, but I can only imagine given all the years she's been with the Amilign. That thought threatens to ignite a rage in me. Somehow I need to soothe her fears and earn her trust, if I am to get her to come with me to The Refuge of the Prophets. I don't know how much she knows about the prophecy and her possible role in it. She thinks I am a random stranger who wants to help her, but at this point, confessing who I actually am, her possible role, and that I was coming for her before she found me might just add to her fear and make her run again.

Ugh, if only Elias were here. He's so much better at this stuff than I am. I'm tempted to throw her over my shoulder and just hightail it there, but Elias warned me that the damage done by that kind of action would be irreversible. I already destroyed some of her trust when I crushed the bracelet without first explaining myself.

Maybe I shouldn't care—it's not for me to worry about, really. I only need to get her there safely. But there's something about her that calls to me. Calls me to protect her and care for her. It has to be what she is. It would be the same for anyone in her presence.

"Nic," I hear her voice drown out my thoughts. "I need to get to my Aunt's house. It's where I grew up as a child. I don't know exactly where it is, but it was somewhat close to a small town in The Range called South Como. Maybe we could start there?"

There's no way I am taking her anywhere but to the Prophets, but somehow I have to get her on board with this plan. Hoping I can gently guide her to the necessary outcome with some questions, I ask, "What about these men you were running from? Do you expect them to continue to pursue you? Would they know about this location?"

I see it on her face when the implications of my words register. A small crack in her composure leaks despair and hopelessness. She doesn't answer me.

"Listen, Lu, I have an idea that will help us figure out how to either get you home or find whomever you're looking for. I have some friends who live in a hidden sanctuary. They are trustworthy and have the means to locate things and people, and I know they can help us. As of right now, it's our safest and best bet, especially if those monks will still be hunting you."

Her barriers come up; she's like a statue as she weighs my words. Trust does not come easy to her. But I can't blame her. She's had no reason to trust in her short life. But she seems to realize she's out of options and, despite her hesitancy, I see her spine lengthen in resolution as she decides.

"Okay, I will go with you, but only because you've left me no other option when you destroyed my bracelet."

Ignoring that last comment, I grab my pack. "The terrain is a little rough, but there will be some good caves we can camp in along the way. Just stay close—there are wild mountain cats and wolves in this area." I didn't need to add that last part, but anything that keeps her from running again is a good idea. I rummage through my pack for a spare T-shirt, since the one I'm wearing is covered in mud from the fall.

I take off the muddy shirt, shaking it out to put in my pack to clean later when I feel the soft, warm caress of fingers between my shoulder blades. A tremble ripples through me at her touch, and I suppress the moan that's fighting to be loosed.

"What does your tattoo mean?" Genuine curiosity colors her words. Her finger continues its ministrations, naive to her effect on me. Like an exquisite kind of torture, I feel her breath against my skin as if it were silk. My heart is beating like a drum in my chest, my fists clenching and unclenching around the muddy shirt, desperate to get this storm inside me under control.

My breath comes in rough bursts; I cough to clear what will surely be a gravelly voice. "Uh, it's a bit hard to explain. I guess the easiest way to describe it is that it represents my identity and purpose. I like to think of it as an outward expression of who I am on the inside."

"What language is this?"

Answering her is the ultimate test of my focus when my mind is clinging to the feel of her skin on mine and the velvety sound of her voice.

"It's the heavenly language." My voice is rough. "It roughly translates, 'I am he who conquers all.'"

"And is this a horse hoof?"

"Good eye; it is. That's what I do...I work with horses."

"Ah, the conquer thing makes sense then." Her hand drops away.

I am all at once relieved and desperate for her touch again. Unable, or maybe unwilling, to analyze that need, I shove it into the recesses of my mind.

"It's beautiful," she says softly.

I quickly don a shirt, taking deep breaths to try and center the turbulent storm in my chest as I turn toward her.

"Speaking of horses, where's Adira?" she says suddenly, looking around.

"She won't be able to follow us where we're going; the terrain is too intense."

"But you just said there are predators out here. We can't just leave her. Can't we take a different path to this place where we can bring her?"

Her concern for Adira just endears me to her more. "Trust me, she'll be fine. She's super resourceful and tough. She's trained to find us or head home. She'll probably meet us at The Refuge."

Hoping that's enough to soothe her fears, I head down the path, eager to get some distance to clear my head and calm the pounding of my heart. It's shaping up to be a challenging journey in more ways than one.

CHAPTER 13

LUCIA

After two fairly silent days of trying to keep some kind of barrier up between me and this intriguing man, pretending the travel through steep and tough terrain is cause enough for my focus and silence, Nic finally breaks the muted expanse between us.

"So, I've been thinking." A hint of amusement colors his tone. "We're going to be traveling together for a while, and it would probably be good to get to know one another, maybe feel more comfortable together. And talking might be better than days on end in silence."

I am still hesitant to trust him or share too much, but I'm beginning to wonder if that's a valid concern, or just a product of my trust issues. So far, he's given me no real reason to doubt him. But despite that, there's still a small voice in me urging caution. After all, I've only ever been given reason after reason not to trust, especially men.

Even so, I don't want my past to define me. I want to believe people can be different than what I've seen. And

Nic's been nothing but kind and helpful to me since we met. Only patient with my lack of athleticism and the snail-like pace I set as we trudge through this difficult terrain. By the look of him, this is his natural environment; he makes everything look easy. I envy the confidence with which he guides us.

"Well," I start, "there's not much to share. I grew up in a small house in a valley near a lake with my Aunt Sid. We didn't have much but we had this incredible garden to grow our own food, and a few animals like chickens and a goat. That's where all my fondest memories come from." I walk forward, my eyes on the trail in front of me, close enough to Nic to smell his uniquely enticing scent of mint and rain. It helps me stay in the here and now, preventing the memories and questions of the past from rising to the surface, reopening old wounds.

"How did you end up in the mountains, running from monks?" he asks.

I hesitate, but it's pointless to be cagey; he obviously saw what happened. "I was taken to live with the Amilign at the age of ten. I decided it wasn't the path I wanted for my life, so I left. Clearly, they disagreed."

I almost run into him as he stops in front of me. Turning around, his wide eyes connect with mine. "How old are you now?"

Hating the intensity and perceptiveness in his gaze, I answer as nonchalantly as I can muster. "I'm about to turn nineteen." My gaze fixes on the dirt I am kicking intently with my foot. I'm uninterested in seeing the pity on his face.

"You lived with those degenerates for almost nine years?" he says in shock. "How did you manage all that time?"

He clearly knows more about the Amilign than most,

and seeing as they are meticulous about the image they portray publicly, that's surprising. Apprehensive of the judgment I am sure to receive for the way I chose to survive, I hesitate. It wasn't tough and brave in the traditional sense. I am not the warrior type he so clearly is. But I refuse to cower to men any longer. I've spent too much of my life forced into a mask of what was expected of me. Now that I am finally free of that world, I'll be damned if I am going to fall back into those toxic patterns that were slowly killing me.

I boldly lift my eyes to his. "At first, they were good at hiding the evil lurking beneath the surface, and I was just a child. As I got older, I began to see through the illusion, but quickly learned that if I wanted any semblance of peace in that place, I would need to be who they expected me to be. Their methods of punishing disobedience or noncompliance are a special form of hell, designed to wipe a person of their will."

My lips thin as a kernel of anger takes root, mingling with the lingering residue of shame. "So I bided my time, wore the proverbial mask I loathed, and dreamed and hoped for a day my life would change." I hold my chin high in challenge.

A muscle ticks in his jaw as his eyes fix on mine. A flash of something across his face—concern or outrage? "I am sorry for what you went through, Lu. You don't owe me any explanations. I shouldn't have asked. We do what we must to survive in hard circumstances, and nobody can judge you for that. But for what it's worth, I think you're incredibly resilient and brave. I don't think I could have survived for so long."

Shocked by his response, I just stare at him. He hands me his canteen of water as he continues, saving me from responding further, "Okay, my turn. What do you want to know?"

With just a few words from him, I feel the wall I've placed between us start to crack and shift, as though it were built on sinking sand. Trying to shore it up, I decide not to think about what his words and proximity do to me, instead trying to focus on what I want to know about him.

"Why were you shirtless in the woods?" The question is out of my mouth before my dumb brain can stop and filter it. My face instantly floods with heat, probably turning a bright red if I could see myself.

I inwardly cringe, but then his laugh catches me off guard. I've never heard his laugh. Deep and rich like melted chocolate, it rumbles through me all the way to the tips of my toes. I smile.

"Of all the questions you could ask me," he says with a smile. "You are an intriguing girl, Lu. I was shirtless because I was chopping wood, and that's hard work that makes me sweat. Taking a shirt off is far easier than doing laundry." That boyish grin makes a reappearance.

"Uh, I don't know why I asked that. It was just the first thing that popped into my head, I guess."

His eyebrows rise. If my face wasn't red before, it definitely is now. I stand there, wishing the earth would open up and swallow me whole.

"Thinking about my shirtless chest was the first thing to come to mind, huh?" He smirks, continuing down the trail. Clearly enjoying my discomfort.

"Ha-ha," I say with an eye roll. "Just seemed random to see a half-naked guy walking out of the woods. But I have a better question for you. You clearly know more about the Amilign than most. How did you come across such knowledge when they do a pretty thorough job of projecting a specific image and fooling most of the world?"

"You know those friends I told you about? Well, they are the main reason I know the monks are not what they seem to be. I have lived most of my whole life with them, so there's not a time when I didn't know what the Amilign were really about. Have you ever heard of the Prophets of The Way?"

Something pings at the back of my mind as though the name is familiar, but I can't quite grasp it. I shake my head, forgetting I am behind him. "No," I quickly say.

"Well, they are kind of the keepers of knowledge, scriptural and world historians if you will, and they'll be able to share more with you than you can possibly imagine. They're actually more like family to me."

Hearing the softness in his tone as he speaks of them, I envy him. It's been so long since I've felt the love of family. I'm surprised that I actually look forward to meeting these Prophets. Maybe they will know about this prophecy I was told about as a child and can shed some light on whether or not I am truly a part of it. If Nic has lived with them his whole life, he may know about it too.

But that small voice of doubt is back, and I wonder if it's too risky to share that kind of knowledge with him right now. Aunt Sid went to a lot of trouble to hide my identity as a kid and told me never to speak of it. I want to trust Nic, but my mind insists on walking me through all the scenarios of how I could come to regret that decision.

"We'll stop here for the night." Nic pulls me from my thoughts. "There's a small cave up ahead that will offer some shelter—it's only a short climb. I'm not liking the look of that sky. I'll get a fire going and make sure it's clear, if you want to rest here for a bit."

I nod and he takes off toward the cavern.

Looking at the orange, pink, and purple canvas of the distant horizon created by the setting sun, I sigh. I don't know what he's talking about—it's so beautiful. At that thought, a crack splits the sky and I tear my eyes away from the beautiful horizon, finally noticing the ominous, dark churning clouds directly above me. I find myself captivated by the movement of the angry sky. The freedom with which it swirls and rumbles, blocking out any stars, silencing all protests from the world around it. In this space, it dominates everything. And then it begins to open itself up.

At first, it feels like thick snowflakes, but then I realize they have more substance than that. Tiny, granule-like pieces of ice are falling from the sky. Hail, I believe it is, though I've not witnessed it myself, at least not since childhood. I hold my hand out as the little pieces of white ice fall and fill my palm. Not big enough to hurt, just amusing and intriguing. I hear a voice in the distance, but I am too captivated to be concerned.

Then suddenly, as if the sky senses my mockery of its power, the pieces of ice begin to shift and grow. It's not amusing anymore as I cover my head with my hands and pebble-like ice pelts me through the rainy, sleet mixture. Through my squinty eyes, I see Nic running down the hill toward me. I begin to make my way to him, slipping in the icy mud now coating the hillside, when another shift in this storm hits and I suddenly feel as if I am being stoned to death. This storm is trying to kill me.

I cry out as a hailstone hits me in the back. Another pelts one of the hands over my head, and as I pull it away, I see the glimmer of dark blood trickling down my fingers. I begin to curl my body over my injured hand, but another ice rock hits me square in the temple and the flow of hot fluid tells me it's not just rain. Before I can fully curl in on myself, I am wrapped in a thick leather covering and being hoisted into strong, sure arms. The warmth surrounding me instantly calms the panic vibrating in my veins, and I surrender to this alien feeling of safety.

The violent pelting dissipates, and I'm placed on my feet in a small, hollow cave with barely enough room to stand. The storm continues to rage on just beyond the overhang of the cave. Rain falls like a waterfall, giving the space we stand in an intimate feel. I sense Nic behind me and I slowly turn. My gaze absorbs him like a sponge. He's soaked to the bone, bits of ice in his dark hair, and those crystal blue eyes with their penetrating stare grab hold of me.

Then, without meaning to, my traitorous thoughts drift to the memory of the feel of his body underneath me, my hands splayed across his chest. His scent of mint and rain permeates the air around me. My face flushes at the heat now coursing through my blood. He stiffens, nostrils flaring as if he can read me like a book, clearly sensing my train of thought. Impossibly, his crystal blue eyes seem to brighten, almost glowing, and in the fading light, it's enthralling. He reaches out a hand, and I place my smaller hand in his as he guides me to a log.

"Sit and let me look at you." His rough voice sends a shiver down my back. I blame the cold. I watch as he grabs a cloth from his pack and gently grasps my chin to turn my head to the firelight. Ever so gently, he dabs at the blood leaking down the side of my face from my temple. I try to look anywhere but at him, but as his breath caresses my face and his scent surrounds me, I am captivated once again. He's completely focused on his ministrations, so I enjoy the rare opportunity to let my eyes drink their fill. He really is the most breathtaking man I've ever laid eyes on, even drenched. The blue of his eyes is a pool I could fall into endlessly.

"Looks like it's a pretty shallow cut. Head wounds are just big bleeders, and that hail hit you just right." His hand leaves my face and I immediately miss the warmth of his touch, which elicits all sorts of questions from my mind.

"Are you okay? You look a bit stunned."

Another piece of my barrier breaks off at his concern.

"I suppose I am. A bit stunned that is. I wasn't expecting that onslaught, and it happened so fast."

"Yeah, those storms come out of nowhere sometimes, and they can change in an instant, causing flash floods and wreaking all sorts of havoc. We're lucky this cave was nearby."

The onslaught continues to rage just outside our small cave, and despite the fire, a shiver violently rips through my limbs. My eyes connect with Nic's over the small fire.

"You wouldn't happen to have a change of clothes, would you?" I sit on the log in my soaking garments, knowing I could never get close enough to the flames to warm up with these wrapped around me.

Nic's wince at my question tells me all I need to know. "Unfortunately, I dropped our packs at the entrance of the cave when I went to make sure it was empty, and they weren't completely out of the way of the storm." He lifts the packs from the small pool of water that has collected around them. He begins pulling items from the soaking pack and laying them out across the dead branches of the log.

"Good news is the bed roll seems fairly dry. So you could put your clothes out to dry by the fire and wrap yourself in the bedroll in the meantime."

My stomach bottoms out at the thought of sitting in my underwear under a blanket with Nic so close. Even though

Nic has been so much more than what I expect from men, and has just risked himself to help me—again—that level of vulnerability isn't something I am ready to experience. Just being in close proximity to him is unsettling enough. I need more barriers between us, not less.

"I'm not that cold, and you built a good fire. I'm sure I'll dry out in no time." And I do my best to believe those words as I sit on the log, trying not to think about how cold I really am.

CHAPTER 14

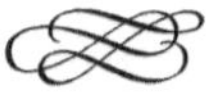

The sky rages all night long. Despite my exhaustion from the journey so far, the effort of trying to keep some semblance of a barrier up between us, and being pelted by ice chunks, the soggy cold of my clothes prevents me from getting even a moment's rest. Instead, I sit on the ground, leaning against the log, my mind replaying all the events of the past few days of my life. Nic sits opposite me, leaning against the cave wall and staring out at the storm.

At some point, the sky begins to shift from darkness to a murky grey to let us know that day has arrived, but the storm rages on.

"Look, Lu," Nic says, "We're going to be stuck here for at least today, it seems. We might as well rest. We both need it. And that is not going to happen if you are soaking wet. It looks like this spare T-shirt is finally dry. You can change into it while your sweatpants dry out, and wrap yourself in the blanket to stay warm. We'll be lucky if this fire lasts another hour, so we should try to get your stuff dry now. We won't be finding dry firewood anytime soon."

I weigh his words and know he is right; survival is what's most important right now. The last thing we need is for me to get sick. I murmur a quiet "Okay."

Nic stands, taking the bed roll to face the opening of the cave. He holds the bed roll across his back from his raised hands, effectively blocking the entrance and any possibility that he might be able to see me. Something bright opens up within me at his thoughtfulness. I quickly tear off my sopping wet shirt and put on the warm, dry one that hangs near the fire. It's so soothing, it makes me question the sanity of waiting so long to switch.

Luckily, the shirt hangs down to my mid-thigh, so I'm well covered. I take the sweatpants off and hang them on the branch nearest the shrinking flames. Hopefully, they will get enough time to dry out before I need to wear them again. All the while, Nic stands stoically in place, holding the bed roll up across his back. I walk up to him and tap his shoulder. He lowers the blanket, still not turning. I grab the edges and wrap myself up in its warmth.

When he finally turns, he is so close, his intoxicating scent makes me light-headed. He must see the daze in my eyes, because concern shines back from his blue gaze.

"Come, lay down and get some rest."

"What about you?"

"I'm not tired. I'll try to keep the fire going as long as possible."

I lie down near my log and it's only a few moments before I am carried away to a dream of open fields, warm sun, and a cute farmhouse. I walk through fields of tall grass that tickle my outstretched hands while the sun's warmth beats down on my face. Closer and closer I get to the place

I've always considered home. Then the sun suddenly disappears, the sky darkens, and I am thrown to my back. Hands grab at me, and the brown-robed monk that tackled me in the woods is back, fighting me—and winning. I struggle and fight, but the more I struggle, the more he wins.

"Lu!" The firmness of the tone pulls me from the nightmare, and I sit up quickly, realizing I have been grappling with the bed roll. The fire is out, and a chill runs down my spine when I realize I am no longer safely contained in the bedroll. My bare legs sprout goosebumps in the open air as I breathe heavily, my pulse hammering away.

Nic kneels in front of me, his concerned gaze absorbing every inch of me.

"It was just a dream, it was just a dream," I whisper softly on repeat.

Nic stands in agitation, his hand scraping through his hair as he paces the small space in front of us. His presence seems to suck all the oxygen out of the atmosphere around him.

"Nic?"

"Sorry, I just...I want to fix this for you, yet there's nothing I can do. It's frustrating."

His words do funny things to me—things that I can't focus on. My mind moves to something he *can* help me with.

"I'm hungry, Nic. Do we have any food?"

"Yes," he says, quickly, looking distracted. He gives me a meager meal of jerky and some dried fruit. "Do you want to talk about it?"

I barely hear his soft question over the rain. "Not much to talk about. It was just a nightmare about the monk who attacked me, and you took care of him."

He nods as he reaches into his pack and pulls out something so precious, I think I am still dreaming. He breaks the small brick of chocolate into smaller pieces and hands the bigger one to me with a wink and a smile. "I've been saving this, but I can't think of a better time to indulge."

We savor the chocolate, its kaleidoscope of rich flavors offering a welcome distraction.

The silence stretches on before Nic finally speaks. "I wish I found you before he did."

I feel another piece of my barrier fall away. "I'm just grateful you found me at all. I didn't expect any help. I can't think about what would have happened to me without you."

At these words, his eyes meet mine and something unspoken seems to come to life between us. Suddenly it feels as if the fire were still going strong in the tiny cave. I move my tongue along my lips, finding the residual sweetness of chocolate left behind. Nic stiffens at the action. Painstakingly, he tears his gaze away and rubs his hand through his messy hair.

It's then that I realize my bare legs are on display. I wrap the bed roll around me and check my pants. They are pretty dry now, if not a bit stiff from the mud I slipped in, but it will have to do. Nic needs rest too, and I can't hog the bed roll.

After slipping the sweatpants on under the bedroll and securing them in place, I hold the bed roll out to him. "Your turn."

He looks at me, one brow lifted. "I'd hardly call that restful sleep."

I shrug. He isn't wrong, I still feel bone tired.

"There's a pretty big spot here that's semi-smooth. We might be able to get some decent sleep, but we'll need to lay next to each other to share body heat now that we don't have a fire. There's no reason for both of us not to get rest."

He says this very matter-of-factly, but avoids eye contact with me as he shifts through his pack. Clearly, he's unsure of what my reaction will be.

And maybe I should hesitate more, but I want to trust him. Frankly, I am too tired to spend any of my tiny pool of rapidly depleting energy running through all the scenarios of how this could end badly if I don't remain on my guard. I ignore the fact that I'm drawn to this man and tell myself the real reason I am not hesitating is because it's cold right now and this is a matter of survival.

"That's great, thanks," I say.

His eyes meet mine with a quick flash of surprise and I'm secretly pleased to be responsible for it. He nods and smiles warmly.

Awkwardly getting into position on the ground, we finally find ourselves lying next to each other but not touching. Keeping a healthy distance I find reassuring and irritating at the same time, which I won't even begin to analyze. After some time, with no real blankets to cover us, the chilled mountain air seeps through the T-shirt and I start shivering. Trying not to wake him, I rub my arms, but that does nothing to warm me. Convinced I'll get no sleep, I lie there trying to prevent my teeth from chattering the way they want to when I feel a big hand reach around my waist and pull me back into his hard, warm chest.

"Lift your head," he says softly.

I do as he says and he slides his other arm, bent at the elbow, under my head, creating a soft, warm pillow. My heart squeezes at the unexpected gentleness and sweet nature of this man, something I have never before experienced. I wish it did more to ease the bitter cold biting into my limbs.

"I'm...f-freezing."

"Turn around, Lu. Press into me."

I quickly flip over, my teeth chattering and shoulders shaking. His hand grasps my wrist as he slides my fingers under his shirt, boldly pressing them to his warm stomach. He stiffens at my icy touch, but he doesn't pull away. Instead, his arm drapes around my shoulders, pulling me closer. I press my face into his neck, his warm skin slowly easing the chill in my bones.

A quiver rolls its way down my spine, taking up residence low in my stomach. My body seems to have a habit of doing that around him. Ever so slowly, my fingers thoughtlessly begin caressing his soft skin, boldly memorizing each ridge of his taut stomach. It's not until a barely stifled moan escapes Nic's lips that I realize I am treading on dangerous ground. Heat lights up my cheeks at the unconscious actions of my hands. Desperate to distract my mind from the overwhelming sensations, the feel of being held like this, his warm breath on the top of my head while his lush smell surrounds me, making me dizzy, I blurt out the first thing that comes to mind.

"I think I've dreamed of Adira."

His breathing shifts, as if he's holding his breath.

Knowing I just crossed one of my boundaries, I push forward. "Pretty sure, actually. And multiple times in fact. I think I maybe dreamed of you too, but there was never a face."

I wait to see what he says, the silence bearing down on me.

"What do you think that means?" he asks quietly, carefully.

"I don't know."

I pause. Weighing my next words, I decide to put it all out there. I am sick of waiting for a betrayal or proof of why

I shouldn't trust him. This information will determine his loyalties pretty quickly.

"Have you ever heard of the Prophecy of the Four Cores?"

Everything seems to freeze at my words. Even the rain dies away, leaving only deafening silence in its wake.

"Yes," he says quietly, still holding me.

I push forward. "Well, my Aunt Sid believed that I was a part of that prophecy—that I am one of the Cores. She's not my blood relative. She found me in a hospital the night I was born. Apparently, my mother died in childbirth and I was born on July 7th, which is part of the prophecy. I also have a small mark at the back of my neck that looks like the Holy Star."

Seemingly incapable of stopping after years of stifling my voice, I continue to verbally vomit everything. I am a pressure valve finally releasing. "I always doubted it. I've never felt like anyone special, someone worthy of a prophecy. But sometimes I wonder if that's why the monks came for me. Why they hid me away and made me go to lessons, tried to convince me I would one day assume an honored position. According to the prophecy, having control of the Cores will put everything in the Amilign's favor.

"And then I wonder about the Horsemen. Are they like real men, or something else? And where are they? Wouldn't the Horsemen be looking for the Cores, just like the Amilign? I don't believe they will stop searching for me." I bite my lip. "I discovered the monks wanted me for dark purposes, which is why I ran. They would probably richly reward anyone who brought me back to them."

And there it is, the burning fear and question that's

been festering inside me. Nic's arm tightens around me, as if he's trying to offer me reassurance through his touch.

"That's a lot of questions, and I'm not sure what to tell you. I know the Prophets will be able to help you with much of that. And I had already assumed that the monks will be fighting tooth and nail to get you back, so I guess we'll need to be on our guard at all times and push harder to get to The Refuge as soon as possible." He says this into the top of my head. "And take this."

He reaches his arm around to the pack by his head, rummages in it for a moment, and then places the cold hilt of a blade into my hand. "I never want you to feel vulnerable again. Keep this dagger by you while you sleep. Even if you aren't trained, sleeping with a weapon in reach will give you some peace of mind."

I grasp the cool steel in my hand, rubbing my finger along the intricate engraving of the blade. He is giving me the power to feel safe and to protect myself, at the expense of his safety. He is offering me his trust. And all this despite my almost constant doubt of him.

But his next words completely shatter me, laying waste to the boundaries around my heart.

"And Lu," he whispers into the night, his tone taking a steely edge. "I would never betray you. And I will annihilate anyone who attempts to take you from me. You are safe now."

It is those last words that have my mind calming and emptying of all thought, my eyes closing as I sink into the deepest and most comforting sleep I've had in years.

And this time, when I dream of the white horse, the dark man riding her has a face.

CHAPTER 15

It's been a week and I wonder if we will ever get to The Refuge, but then a secret part of me isn't eager for this journey to end. I've never had this kind of freedom, and experiencing the beauty of the world in tangible ways that overcome my senses is euphoric. It's like this world is my greenhouse, magnified just for me. It's a small taste of freedom, and yet I know I could never go back to the life I lived before, it would break me beyond repair. That thought sobers me.

I walk behind Nic as he expertly guides us through a canyon, trying to puzzle him out. He looks like he's trained for years with purpose to achieve his physique, yet I found him randomly living in a cabin in the woods. What was he doing out there? He says he works with horses—is that all he does? It has to be something physical for him to look like he does. He seems so at ease out here. Maybe he travels this path a lot? I wonder why.

"You okay back there?" he asks, peeking over his shoulder. "You're awfully quiet."

"Yeah, I guess I'm just trying to puzzle you out."

"Oh really? Well, let me hear it. I'm an open book." His eyes dance with amusement.

"Okay, first off, what were you doing at the cabin in the woods? Do you live there normally? You said you work with horses—is that like a job or does it entail something more? How do you know your way through this area so well? Do you do this a lot? Um..."

I pause. "I could keep going, but I'll stop there."

"Wow, that's a lot of questions stirring in that busy mind of yours," he comments. "Not quite sure where to start." He starts leading us up a trail out of the canyon. "It's going to start getting steep here so watch your step and stay close."

He's quiet for a while, and I wonder if he actually is an open book. Maybe he has something to hide and I am stupid for trusting him so quickly. My mind is ready to run away with that thought when he speaks.

"I like time to myself, so sometimes I take off for that cabin. I kind of work as a stablehand and trainer for the Prophets, along with doing other stuff, and it can be a nice break and change of scenery to take the horses out on longer trips. I suppose I have a bit of a restless spirit. I've done a lot of traveling over the years, and I guess I'm just naturally good with direction, especially when it comes to finding my way back home."

Some of the monks at the ashram took care of horses too, but none of them were anywhere near in the kind of shape Nic is in, like he was carved out of stone and then given life. Even his profile as he turns is exquisite, the line of his jaw almost perfectly chiseled.

Realizing this is a dangerous path to wander down, I

attempt to refocus. "So you really like working with horses?" I ask. "You seem to have a special connection with Adira."

His tone warms as he replies, "Yeah, she's special. One of a kind. I love animals and especially horses. But Adira is in a class all her own."

"She is," I say genuinely. "I've never seen anything like her." Recalling my dreams of her, I realize I never heard what Nic thought of my confession. "What do *you* think it means that I dreamt of her? You never said."

"Probably just coincidence," he says a little too quickly. There's an awkward silence and he doesn't look back at me. He's avoiding the question, and it surprises me. I sense he knows something he isn't telling me. He probably knows more about a lot...the prophecy, my dreams, and maybe even me. That old, familiar confusion is back.

"What do you know Nic? I know there's something you're not telling me."

He stops and slowly turns. The jovial look is gone from his face, a more serious expression in place. "I think you should let the Prophets interpret your dreams. They'll be able to give you the truth."

The coolness in his words starts to sink in; he's pulling away from me. "And you won't give me the truth, is that it?" My eyes narrow.

"I don't know what you're talking about," he mutters, tearing his eyes from mine.

The broken eye contact is what does it, a universal sign of lying. I find myself flustered by his sudden change in demeanor. "What aren't you telling me?" I demand. "I am not stupid; it's written all over your face. You're keeping something from me."

His face grows even colder, and as if it's physically

happening, I see a shield coming up between us. But I can't tell if he's shielding me or himself. "I think you already know, Lu. If you are a Core and you dream of a horse and a rider, then you must know the significance. The Refuge, where we are headed, is not just home to the Prophets. It's home to the Horsemen as well. They too are like family to me. But I can't give you more than that. I can't give you what you need. You'll get all your answers when we get there."

"Can't, or won't?" I seethe.

He just shrugs.

I'm confused by his reaction. Is there something about the Horsemen that he's not allowed to share? A nagging doubt says that it's because of me; there's something intense between us and I'm guessing it shouldn't be there if I am to connect with a Horseman. But the prophecy doesn't clarify what type of connection.

There are many different types of love, right?

Whatever it is, something has him shutting down, but I've pushed as far as I can. Annoyed by his vague response and how I am no closer to understanding anything, I push past him, stomping up the trail.

"Slow down, Lu, this is a dangerous trail." he shouts at my back.

I continue to ignore him. I am sick of always being in the dark. Never having answers. Always having to work so hard to find the truth. Not having anyone to trust. It's exhausting. And even Nic, whom I started to trust, is keeping something from me. My anger and frustration just keep building.

I barely hear Nic's cry of warning as small rocks slide down the steep embankment to my right, pebbling my legs. The ground vibrates, a growing thunder reverberating all around me. I lift my eyes just in time to see huge boulders and jagged rocks rolling right for me, gaining unimaginable speed.

Paralyzed with fear, I'm rooted to the spot. It's as if my brain has short-circuited. I know I need to move, but I can't seem to organize my thoughts enough to decide where or how. This is it: this will be how I die, having never really lived.

And then I am flying. A massive force barrels into me from behind. The weight pushes my body into the ground, covering me. A fiery pain lances through my ankle, shooting up my leg. I close my eyes, dust swirling around me, waiting for the crushing weight to steal my last breath, as the ground shakes in a deafening roar.

Will it ever stop? A gentle breath on my face has me opening my eyes to Nic's piercing blue ones absorbing me as if I might disappear. I realize his hands are under my head, protecting me from the fall while he uses his body as a shield to protect me from the rocks. I try to ignore the way his actions cause small buds of light to bloom and open like flowers inside me. I break his intense gaze and notice that we are protected by a protruding boulder that's acting as a sort of shield or overhang; it's the only reason we're still alive. That, and Nic thinking fast on his feet and saving me yet again.

Another near-death experience sits like a heavy stone in my gut. And like a guiding light in a storm, my eyes find Nic's again, and he anchors me. A siren's call I can't resist, my hand moves from between our chests to cup his strong cheek and jaw.

The destruction finally stops, and the dust settles. The blue of Nic's eyes is a bright, glowing hue as the sun begins to break through the settling dust. He makes no attempt to move as he intently soaks me up with his gaze. He just lies there, his weight being held up by his forearms so he doesn't crush me, his hands still protectively cradling my head.

Both our hearts pound in tandem. Those impossibly thick lashes lower, and his gaze dips lower, so intent on my mouth that it is like a caress. I shiver. I find my gaze moving to his lips, wishing them closer, imagining the feel of them softly touching mine, shocked by how much I want my first kiss to be with him. This man that draws me near and infuriates me at the same time.

I feel Nic tremble, and I think it's because of this heat growing between us until he grunts and a flash of pain moves across his face.

A drop of blood rolls down the side of his neck to his jaw.

CHAPTER 16

LUCIA

"You're injured." I pale, snapped out of the moment at the sight of his blood.

"I'll be fine." A sheen of sweat covers his brow. "It's just a couple of scratches. Are you okay?"

I don't really believe him, but I answer his question. "I am, thanks to you."

He slips one hand at a time out from under my head, and slowly lifts himself up. He extends a hand to pull me up too. I grasp it and step forward, only to feel a fiery pain flare through my ankle. I fall forward into his arms as I let out a gasp, my breath stolen by the intensity and shock of the pain.

Teeth clenched, I stand on my uninjured leg and struggle to calm my breathing. Nic guides me to sit on a nearby rock and inspects my leg.

"I'll be gentle, I just need to see where the problem is," he says.

I don't doubt him. Even with unanswered questions, I know he'll take care of me.

He grasps my knee, gently moving his hand down my leg, applying slight pressure until he reaches my ankle and I gasp. "I think your walking days are on hold for a while. Looks like you have a sprained or broken ankle. Could have happened when I tackled you to the ground or you could have been hit by the rock slide." An apologetic grimace on his expression.

"Don't Nic," I say. "I am only alive because of you." I don't say how he'd probably be better off without me. All I seem to do is slow him down and get him into trouble. A wave of despair threatens to overwhelm me as I look down at my swelling ankle. Now we'll be stuck here for who knows how long. Sitting ducks for the Amilign.

I fight back the tears that threaten to spill over. Nic gently lifts my chin with a finger, bringing my eyes to his.

"We've got this. I'll carry you out of this canyon, and when we get to the rim, we'll go from there. One step at a time." He smiles.

So much confidence shines in his eyes that I can't help but feel hope. He grabs me by the waist and lifts me. My hand moves to wrap around his shoulders when I see his mouth tighten. He barely hides a wince.

"Wait, you *are* injured!" I exclaim. "You're not going to be carrying anyone!"

"It's not that bad, really," he says. "Just some scratches and scrapes from the rock slide. Nothing that will hinder me from getting us out of here."

"I don't want to hurt you more, Nic." I hesitate with a hand on his shoulder for stability. His hands still hold my waist.

"You won't," he says confidently. "A piggyback ride is

probably out of the question, but I can carry you in my arms."

Before I have a chance to protest, I am hoisted into his arms as if I weigh nothing. Unsure what to do with my hands, I try to fold them in my lap. Feeling awkward, I start fidgeting with my fingers.

"Relax, Lu, you're as stiff as board." He smirks. "I promise I won't drop you. Tell me, how's your ankle feeling?"

I know he's trying to distract me. "It's better now that I'm not trying to walk on it," I say. "And I want to thank you, for everything. That's the third time you saved my life." I don't tell him how I am coming to rely on his soothing presence, how I am starting to crave his nearness, how my eyes always search for him when he's not close.

"You don't need to thank me. I'm just happy I could be here to help you." He says quietly, his breath gently brushing across my face. He continues the upward trek.

In no time at all, the comforting lull of his pace and his lush scent settles me, and I relax in his arms. I find myself resting my head against his chest and neck, the pounding of his heartbeat adding to the rhythm of peace that starts to fill me, despite the aching of my ankle. My hand, acting as if it has a mind of its own, reaches up and presses against his chest, against his heart. I feel a shudder run through him, and the next step he takes falters a bit.

Is it possible that he's as affected as I am by this intensity between us? He's probably just exhausted from saving my life, getting injured, and then being forced to carry me out of this canyon.

Almost to the top, he gently sets me down on a rock. "I'm going to check and make sure it's safe up there, and that we're not walking directly into the path of some monks. Wait here; I'll be right back."

I nod, my mind a flurry of thoughts. I hate how affected I am by Nic. I hate how there are things I know he's not telling me. I hate how despite all that, I am still drawn to him and somehow I want to trust him. I feel safe with him. And I hate that I wonder about this connection with him in the back of my mind, and what it means for my prophesied bond with a Horseman.

Nic returns smiling. "Coast is clear, and we're in luck! You won't believe who's found her way back to us just when we need her."

"No way!" I exclaim. "Adira is up there?! Wow, that horse is incredible. Now we can get to The Refuge quick so you can be done with all this tedious protection duty and return to your life."

He deftly lifts me into his arms, the swiftness of the action causing me to gasp.

"Nothing about you is tedious, Lu." A wry grin on his face; clearly, he enjoys catching me off guard.

And that's when an idea starts to take form. Two can play at this game. I think I know just how I can catch him off guard and test my theory on whether or not I affect him as much as he does me.

I lift my hands and slowly slide them up to his neck, careful to avoid his back. His breath hitches. Gently grasping his neck, I pull myself closer, my nose pressing in under the curve of where his jaw meets his neck, my lips gently grazing the skin there. A deep, shuddering breath powers through him as he sharply inhales, his muscles tensing under my hands, his heart pounding. His steps falter as he tries to keep moving forward.

My heart does a happy little skip. I breathe in his scent

deeply and tell him in as seductive a whisper as I can manage having zero experience with such things, "You smell like..." I pause. "Horse," I finish with a grin, relaxing back.

A deep, genuine laugh rumbles through him. It's contagious, making me smile as he brings us out of the canyon. The setting sun has turned the sky an incredible shade of gold and orange. Coming out of the dingy shade of the canyon into this light only emphasizes its heaven-like beauty. I stare at it, awed.

"Absolutely beautiful," Nic says.

I look up to find his attention is fixed on me. My cheeks flush.

"Your smile is incredible. My new goal is to make you smile as much as possible."

Adira chooses that moment to come trotting over from behind a brush. Nic sets me on my good foot with a hand on my waist to stabilize me. I reach for Adira and she nuzzles my hand with her soft nose.

"Your timing couldn't have been more perfect, sweet girl," I say to her softly.

Nic turns slightly to pat Adira and I get a glimpse at his injured back. His shirt hangs in blood-soaked tatters; deep gouges layered with dirt leave his back looking like a gruesome canvas right out of a horror story.

"Nic!" I practically yell. "You are seriously injured!"

He startles and turns his back away from me. It's almost as if he's forgotten about his wounds, which he couldn't possibly. He steps out of my reach so I have to keep a hand on Adira for stability.

"It looks worse than it is, I promise," he says avoiding eye contact. "It was lucky we were shielded by that boulder, but it wasn't quite tall enough to fully protect my back."

"Really," I say incredulously. "Because it looks like someone took a meat cleaver to your back!"

He takes his shirt off and turns. "Look, just some deep scratches. I tend to bleed a lot when I get any sort of minor injury. It's mostly old blood."

Standing near Adira's back legs, he's too far away for me to closely inspect him and there is a lot of dried blood. But some of these wounds look like they are a few days old, not hours. Is it possible he had previous injuries on his back that tore open in the rock slide and he doesn't want me to know? What has this man been through? It's hard to believe he wasn't more severely injured just based on his shredded shirt.

More secrets and more mysteries I won't get answers to, at least not right now.

"Okay, if you're sure," I say hesitantly, my eyes narrowed.

He nods, avoiding eye contact again.

Irritation flares to life, waring for a place alongside my growing hurt. One moment he does something incredibly gallant and sacrificial, like covering my body with his in a rockslide, and the next moment he's all half-truths and avoiding eye contact.

As much as I find myself drawn to him, he's hiding something. I need to be cautious. It'll be good when we get to The Refuge so I can get some space from him. I'll have my questions answered and get my head on right. And maybe all these doubts will go away when I meet the Horsemen. Because depending on what the Prophets say about this prophecy and my role, Nic may just be a complication that I don't need.

What I desperately need is distance, but seeing as I can't walk and we'll both be riding Adira until we get to

The Refuge, distance is the one thing I won't be getting. I say a quick prayer to Elohim to make our travels swift, keep us safe, and guard my heart, because despite all the dangers we've encountered so far in this journey, I fear I am more at risk now than I ever was before. The risk to my vulnerable, exposed, and desperate heart, I fear, is an injury I won't soon recover from.

CHAPTER 17

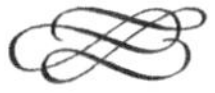

LUCIA

We've been traveling for almost two weeks now, and the constant ache of my body from hours on end riding on Adira's back is an unwelcome companion. I am getting better and better at stifling the groan every time Nic helps me dismount. He says we should be there by tomorrow night, and I can't wait.

We've fallen into a comfortable and yet potentially dangerous rhythm during that time. Stopping at dusk, me rubbing down Adira while Nic lights a fire and cooks us fish he catches or rabbits he snares. Sleeping under the stars on the shared bedroll. Our bodies seem to naturally find each other in sleep, drawn together like two magnets. We often wake unintentionally intertwined; either I am sprawled across his chest or his body is wrapped around mine. At first, it was awkward, but as the weeks have gone by, it's become an accepted and, I daresay, welcome norm in the mornings.

I often feel his gaze on me, as if he is trying to memorize

each brush stroke in a painting, his eyes intimately devouring every movement. And I've come to realize I have a keen awareness of his presence, like the scent of rain in the air before a storm. I know he's near, returned from whatever task he was completing, before I even lay eyes on him.

Taking a breath, I shove that new awareness and all that it stirs within me away. I've created a sort of invisible boundary to separate all the "Nic stuff" from the rest of me. Like if I can keep all these unexplored feelings and emotions in a little box or behind a wall, then they can't touch me.

As I have watched him these past few weeks, I'm amazed at how adept he is at surviving without anything. We lost most of our meager supplies in the rockslide, other than the small bedroll Nic was able to salvage. Even our extra clothes. Nic's been shirtless since the rock slide and I can't say I mind it, but I don't know how he isn't bothered, especially at nights when it can get chilly. After two weeks of wearing the same thing, I have a new appreciation for soap and clean clothes not just rinsed by river water.

Despite there being things we avoid talking about, kind of like neutral zones, it's been nice having someone I can share my thoughts and dreams with too. Nic is a great listener and seems genuinely interested in my life. We talk about our favorite memories; the people who are special to us and have had an impact on our lives. I tell him about my love of gardening and bringing life to things, and about my only real friend, Ansel, and how we met. He shares with me his love of all animals and nature. How he never feels more connected to the world and Atik Yomin, the name of Elohim that means Ancient of Days, than when he's immersed in the wilderness.

His admission resonates deep within me. When he talks

about The Refuge and what it's like, my eagerness to reach the sanctuary grows.

I surprise myself when I share that my dream for the future is simply to be able to make my own choices. An inner hope I've never said out loud, not even to Ansel. I lived for so long with no control over my days or future. I was told by the monks where to go, who to be, what was expected, and what future I would have. Not even given the simplest choices regarding what I could wear. The first choice I made for myself was to flee the ashram, and it was the most empowering moment of my life. I look forward to a day when I can choose things for myself.

I'm nervous about telling Nic such a deep secret, afraid of the pity I am sure to see in his eyes. But he only looks at me with respect and, surprisingly, a level of solidarity. It only makes me more curious about him, wondering if he too feels stuck sometimes.

The conversation helps distract me from the heat and tension that constantly seems to want to rise between us, no matter how much either of us tries to avoid it. My ankle heals enough that I can hobble around on it, but long hikes are still out of the question, so I am forced to rely on Nic. And I know he hates seeing me hobble or struggle in any way, so he's always there to help even if I can manage without him.

Even now, as we ride in search of a place to stop for the night, our conversation flows so easily. It's extraordinary, how easy it is to be in his presence, when I've never been comfortable around men. But with Nic, it's as if we've known each other for years rather than a few weeks.

I feel Nic's hand on my waist. I am wedged between his legs on Adira, my back pressed against his chest, his breath in my ear. With his back injured like it is, despite his protest that he's fine, it's better for me to ride with him this way. Occasionally, I feel him adjust his grip on my hip, as if he's reassuring himself he's got a hold on me.

I try to avoid evaluating how that makes me feel. Just another thing to bury away in my mind. Because to my dismay, I am coming to crave it. I tell myself it's because he makes me feel safe and protected. But the truth is I am coming to crave *him* and that terrifies me.

I crave the small touches and heated glances from him. The way they warm my blood and cause sparks to dance across my skin, sending shivers down my spine. But just as much, I crave the depth of his words, the rumble of his laughter, the light in his eyes when he smiles. I crave knowledge of his soul.

But those are thoughts I don't dare admit to the light of day. They are dangerous. So instead I shove them deep down and bury them under a wall. A wall of playing it safe, for the sake of protecting myself. Even as I do this, I realize this growing thing between us is like the persistent crashing of a wave and it won't be held back for long.

We come to a stop in a small clearing surrounded by trees, a creek running through the center. Its picturesque charm captivates me.

"Well, this is as good a place as any. And a great spot to try to catch some fish," Nic adds confidently.

His warmth disappears from my back as he slides off Adira. I brace myself as his hands reach up to gently grasp my hips, lifting me from her back. My hands are on his shoulders as he begins to lower me when suddenly Adira sidesteps, shoving me into his bare chest. His arms come around me tightly to keep me from falling; my chest is level with his face.

My face flames red as my body slides against his. Carefully and painstakingly slowly, he lowers me to my feet. My body hums like a tuning fork from the contact, and his eyes catch mine. My heart pounds in my chest; I am a butterfly trapped in a net. Neither one of us moves as our eyes lock on each other.

As seconds turn into minutes, I find my eyes drawn to his full lips. I long to feel them against my own. Another craving I should suppress—I *need* to suppress. But the longer I stand here, the less I remember why. My excuses are like popping bubbles, quickly disappearing. I decide to choose this moment for myself, damn the consequences.

Reaching my hand up to his jaw, I move my thumb boldly across his bottom lip, his hair brushing my fingertips. He closes his eyes as he takes a deep, ragged breath. His eyes open, hooded, and the blue glows with an intensity that steals my breath. His arms tighten around me, drawing me against him, up onto the tips of my toes. One of his hands trails up my back, leaving shivering heat in its wake, and grasps the nape of my neck under my hair. His eyes consume every inch of my face.

He has this way of looking at me that leaves me feeling stripped bare, and I feel fully possessed by him in this moment. No space between us. He lowers his head to mine, his forehead pressed to mine. We breathe in each other's breath. I can almost taste him. We stay like that for what feels like an eternity. I both want and fear the next step over the line. The irrevocable change that is sure to follow.

Finally, ever so gently, his lips press against mine. My arms come around his neck. It is the work of a moment, but I know I am forever changed by this kiss, this man. It feels as though a piece of me I didn't know existed is bursting forth from my chest, peeling the layers of my old self away and making way for this new, shiny, electrified creation in its place.

There is no going back.

The kiss begins to change, a desperation to it taking hold. Like a drowning man seeking air, it's all-encompassing. I feel like a tinderbox and he's the match. Kissing me with such a fervent hunger, my senses are on overload. He pauses for air, only for his lips to begin a fresh assault on my neck, burning a path along my collarbone, across my throat and up my chin, until I'm gasping for breath and his lips claim mine once again.

I've never been held by a man like this, my feet barely touching the ground, not an inch between us.

Then, without warning, he's gone from me, leaving me cold, the space around me vacant. Only dim embers exist where there was just a blaze, and they quickly turn to ash. I open my eyes and find his back to me, just out of reach. The muscles in his back flex in tension as he runs a trembling hand through his hair.

"I'm sorry, that shouldn't have happened."

My heart starts to fissure. Surely he can hear the loud cracking in my chest? I stare at his back, struck silent by his words. How can his response to something so incredibly life-altering be regret? Doesn't he feel what I am feeling?

But I saw his reaction; he is just as affected as I am. Why is he responding like this? Is it because of who I am, and his friendship with the Horsemen? He is typically light-hearted and jovial in nature, but now he turns to face me, his face somber and stoic.

"I'm sorry..."

"Stop saying that," I interrupt, angry. Angry that even in this, I don't get a choice. That he's taking that from me. "I don't want an apology from you. Do you know what I think?

I think you're afraid!" I place my hands on my hips, my eyes narrowing.

"Afraid?" he says incredulously.

"Yes, afraid. I think that kiss affected you like it did me and it spooked you."

"You know nothing, Lu, absolutely nothing!"

"Well if that's true it's because you tell me nothing!" I shout at him, throwing my arms wide.

He's practically steaming now. He looks like a dark god, his skin glistening in the fading light, the blue of his eyes dimming, taking on an eerie shade I've never seen in them before. "You live in your little bubble, thinking you can demand whatever you want, but you know nothing about what's at stake. You don't even have to think past today if you don't want; you have no reason to. This is bigger than you can possibly imagine. It's not just about what you want in a moment with your selfish desires and childish dreams."

I stagger back as if he's given me a physical blow. I get the feeling his words are not just meant for me, like he's projecting his own struggles, too. But despite that knowledge, a knot forms in my chest, pushing its way up my throat, making it impossible for me to speak. A shiver makes its way down my spine...hurt, along with a bite of desolation.

I turn my back on him. With as much steadiness as I can muster, I hobble away from him to the creek and sit down on the pebbled shore. I submerge my feet in the icy cold of the mountain stream, the stabbing pain attempting to distract me from the hurt and despair that threatens to overwhelm me. My mind is a dark storm.

I stand by my theory that he's scared. Maybe I am being selfish, wanting him the way I do when there are so many unknowns. Knowing it will only hurt that much worse later if we have to walk away from each other. Maybe it's his loyalty to the Horsemen that has him apologizing and then responding the way he did.

But I can't change the nagging feeling that there's more going on here. It seems no matter where life leads me, the elusiveness of choice will be an ever-present misery. Will my life always be dictated by forces outside my control?

My swollen lips are a tangible reminder of a moment that will run on a reel in my mind, even if my heart will continue to crack at the memory. So I try to do what I do best and build my walls up again so nothing can touch me.

But I have been unmade by that kiss. My ability to build walls against him is demolished. I hate that I was right to resist trusting him, at least with my heart. Part of me, deep down, must have known. If I am a Core, destined to have some form of love with a Horseman, then maybe Nic is right to push me away. But if he's right, why does it feel so wrong? I stare up at the now grey sky. It's fitting that it should start weeping alongside me. Its rainy tears mixing with my own.

I stay there until nothing but darkness surrounds me. I pull my knees up to my chest, my cheek resting against them. The sounds of nighttime lull my eyes closed. Warm hands lift me into the air, my cheek resting against a bare chest. I sigh, even though I shouldn't. I hate that my traitorous body still responds to him.

He brings me to the fire and lays me down, covering me with his portion of the bedroll. I open my eyes. His eyes, now crystal blue again, are downcast, his expression morose. He lifts a hand as if to stroke my hair, but then pulls back, dropping it to his side.

He looks at me, as if wanting to say something. He finally sighs, his shoulders sagging, and turns away. Just beyond the glow of the fire, he leans against a tree, keeping watch.

My last thoughts as I drift off to sleep are of the lost and broken look of wanting on his face, warring with his control. I think of the crystal blue eyes that seemed to grow dark as harsh words fell from his mouth. And I wonder what is going on underneath these layers he's trying to build up.

Tomorrow is the day I will finally find out. The day I will have answers.

CHAPTER 18

It's a quiet ride. The heat of Nic's body against my back is a special kind of torture.

We arrive as the sun is beginning to set. I never would have been able to picture this place in my mind. It looks as though it was once home to an ancient indigenous tribe. A combination of clustered sandstone and mud-brick dwellings appear as though they've been carved out of the cliff face. I don't see how this place is livable now, but as we get closer, I notice new improvements and enhancements subtly hidden.

"It's far more than you can imagine," Nic says, breaking the silence. "It serves as a good cover to hide what's going on deep within."

"Are those *windows*?"

"Yes, as you can see, they're hidden beneath greenery and angled in such a way to prevent glare from the sun. They're also a special kind of anti-reflective, colored glass that, from a distance, matches the cliff, but just in case, there are shields that can slide into place over the windows. You would be none the wiser that anything was here. This place has all the luxuries too, solar power and even running water. The Refuge is not just what you see on the cliff face; it extends deep into the mountain and is structurally reinforced."

There's such pride in Nic's voice, I can't help but smile in awe. It's truly magical, and I can't wait to explore the place.

As Nic leads us closer to the façade, he slips off the horse. I try to ignore the feel of his hands on my waist as he lifts me down, but they're like a brand on my skin. I avoid his eyes as I look around.

A man walks out of one of the cliff openings. He has grey hair and a scruffy beard. His kind, weathered face is abundant with crow's feet and laugh lines—the marks of a life well lived. He is older but not weakly so. He seems confident and hardy, like he has been toughened through life experiences. He reminds me of a piece of worn leather: strong and resilient, but more pliant and with a depth of character.

"Finally!" the man says. "I've been dying for you to get here."

He seems unsurprised by my presence, which I find curious.

"It's a long journey, Elias," says Nic, "you know that, and I came across someone in need of my help. Elias, meet Lu. Lu, this is Elias. He's one of the Prophets I told you about."

Elias raises a curious eyebrow in question, his gaze intent on Nic. Nic purposely ignores him.

Curious, for sure.

I reach out a hand to Elias. "Nice to meet you."

"Nice to meet you as well, Lucia. We are happy to have you with us. There is much for us to talk about." He wears a mischievous smile.

My jaw hangs open. I never told Nic my full name, which either means this man knew who I was before this moment, or can read minds. I highly doubt the latter.

Then the realization hits me. What if Nic didn't just stumble upon me as I first thought? I turn my gaze to his, but he won't look at me. Instead, his eyes burn a hole into Elias.

But Elias has a small smile on his face as he takes my hand, looping it through his arm. He turns his back on Nic to lead me into The Refuge.

"We'll leave Nic here to deal with Adira. I am sure you have lots of questions that can't wait, Lucia" he said with a wink.

I like Elias already. And despite my doubts, I have the feeling that I've finally arrived where I was meant to be all along.

As Elias walks me through the ancient, carved outer doorway, we come face to face with a solid black door. He punches in a number on a keypad and the door slides open. The contrast between ancient times and new technology is stark.

As we walk in, I'm surprised at how bright it feels. I expected a dingy dungeon sort of feel with all the rock and sandstone. Instead, there is warm lighting throughout. Regularly spaced windows, placed high in the walls and ceiling, are covered with glass that seems to glow from within. A question forms on my brow.

"It's really quite ingenious," says Elias. "The light is essentially collected, and the power of the sun is used in the evenings to light up bulbs throughout The Refuge. During the day, we have these series of mirrored tunnels or openings in the ceiling and high areas of walls that bring in the natural light, kind of like an amplified skylight. With the honey-colored glass, it provides a unique atmosphere. It's as if the golden hour of sunset is always upon us in this space. Elohe Tishuathi has provided for us in such incredible ways."

I glance up at him as he speaks, noting the reverence and awe on his face. "Elohe Tishuathi?"

"Elohe Tishuathi is our Salvation, our source. He is also more commonly known as Elohim."

He leads me to a library that radiates warmth with its plush rugs, warm candlelight, bright windows, and dark wood throughout. It's a place I could find myself easily spending much of my time. He shows me to a corner with two high wingback plush leather chairs the color of chocolate, and a rug so soft and plush I could sink my feet into it. As he sits down, he gestures me toward the chair opposite him.

"So, Lucia, you must have a lot of questions for me." His expression is patient.

"Well, honestly, I am not even sure where to start." I want to know more about Nic, but I don't think it's a good idea for my first question to be about one of the stablehands sent to retrieve me. But that gets me thinking.

"I guess the first prudent question is how do you know who I am? I only told Nic my name was Lu, so I'm guessing you knew who I was before all of this."

"I suppose that is the question of all questions, isn't it?" he says with a soft smile. "I imagine my response will answer many of your questions, and possibly create many more. Before I answer, though, I would ask that you allow me time to fully explain everything before you make up your mind about anything."

"I think I can do that."

"Good, thank you." He takes a deep breath, settling deeper into his chair. His expression is thoughtful. "I've known you since you were a few days old, sweet Lucia. In fact, I even held you in my arms, rocked you to sleep, and fed you bottles for a brief time. I've always been so very invested in your life, even if it's had to be from a distance. I think one of the hardest decisions Elohim guided us to was for Sidora to take you to live far away from us, knowing that there would come a time when you would be taken into the very heart of the darkness. Far from where we could protect you."

It feels as though the oxygen has been sucked from the room.

"I know this comes as a shock to you," Elias continues, "but there are reasons why things had to happen the way they did. We have Prophets in this Refuge who are gifted by Elohim in regards to visions, and He often guides our path through them. It was confirmed by all of them at the same time—which rarely happens—that you needed to be raised away from this place, as much as it broke all of our hearts to do so. Sidora was the one who found you at the hospital and was already committed to you, so she offered to be the one to raise you far away from this place, her home.

"It was years later when, once again, these Prophets all saw the same vision that warned of the Amilign coming to collect you. They saw in this future that for you to become who Elohim and this world needed you to be, you would have to take this path through the darkness. And not just that, but any effort on our part to change this course or shield you from it would not only lead to heartbreak, but world-altering destruction.

"It can be hard for us to understand, and in many cases, our minds cannot comprehend the ways of Elohim. We see only from our perspective of humanness, from our self-focused nature. Whereas, Elohim sees the infinite and all-encompassing; everything individually and all at once; past, present, and future. When we cannot understand His ways, we can trust His heart, which is always for our good. And just as pottery cannot be made into the beautiful and strong masterpiece it becomes without first being molded and then placed in the hottest of flames, so too we cannot be shaped into our destiny without first being forged in fire."

He pauses and gazes at me with concern, waiting with bated breath for my response. I stare at my hands, trying to soak in all his words and the blow that was dealt. I feel incapable of forming words.

He reaches out both his hands, surrounding mine with his bigger, more world-weathered ones. I look up into his grey eyes.

"You have been so very loved by us in this Refuge, and prayed over daily in the years you spent away from us. Not a day went by that you weren't in the hearts and minds of many. And it was Elohim that led us to send Nic to collect you. We were shown a countdown of a timeline in which your time spent in that dark place was over and would tip into a dangerous path for you."

My voice cracks as I finally speak. "But Nic didn't collect me. I escaped from that place myself. He found me in the woods and saved me from an attack from one of the monks, but I got myself out of that place."

"And in doing so," Elias replies, "you fulfilled the will of

Elohim, even if it is hard to see. He pressed upon you to leave that place and guided you through. As a child of Elohim, you've been given the gift of Ruach. Roughly translated, that means breath of the Creator, but it truly means His very spirit. You see, His Ruach lives in you, to guide you. We find the urging of our gut often gets credited to our feelings, because humanity's biggest weakness is pride, when in most, if not all cases, it's the guidance of Elohim.

"Do you not find it unusually convenient that of all the places in that vast mountain range, you ran in the direction of Nic? And do you know, that cabin he stayed in was built by him for the purpose of this journey alone? Curious, don't you think?"

"But I am not prophecy material," I insist. "I am not a warrior. I didn't do anything with my time in that place but try to blend in and stay hidden, and honestly wish to be anywhere else." A tear rolls down my face, memories rushing to the surface unbidden.

A knuckle reaches up and wipes it away, then lifts my chin. "Child, you are chosen by Elohim Shomri, our Protector, and you did exactly what you were meant to. You survived the darkness, not by drawing attention to yourself and laying the foundations of your own destruction, but by fooling them into seeing you as a compliant pet. You gained knowledge of them and their ways in a way only you could. Even if you can't see it, I see a strength and resilience in you that could only come through surviving the flames."

As his words settle around me like a blanket, one thought stands out in my mind. "What about my Aunt Sid? If you know her, she must be here."

"I am sorry, my girl, but she is not at The Refuge. She came back to us after you were taken, her heart shattered. It went against everything in her not to fight the Amilign when they came for you. She stayed here a few months, but the loss of you and knowing where you were slowly ate away at her, chipping away at her soul. We knew she needed a new mission, something to focus on, as it would be years before she would see you again. For the past seven years, she's been hunting for knowledge of the other three Cores. Occasionally, she'll come by and give us news, but mostly she stays away. She does head to the farm sometimes, I think to feel close to you."

I deflate like a balloon. But having answers to the questions that have plagued me for years fills me with a peace that calms my restless soul. I have so many more questions to ask, but we've been traveling all day. I'm starving and in desperate need of being cleaned up. It must be all over my face, because without any prompting, Elias speaks.

"Let me show you to your room so you can get settled. There's a shower, and I'll have some food sent up. I'm sure you are exhausted, physically and mentally. I'm not going anywhere, and will be happy to answer more of your questions later. I also have quite a bit to show you around here. I would love it if you would one day be able to think of this place like your home."

Home will forever be the farm I lived on with Aunt Sid. But Elias is so genuine and hopeful as he stares into my eyes, I can't help but smile back at him.

"And, if I'm not mistaken, your nineteenth birthday is only a few days away. So in honor of your safe return and to celebrate the gift of your birthday, we are going to have a celebration tomorrow with great food, cake, and music." He winks. "A sort of welcome home."

My thoughts are a jumbled mess as I follow Elias quietly through The Refuge, until he stops in front of a wood door. I don't see any other people, but maybe Elias sensed that I needed some alone time before meeting others and told them to stay away. He turns to me, placing a hand on my arm.

"We are so very grateful to Elohim to have you returned safely home, Lucia. I know I am a stranger to you, but I very much look forward to getting to know you."

I sense he wants to hug me but holds back. He nods, smiles, and leaves me alone with my thoughts.

As I enter the room, I'm surprised to see it looks fairly normal. I'm not sure what I was expecting, but a plush carpet covers the middle of the floor. A large bed sits in the center of the room, a dresser next to it. To the right is a door I assume leads to a bathroom.

I am most excited that I have my own window. The room is cozy, and I can't wait to shower and fall into the fluffy bed. A knock at the door sounds. I turn to answer as it swings open. Nic stands there, holding a plate.

Butterflies return to my stomach as we stare at each other. He finally clears his throat and holds out the plate.

"Elias wanted me to make sure you got fed."

"Thanks," I say, reaching for the plate.

He turns to leave.

"Wait," I say, surprised by the indignation I feel. "Why all the lies, Nic?"

He steps back, startled by the abrupt question. I don't know why though—he had to know it was coming.

"I—"

"You clearly knew who I was when you saved me from the monk. You were sent there to get me. Is it really so hard for you to be honest?!" I put the plate on the dresser and walk forward. My presence pushes Nic back to the opposite wall outside my room.

"I can't possibly understand what reasons you had to

keep me in the dark about so much. Especially after all we shared with each other. Or was that just more lies? Was anything that happened out there real?" My cheeks flush at the last question that slipped out.

He just stares at me, his chest rising and falling sharply.

"You know what, just forget it. I don't know why I would expect a truthful answer from you anyway. It's what I get for trusting you, I guess." I turn, heading back into my room. "You'd think I would learn after all these years."

Right as the door is about to click shut, I swear I hear him say with a sigh, "It was real."

CHAPTER 19

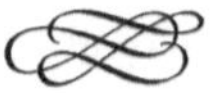

LUCIA

I wake to a soft, golden light shining through the tinted glass of the small window, filling the room with a peaceful glow. It feels so good to wake in a bed after weeks of sleeping on the hard ground. I attempt to shove down the painful memory of Nic's nearness in the mornings, but my mind has grabbed hold of it like a magnet. How he would lie close on super cold nights to share body heat and I would wake in the morning with his hands wrapped around me, my face buried in his chest, his scent surrounding me. Those thoughts are like a vise around my heart.

I throw the covers off and immediately head to the shower. I need a distraction from the loop of my traitorous thoughts. Quickly drying off, I dig through the dresser and pick out some tight but stretchy and soft blue athletic pants, and a bright yellow T-shirt that's a little big. I knot it at the back. Already my spirits are lifted.

Brown is officially banned from my wardrobe.

I decide to head out of my room instead of lingering. I

figure I will eventually run into someone who can point me in the right direction. I'm looking forward to getting a full tour of this place today, and hopefully spending some more time with Elias.

I open the door to a big, muscular man leaning against the wall opposite my room. He has dirty blonde hair, longer on top but buzzed short on the sides, with scruffy, few-days-old facial hair covering his chiseled jaw. He wears a form-fitting black T-shirt and black military-style canvas pants. His hazel eyes are bright, a sideways smile fixed on his face. I stop in my tracks, hoping my jaw isn't hanging open as I stare. He's not what I was expecting for a Prophet. He's absolutely gorgeous.

He pushes off the wall, sticking a hand out. "Lucia, I presume."

I step forward, taking his hand. "That's me."

He pulls me closer, boldly threading my hand through his arm as he turns down the hall, leading me with him. "I'm Mordecai, but everyone calls me Cai. And I am here to get you fed and give you a tour."

"Nice to meet you Cai" I glance sideways up at him, taking in his immense height and build. This guy has to be even bigger than Nic, which is saying a lot. He must feel my eyes on him because he turns his head and winks. My face flushing, I ask, "Are you a stablehand too?"

"Too?"

"Yes, like Nic."

"Nicanor?"

"I don't know a Nicanor, just a Nic, but I suppose that could be his full name. He hasn't exactly been forthcoming with me."

His lips twitch as he tries to stifle a smile. He finally says, "I'm a Horseman."

Stopping abruptly, I grab his big arm and turn him to face me. Or more like he lets me turn him, because there's no way I could make this wall of man do anything he didn't want to.

Now he has a huge grin on his face, and if I thought him handsome before, he's devastatingly so now. "Surprised?" he asks.

"I just...I've never met a Horseman. But my Aunt Sid told me about you and the prophecy when I was a child. I suppose I feel a bit like I am meeting a fantasy."

His eyebrows rise at my choice of wording, and he smirks. My cheeks heat. Man, I have a talent for putting my foot in my mouth around gorgeous men.

"Well, lucky me to be the fantasy of a rare beauty such as yourself." He winks. This guy is a bold tease if ever there was one, but I sense a playfulness within him.

Grabbing my arm again, he leads me back down the hall and into a big, open room filled with tables and chairs. One whole side of it is solid stone, as if it was chiseled out of the cliff with rudimentary tools. It's natural and rough looking, almost harsh. But in the stone, spaced evenly, are tall, slender, amber windows that allow a warm golden light to fill the space that contradicts the stone, making the room feel spacious. Along with the elevated ceilings, the room is open and inviting.

The other walls are a soft, sage green hue with dark wooden tables, benches, or chairs sprinkled throughout. Cinnamon and cardamom fragrance the air and draw me into the room, like the warm embrace of a long-lost family member. Quite a few people sit sprinkled throughout the tables, talking and eating. Their conversation and soft laughter create an atmosphere of connection and joy that I have not experienced before. I get the sense this room is so much more than an eating space for the people who live here.

Cai leads me to a table in the center of the room, pulling out a chair for me.

"I'm sure you have a million questions burning in you, Lucia. I'm going to go grab us a couple of plates for breakfast, and when I get back, we can eat and you can ask away."

"Really?" I'm surprised by his openness after my experiences with Nic. "You don't mind?"

"Not at all, but I'm starving, so food first," He winks, then turns and weaves through the tables to what I assume is the kitchen area.

Glancing around, I notice some people looking at me curiously. They smile when I notice them and return to their meals. No one stares rudely or anything. If what Elias had said is true, I imagine some of these people know who I am. It's a little disconcerting when I am used to being ignored and easily blending into the background. I much prefer the safety of being invisible.

Cai comes back with an ungodly amount of food. My jaw hangs open as he sets three huge, overflowing plates on the table. The one he puts in front of me is more than I am used to eating in a day, filled with some things I remember from my childhood.

"Pancakes!" I exclaim.

That smile again. "Yep, and sausage, scrambled eggs, strawberries, and my personal favorite, Seb's famous cinnamon rolls. Didn't know what you liked to eat, so I brought a variety."

"Thank you," I say, biting into a perfectly ripe strawberry, the juicy sweetness erupting on my tongue.

Digging into his horde of food, Cai takes a bite of a cinnamon roll that has him moaning in pleasure. I smile at the simple joy on his face. Chasing it down with a sip of coffee, he looks at me. "So, lay it on me, Lucia. What questions do you have?"

"Do the other Horsemen live here too?"

"Yes, at one time or another. It's rare we'll all be here at the same time, but it does happen. We're either training or helping the Prophets with something. Two of my brothers are out at the moment."

"And the third one?"

"Oh, he's around here somewhere."

A question that's been burning in me for quite some time pushes to the forefront. "I assume you know that Elias believes me to be a Core. What do you think of all that, and the prophecy?"

His expression is contemplative as he says, "First, there's no 'believes,' Lucia. You *are* a Core. It might be hard for you to believe, but there's no doubt in my mind, or Elias's, for that matter. I suppose a part of who I am senses it. And Elias...well, being who he is, is in tune to such things as well. Not to mention you check all the prophecy boxes."

He pauses to take another bite of his cinnamon roll and I smile as he tips his head back and closes his eyes, once more groaning around the taste. He chases it with another sip of coffee and looks at me again.

"And overall, I'm grateful for the prophecy. I am the Red Rider, the Horseman of War. I am, in my nature, a strategist as much as I am a warrior. And I know that without the prophecy, whether I wanted to be or not, there would come a time when I would be leashed to hell, and all would be lost. I know some who would rather stick their head in the sand about this, but all information helps you strategize better when it comes to winning a war, even if it may be something you don't want to hear. Being leashed by darkness is not something any of us want. Being matched with my Core is a great gift from Elohim to prevent this world's complete fall to darkness, and I see it as the honor and blessing it is."

Another question sticks in my throat as I muster the courage to ask it, but before I get a chance, Cai speaks.

"And in case you're wondering, I do not believe you are my Core, Lucia. When a Horsemen finds his Core, besides the overwhelming draw he feels to her, his seal will change."

"Seal?"

"Yes, all Horsemen bear a heavenly seal, like a tattoo. It's the seat of our power and strength, the location of our mount, and it changes when we connect with our Core. It becomes more elaborate, and we think it will incorporate some sign of the Core each Horseman connects to."

"Wait, you *think*? You don't know?"

"Well, the prophecy is at times vague, and none of us have found our Cores yet. In fact, you are the first Core I've ever met."

My eyes widen in surprise.

"And yet you are sure I am not your Core?" I'm genuinely curious.

"Yes, other than a natural desire to see you protected and safe, as a Core and sister, there's nothing more. And from what I understand, the "more" will be made known very intensely. Also, my seal hasn't changed."

It's such a breath of fresh air, being around someone who answers my questions with simple honesty. It makes me so curious to learn more about the Horsemen.

"So, are there any special benefits to being a Horsemen? Like do you have powers or something?"

"Powers?" Cai chuckles, almost choking on his food. "I am not a superhero, Lucia, although I can't say that wouldn't be awesome. We are strong, probably stronger than average men, but we also train very intensively and are pretty hard to kill. We have the power of our mount, being able to call on them when in need. And when riding our mounts, we have the ability to distance jump, essentially like teleporting, as long as we've been to the area before."

"Uh, yeah, sounds to me like you have superpowers." I smirk, a thrill shooting through me at the idea of having that kind of ability. "I mean, I can't imagine being able to do that. If I could, I would have fled the ashram long ago."

Silence hangs in the air for a beat, before I push forward, not interested in receiving any pity or discussing my history at this moment. "And what do you mean 'call on your mount'?"

I can practically see the lightbulb turn on in his mind. Instead of answering, Cai abruptly stands. "I've got a great idea! I'm going to introduce you to Ginger!"

He comes around the table, grabs my hand, and practically drags me from the dining hall. I rush to keep up. He steers us through a hall to the black door I came through yesterday. He pushes a button and leads us outside, through the indigenous ruins that surround the entrance to The Refuge. We keep walking until we enter a grassy clearing surrounded by trees.

"You'll love this," he grins. His joy is contagious and makes me smile. He takes his shirt off facing me, and I try not to blush at his gorgeous physique. He bows his head, closes his eyes, and whispers, "Lavo Veshuv."

In a flash of golden-red light that seems to come from behind him, a gigantic and exquisite sorrel red horse suddenly appears before him.

I lift a hand to my mouth, gasping in shock and delight. I've never seen anything like this before.

He turns to me and says, "Ta-da! Lucia, meet my girl, Ginger."

Words fail me in the presence of this majestic, other-worldly animal. I extend a hand to her as she takes a step forward. My hand touches her soft muzzle.

"What was it that you whispered?" I ask Cai.

"It's from the ancient holy language. It means, 'Come forth.'"

The red of her mane is like fire, and almost glows. It reminds me of Ansel, and a pang of sadness hits my heart at the thought of how much I miss her. She would love this place.

"You okay?" Cai asks, his tone concerned.

"Yes, sorry. It's just Ginger reminds me of a friend I miss, my only friend, really. She's a redhead, too." A soft smile on my lips.

"Not your only friend anymore," he says with a grin. "You've got me now, too. Before you know it, you'll have more friends than you know what to do with."

Before I know what I'm about, I throw my arms around Cai and hug him, forgetting he's shirtless. Even so, he squeezes me back. Cai feels like a big brother to me. I now understand what he's saying about his sense that I am not his Core. I would imagine it wouldn't feel like hugging a sibling, probably more like what it feels like when I touch or hug Nic. A heaviness weights my heart at the thought.

Suddenly, an animalistic bellow tears through the silence, causing Ginger to rear and raising the hair on my arms. Cai puts a hand on her neck, calming her, his expression serious as stares off in the direction of the noise.

"What was that?"

"Not sure, but it's as good a reason as any to head back inside." He strokes Ginger's neck.

"Thank you, Cai, for being so forthcoming with me. It's been so nice to have an open conversation with a friend."

"You don't need to thank me. I am happy to spend this time with you. And you won't get rid of me that easily. Elias is expecting us, or should I say *you*. But I am going to stick around so I can give you a grand tour after the meeting before we all have to get ready for the big shindig tonight, so long as you're okay with that."

"That all sounds amazing," I say, genuinely pleased.

I watch as Cai closes his eyes again and whispers, "Baim Lyy." Ginger disappears in a flash of golden-red light. He throws his shirt on again and then sticks his elbow out to me. "Shall we?"

With a smile on my face, I thread my arm through his and we take off. This place might feel like home before I know it.

CHAPTER 20

"Come in," Elias calls from the other side of the door before we even knock.

"I still don't know how he does that," Cai whispers to me as we enter.

A smile lights my face at the familiarity between the two.

"Cai," Elias says, "before you sit and make yourself comfortable, I want to make sure Lucia is okay with you sitting in on this."

"I—"

"And before you answer, Lucia, I am going to make a hard request of you, but it will help us to know as much about your experience as possible."

Unease fills me, but I nod. Cai reaches out and grabs my hand, squeezing as he leans down. "I know what he's going to ask, and I'd like to be here as support if you'll allow me. Solidarity in numbers and all that jazz." He smiles reassuringly at me.

I nod again, waiting for the proverbial shoe to drop.

"If you are willing," Elias says, "we would like to hear of your time at the ashram. I know it may not be something you want to relive so soon, but your knowledge and experiences will give us a better understanding of what we are dealing with."

A bit relieved by the request, I swallow and nod. I'm not exactly surprised by his request; I knew at some point, this would happen, and it's best to get it out early so I can begin to put it behind me.

"I'm willing to help however I can."

Cai reaches out with another reassuring hand squeeze as we all take our seats, Elias in the wingback chair and Cai and me on the sofa.

"I'm not quite sure where to start," I confess, starting to fidget at the attention.

Cai's big hands cover mine as he says, "You don't need to be nervous with us, Lucia. We have no expectations."

"Why don't you start with what your day-to-day was like?" Elias suggests.

"Um, okay," I take a breath to gather my thoughts. "It was extremely boring. Most of my days were filled with lessons. When I was younger, the lessons were about world history and the state of the modern world. They presented the Amilign as saviors to our distraught and broken world. It wasn't until I turned eighteen and my lessons took an uncomfortable turn that I started questioning things.

"Recently, the Feminea Potentia came to stay for a few weeks, and I made a friend who opened my eyes to the truth. For the first time, I questioned what I'd been told and imagined leaving that place." I pause to take another deep breath as unwanted memories flood in.

"What were the lessons about, to make you change your thinking?" Elias questions.

"The monks started talking about a woman's body, describing certain parts in relation to her physical nature. It was extremely uncomfortable, and I came to dread it." I look down at my hands, picking at my fingernails.

"What gave me the final push to leave was when I discovered a paper in one of the monk's desks that outlined the details of the role of a Bolster Sage. The words 'Breeding Servant' were written just below that, and it included details on training, an ovulation timeline, and a non-ovulation rotation, whatever that means. I didn't necessarily understand most of that, but 'Breeding Servant' was pretty clear."

All of a sudden, the sound of splintering wood fills the room. I look up to see Cai's hand gripping an annihilated couch armrest, the wood shards poking out in all directions from underneath the fabric. His jaw is clenched so tight I'm surprised his teeth haven't cracked. I look to Elias, and his expression isn't much better. The bleak desolation leaking from his eyes is almost tangible. He's clearly unsurprised by Cai's reaction and strength.

When Cai said Horsemen were strong, he really meant it.

"I am sorry, Lucia," Elias says, "so very sorry that you went through that. We had suspected for some time that the Amilign have designs on the Cores for more than just preventing their connection to a Horseman. You see, each Core represents an attribute of Elohim's love. In essence, they are the central core of pure, real love from the very heart of Elohim. After lots of digging through our ancient scriptural texts, we discovered the four Cores represent the love elements of Protects, Trusts, Hopes, and Perseveres. Each one of you embodies one of those attributes.

"Through the sacrifice of far too many of our spies' lives, we discovered that the monks also have plans to damage or corrupt you beyond repair based on what attribute you represent. That is how they plan to prevent the connection to the Horsemen. Specifically, with you, it seems they had plans to use you to breed an offspring they hoped would hijack the power of Heaven within you. After hearing your experience, it only seems to corroborate those assumptions." Elias sighs as if the sharing of such information weighs heavily on his soul.

My pulse is a steady beat in my ears. *Breathe in, breathe out, you are safe.* I say it to myself over and over. When I no longer feel like a spool of thread unraveling, I push on.

"Does that mean you know what Core I am?"

"Unfortunately, not quite, though I have my thoughts on the matter. In some way, all of the Cores could be corrupted or damaged through that kind of abuse. I am certain it will be brought to light at the right time." Elias reassures me.

"Do you want to stop?" Cai says in a rough tone. His voice has me looking up from my hands to his face. Ice chills his gaze. This is not the playful Cai I'm used to. This is the Horseman of War looking back at me.

"No, I need to just get it all out." I swallow; the intensity of his gaze feels like a laser. He must see the action and sense the tension in me, because he closes his eyes and takes a few deep, calming breaths. When they reopen, warmer, softer eyes stare back at me. He nods.

"When you weren't in lessons, what were you doing?" Elias asks. "Did you see any prisoners? Do you know the names of the monks that you had to deal with?"

"I never saw prisoners; I wasn't allowed past certain doors. But right before my friend left, she broke into one of the doors and discovered an entire lower level of the ashram. She overheard a discussion regarding what sounded like a secret weapon that was almost ready called the Silent. She said she heard screams, and the monk was wiping blood off his hands."

Both men's eyes meet in concern. The air between them is charged with dread. Elias finally breaks eye contact and looks at me. I push on.

"That could be where any prisoners were kept. But I wasn't given much freedom. My room was windowless and small. It was somewhat claustrophobic, not being able to know what was going on in the world. I avoided being there at all costs, unless I was sleeping. But I had to be cautious about what I did or said, or they would punish me. Nothing really physical, other than the one time when I was twelve and Cain broke a rod over my back."

As if in chorus to my words, more wood cracking and splintering fills the air.

"Cai, do you need to leave?" Elias asks sternly.

Cai stands like a statue, fists gripping what was left of the couch armrest. When he gets his emotions under control, he looks to Elias. "No, my apologies. I was unprepared for the intense urge to war I would feel just by listening."

Cai turns his gaze on me again. "And to you, Lucia, I am supposed to be offering you comfort. Doing a great job of that, aren't I?" Contrition laces his voice as a pained half-laugh escapes his mouth. "I'll just stand over here so Elias still has some of his couch left when I leave."

"Please continue, Lucia," Elias says softly.

"Okay, so after that one time, anytime they wanted to

punish me, they would send me to a room they called the 'Den of Consciousness.' It was filled with some sort of smoke that altered your mind and will. It was what I dreaded more than anything."

"Must have been some kind of hallucinogenic, mind-clearing drug," Cai says in a rough voice.

I nod. "I constantly felt like I was walking a tightrope of doing what was expected and pretending to be what they wanted me to be, all so I could avoid that place. If I ever slipped up, or if they came up with another reason to punish me, like I didn't have something constructive to do or I didn't seem meek enough on a given day, they would send me there. That place strips you of all that you are, making you a compliant, moldable tool for their use. I know I lost memories and pieces of my childhood in there. I only ever spent a few hours in there at a time; the longest was twelve hours.

"But it took me days to feel myself again. I still wonder if pieces of myself were left behind, never to be found again. If anything gives me nightmares from my time there, it's that place." I finish quietly.

"I think that's probably enough for now," Elias says, his gravelly voice betraying his anger. "I am so sorry to make you relive that. We have never gotten a spy inside the mountain ashram, which is the main fortress of the Amilign, so every piece of information is helpful."

"Wait, you wanted names. The main monks that I encountered were Tavarious, Cain, and Amon. I met Legion, the Master Sage, when they took me to the ashram as a child. With his fair hair and skin, I stupidly thought him an angel or something. But even as a kid, I remember there being something off about him. Something not quite natural. Another name that was spoken in hushed tones was

Drystan, but I never met him. I got the feeling he handled the darker and dirtier side of whatever the Amilign do."

"Thank you, Lucia."

"I did have one question, Elias. You mentioned something about hijacking my offspring. What would make the Amilign think any child I had would swear allegiance to them? I mean, just because one of the parents is evil, doesn't mean the child will be, right?"

"You are right, but there's one thing I didn't mention to you. I was hoping to spare you this piece of information," Elias sighs and then presses on. "It was discovered years ago that the Master Sage, Legion, is in fact an upper-level demon, and as such, he can make himself as appealing and tempting as possible. That's probably the 'something off' you felt about him. In fact, many of the higher-ups within the Amilign are part demon, just lesser demons. They're called vessels. So any child you had would be a demon-bred vessel first. The demon always overrides any humanity."

I stare at him, taking in those words. I don't even know what to say in response to that. The thought of what was intended for me is a rabbit hole I can't go down. But it threatens to take me captive anyway. Just when I feel like my mind is preparing to run away with the what-ifs, Cai grabs my hands off my lap and pulls me to my feet.

"Come on. I have one more thing to show you before we need to get ready for your party."

We say a quick goodbye to Elias, and Cai leads me through the warm halls of The Refuge, out the main door, through trees, and down a winding path. Just when I begin to wonder where we could possibly be going, the path opens up and all the worries swirling in my mind moments ago dissipate like a fog exposed to the warmth of the sun. Before me, a beautiful garden sits, flush with life. Surrounded by a rustic-looking fence to keep animals out, it's far bigger than the garden I had as a child at the farm. From here, I can see zucchini, pumpkins, different varieties of peppers and tomatoes, cucumbers, and lettuce. Raised beds filled with berries line the fence.

I turn to Cai, my mouth hanging open. His eyes are alight with mischief as he smiles at me.

"How...what...I..." I stumble over a response.

"A little bird told me that gardening holds a special place in your heart. So I thought you would love to see ours. And turns out, our head gardener Willy would love some help."

At the mention of the name, a beautiful, middle-aged woman with a kind face and curly red- and grey-streaked hair stands up, putting her hands on her generous hips. "Did someone call my name?"

"Hey, Willy, I want to introduce you to someone." Cai smiles.

She walks toward us, taking her gloves off, shoving them in a large pocket on her apron and wiping her hands on the fabric.

"Lucia, meet Wilhelmina, more commonly known as Willy. Willy, this is Lucia, she's—"

"No need, Cai, we all know who Lucia is," Willy reaches for me, grabbing one of my hands between both of hers. "It's so nice to finally meet you, sweet girl. We are all so relieved to have you home safe."

"Lucia here has a deep love and skill for gardening, Willy. I told her you would love the help."

At Cai's comment, Willy's face lights up even more. "Absolutely," she says. "You are welcome here as often as you wish."

"Thank you so much Willy," I say softly, still a bit

awestruck by the magnitude of this garden and the emotions it's eliciting from me.

She nods with a knowing smile and disappears back into the greenery.

Tears begin to roll down my face unbidden. It's not only because of the realization that I get to be a part of growing and nurturing things again, which is the only time in my life I've ever truly felt like I had a purpose, that I was useful. But there's only one way Cai could have learned this about me.

Nic.

CHAPTER 21

Cai walks me back to my room, dropping me off at my door, with a quick side hug and a reminder that he'll see me in an hour. It's been an emotional rollercoaster of a day, and I'm really looking forward to my first party. It feels like another step in the direction of my new life and I can't wait.

Walking through my door, my eyes immediately go to a beautiful, royal blue dress laid out on my bed. The satin bodice is overlaid with chiffon. I try it on and it's absolutely exquisite, like nothing I've ever worn before. Surprised that it fits me perfectly, I turn to the mirror. It has a sweetheart neckline, with small cap sleeves and a low back. The skirt is long, touching the floor, with a split that reaches my thigh. It was the softest most beautiful thing to ever adorn my skin. Not sure what to do with my hair—I've never been allowed to wear it down—I decide to leave it in loose waves.

A light knock at the door startles me. Cracking it open, I peek around the door. Elias stands on the other side, holding a pair of lovely, black, strappy sandals.

"Not sure if these will fit you, but I wanted you to have the complete look for your first big celebration." He hands me the shoes with a smile.

"Thank you," I say, genuinely overcome by his thoughtfulness. I place the shoes on the floor, then step into them. Just a hair too small, they'll be fine for one night. I look up at Elias as a tear runs down my cheek.

"Oh my sweet girl, why the tears?" His voice is laced with concern; he reaches up to wipe my cheek with his thumb.

"I just...I've never had anything like this. I honestly didn't know if I would ever have experiences like this. I am just so grateful to be here. It almost feels like a dream to me."

He takes my hand in his, and I look up into his sad eyes. "I'm sorry you had to go through what you did. It hurts my heart to think of you alone in that place." He sighs. "But you are home now, and this is very much real. This celebration has been a long time coming; we are all so happy to have you returned to us. So let's go celebrate your birthday and your homecoming, Lucia, and you can meet everyone."

Elias walks me into the dining hall. All but a few tables against the wall have been removed. Music is being played by a few musicians in the corner. As I walk into the room, applause erupts, along with cheers. I freeze, overcome, not used to such attention. Elias smiles at me, easing any tension.

I scan the room. Many kind faces smile at me, but my eyes search mutinously for Nic. Instead, Cai walks toward me with a big grin on his face. He stops just in front of me, holding his hand out. "May I have this dance?"

"Yes, but I'm warning you, I have no idea how to dance." I place my hand in his.

"Why do you think they sent me in? You can hardly crush *my* toes." He winks.

I laugh as he begins to move me across the floor; the song is quick and upbeat. I can hardly believe I am having my first dance. Cai twirls me, my dress spinning around my legs. Carefree joy bubbles up inside me and I throw my head back in laughter. And yet tendrils of grief tease the back of my mind, that it's not Nic here with me. I swear I feel another crack in my heart appear.

Cai looks at me knowingly as we finish. "Come on, the only thing that makes a celebration better is cake."

I laugh again as he leads me to the table with the cake. A young boy hands me a plate with a slice, smiling at me as his face turns red.

"Thanks, Laz." Cai ruffles the boy's hair. Laz glares at him and shoves his hand off as I take a bite out of decadently delicious chocolate and strawberry cake, trying to suppress a moan.

"Lucia, meet Lazarus, otherwise known as Laz."

"Hi Laz, it's nice to meet you."

"You too," the boy says quietly.

"Laz here has been talking nonstop about your homecoming for weeks," says Cai, amusement on his face.

"I have not talked nonstop," the boy says indignantly to Cai, his dark eyes flashing. He turns to me and his demeanor becomes excited. "But I've heard the stories of how Sidora found you, then you growing up away from here and living in that house of demons. It's got to be so exciting! Better than being here day in and day out."

I struggle for words. "Well, I didn't think it was exciting, just the opposite, in fact. I couldn't wait to get away from there. If anything, being here is far more exciting than anything I've experienced in my life so far."

"Pick your jaw up off the floor, Laz. I told you how good you had it. You're too young to be so disgruntled already. But I've got a good remedy for that. We'll get you out to spar with me soon and burn off some of that restless energy." Cai tousles the boy's hair again, despite Laz's clear loathing of it. Cai throws our plates away and grabs my hand, leading me back to the dance floor.

This time the song is a slow, romantic melody that drifts through the air. Cai grabs my waist, my hand tucked into his, and pulls me into his chest as he slowly sways across the floor. I've only ever been this close to Nic. It should be easy to stay focused on Cai but all I can seem to think about is Nic. The memories he's drawn on my mind will never be erased.

Cai reaches up to move a strand of hair that has fallen across my eyes, and at that moment, another animalistic bellow roars through the hall, stopping the music and everyone in place. We turn toward the source of the sound and I see Nic standing there, rage pouring from him, his normally blue eyes pools of endless black. I realize that Nic must have been the source of that noise in the woods earlier. I was almost in the exact position with Cai that I am now.

My mind tries desperately to quantify what I am seeing. His body shakes with tremors, his fists clenched at his sides. He rolls his neck and shakes his head, as if trying to clear something from his mind. His black eyes are intent on me, and I'm surprised that even in this state of chaos, and the sheer terror he elicits from around the hall, my heart responds to him, lighting up like an ember exposed to a strong wind.

Elias steps toward Nic, placing his hands on his shoulders and speaking in low tones. Nic's unusual eyes flicker between black and blue in response to Elias's words, but his gaze is still locked on me. I sense such pain and turmoil in his eyes; he's struggling for control and he's hurting. Something is wrong with him—my heart cleaves in two at that thought.

Letting go of Cai, I walk up to him. I can feel all eyes on me. Surprisingly, I don't care. My only concern is for Nic.

Elias steps aside, one hand still on Nic's shoulders as he hears me approach. I instinctively reach a hand up and place it on Nic's chest, over his heart. A shudder racks him from head to toe. His eyes close, his erratic breathing fights to slow.

"Get closer, Lucia," Elias whispers. "You soothe him."

Confused by his words, yet unafraid, I step right up to him. My head at his chest, my hand still over his heart. Instinctively, I lean into him, resting my cheek against his chest. I hear his pounding heartbeat begin to slow. I take slow, deep breaths, subconsciously willing my calm into him. As his heart begins to calm, I feel his arms reach up and surround me. He holds me to his chest like a drowning victim clings to a life raft. One of his hands slides through my hair, sending shivers through me. It feels like coming home.

All too soon, he begins to pull away from me. His eyes avoid mine. It takes everything in me to stay in place instead of pressing up against him again.

"I...I'm sorry for the interruption."

He turns, leaving the hall swiftly, the silence deafening. From the corner of my eye, I see some of the people shake their heads. I turn to look at Cai, and for the first time, his eyes are downcast, his expression bleak.

Elias must signal to the musicians because they start playing again, but I see him sneak out of the hall after Nic.

As Cai approaches, I turn to him. "I need a moment." Somberly, he nods.

I leave the hall, intent on heading back to my room and just breathing for a moment, trying and failing to quench the flame burning its way through my veins, when I hear voices down the hallway. I am so over all these mysteries; it's time to get some answers. I tiptoe up to the corner, staying hidden.

"You cannot keep this up, Nic—you are losing yourself. Can you not see it?"

"I don't see how I have another choice here. Can't *you* see that? Do you think I want to be struggling like this? It's only when I'm around her that this happens. If I were to leave or just stay away, it wouldn't be a problem. I know you don't agree, Elias, but I don't see another choice."

"I love you like a son, Nic. It kills me to see you like this. I always knew that surrender would be hardest for you, your nature being what it is. But you must remember that Elohim gave you a mind *and* a heart. And you are only at your strongest when using both in tandem. "

"I know, and I love you too. I just need some space and time, you'll see."

"Well, you're right about one thing, we *will* see, but I fear it may be too late at that point. Be warned—we often come face to face with our own destruction on the path we seek to avoid it. Please, consider my words, I beg of you."

I hear them embrace, then a muffled, "I will."

I turn and swiftly head down the hall, my thoughts too chaotic to return to dancing. I retreat to my room. What possible risk could Nic be referring to? And what is with his eyes and the intensity? Elias said he was losing himself.

Whatever it is, I am determined to find out the truth.

CHAPTER 22

LUCIA

It's been a whole month since the night of the celebration, and since then, Nic has managed to avoid me completely. Cai is quiet and oblivious whenever I ask about him, quick to change the subject. I am no closer to the answers I seek.

But I've gotten to know some of the people here at The Refuge, making this place slowly start to feel like home. Most are Prophets and the families of Prophets, like Seb and Isa, the twins that run the kitchens. At twenty-two, they are only a few years older than me, and their love of cooking, baking, and creating gives me an instant connection to them. They've made me feel welcome by delivering surprise concoctions and treats to my room.

"The way I figure it," Isa drawls, "you need to make up for lost time, having had to live without comfort food for far too long. That's just inhuman! You deserve a little spoiling, and I plan to deliver."

"Best not to try to argue or talk her out of it Lu," says

Seb. "When my sister sets her mind on something, she will stick with it come hell or high water."

"Like you're one to talk, Seb!" Isa scolds. "Heaven forbid I try to change the spices on your precious cinnamon roll recipe. You know it would do you good to try something new, you might just love it."

"Now, now, ain't nothing in that recipe that needs changing. When you achieve perfection, you leave it be." Seb smirks.

I wave my wordless goodbyes as I quickly stuff a cinnamon roll in my mouth on the way to the garden. Their banter is one of the reasons the kitchen has become a favorite hangout of mine. That, and all the delicious recipe experimenting I get to sample. Seb and Isa came to live here when they were children with their dad, who is one of the Prophets. He foresaw the destruction of their town and fled to The Refuge. Tragically, being gifted with prophecy didn't prevent the death of their mother when they fled. It seems there's not a family or person here who is untouched by abuse or loss. Even Willy, who I've been spending much of my time with in the garden, has a grisly and telling scar that marks her neck and a history that haunts her eyes when she thinks no one is looking.

If there's a place at The Refuge that has quickly stolen my heart in my time here, it's the gardens. Nothing else has done so much to make this sanctuary feel like home. I am in my element out there with Willy, and she's been so kind to quickly bring me into the fold. Working in the garden with Willy is calming and relaxing, and I suppose part of the reason why is that Willy is quiet-natured. Perfectly content to work alongside me, without the need to fill the space with words. Both of us soaking in the peace the work offers us, the birdsong a musical chorus for our souls. Hours fly by like minutes out here.

I sense there is so much more under the layers with Willy, things she's not ready or willing to dig up from where she's buried them. Her scars tell of a past life of violence. There are only a few superficial things I do know about her from the few conversations we've had.

"You don't by any chance know Sidora do you?" I ask as we both hang up our aprons for the day, stowing our gloves.

She turns and faces me, a warm look of fondness on her face. "I do, she saved my life. When I first arrived here, I was not in a good way. She stumbled upon me just outside The Refuge. If it wasn't for her, I don't think I'd be here." Her eyes get a faraway look in them, as if she is being pulled into the memories that she's worked so hard to bury.

"Really? I miss her so much. I just wish I could see her again. Talk with her," I add wistfully.

Willy turns her eyes back to me, an ache in them as she speaks. "When we met, she was just returning from you being taken by the monks. While I was recovering, she checked on me often and we spoke. Well, *she* spoke, but she told stories of you and your life together at the farmhouse. Her love and fondness for you saturated every conversation, Lucia. I have no doubt if she could be here for you, she would. In fact, Sid is the reason I started working in the garden. She thought it would be a healing place for me."

"And has it been?" I hesitantly question, as I know her past is a topic she avoids.

She is quiet a long time, looking off into the horizon, so I wait. Just when I begin to think she won't answer, she looks at me, and the pain and horror reflected back at me in her eyes tells me everything I need to know. Without any prompting, I pull her into a hug. I cling to her as if I can anchor her to the here and now and keep the nightmares at bay.

When she speaks, I'm not sure she means the words for me, but I hear them nonetheless. "There are some things too broken to heal."

And my heart cracks a bit more. I think in some way, Willy and I need each other. She reminds me of my Aunt Sid, easing the pain of missing her, and I think there's something about being near me that soothes Willy too.

Parting ways with Willy, I head back into The Refuge to meet up with Elias. Many kind faces smile at me as I make my way to the library. I've realized in my time here that there's a level of solidarity among the residents. The kind that comes from a familiarity with suffering.

A select few of those who live in The Refuge are orphans of this world, as Elias would say. Like young Lazarus. Found on the streets of one of the few big cities left, living in a makeshift large cardboard box at a mere six years old. He didn't have a name, so Elias named him Lazarus, like the story in the ancient Scriptures of the man Lazarus, who was dead but given new life. So too was Lazarus given new life when he was given a home and a family with the Prophets.

Laz has grown on me, like the younger sibling I've always wanted. He's hungry for news of places beyond The Refuge, so I've shared with him stories of my childhood with Sidora and of my time in the ashram. He is especially interested in how I escaped and found Nic. I keep those stories brief; like digging at an old wound, they contain thoughts and feelings that need to stay buried.

I have come to truly enjoy my time with Elias, learning about all the details of the prophecy. He explains to me how each Core was created by Elohim, in a way as a weapon.

Not in the sense that the world would assume, but as a heavenly weapon of the heart of Elohim. The greatest power of all: pure love.

Elias has his theories about which Core I am, but he says it may not be fully revealed until I connect with my Horseman. I don't ask him if connecting with a Horseman means romantic love or something else. I am not ready to admit I still hold out some twisted form of hope with Nic. I ask him when I will meet the others and he says that will come in Elohim's time. I don't understand how he can be so calm when it seems so much is riding on the Cores connecting with their Horsemen. But he just says, "Elohim's timing is perfect; we wait on Him."

Finally walking through the double doors of the library, I join Elias in what's become my favorite resting spot. Comfy wingback chairs sit near one of the warm, amber windows. A low round coffee table sits between them, surrounded by scattered scrolls and dusty parchment while we discuss another vague part of the prophecy.

"The gift of Heaven will be unknown to them until activated." I read, then look at Elias. "That's it? What's a *'gift of Heaven'* and how will we activate it?"

"Unfortunately, our scholars have been unable to determine what a gift of Heaven is specifically. But as for the activation part, we believe it will tie into the connection between a Core and her Horseman. It's not clear if the connection is formed through touch or something deeper, like acceptance within the heart. However, recent information has been revealed to us, leading us to believe it has to do with the heart, which would also make more logical sense with the Cores themselves being of the heart of Elohim."

My brows pinched as I let out a sigh of frustration. "I don't know how you can stand it. Parts of this prophecy are so vague. Why can't it just say 'Go here, and do this, and this is what will happen'?"

A deep, belly laugh bursts from Elias that fills the quiet library. The laugh lines on his face crinkle, causing me to smile.

"Ah, Lucia, there is a purpose and growth to be found in the journey. It is through the seeking that we often discover the depths of who we are and who we are to become. Easy almost never equals worthwhile."

I frown. "What about this part: *'They will be brought to the world on a day made holy by its twin of seven. You will find them with three of sevens; a unique mark of Heaven they will bear.'* Seems like a miracle that Aunt Sid was able to find me if these were the clues."

"Sidora has studied the prophecy and historical texts alongside us for years, so for her, it was not quite the challenge it would seem. For example, seven is Elohim's holy number. So *a day made holy by its duo of seven* can only be one day, July 7th, the day you were born. Now *three of sevens* signifies that more sevens would surround your location, revealing who you are. Sidora found you in the newborn ward of a hospital on 7th Street in one of the remaining big cities where she frequently did reconnaissance. You were in the number seven bassinet, and your time of birth was listed as 7PM sharp.

"Now, the mark of Heaven was tricky because that could be anything, but lucky for Sidora, she found a small birthmark on the back of your neck in the shape of a star, much like the Holy Star of old sent by Elohim as a guide. Fitting, that symbol would act as the final guide to finding you." He smiles.

I sit in silence, his words a weight around my neck. It's a lot to live up to. Part of me thinks it would be amazing to be linked to a Horseman, and have a love that is a gift straight from Heaven and Elohim Himself. After the life I've lived so far, I wanted nothing more than to find my true purpose. But I can't help all the doubts that surface. I'm not any different than anyone else out there, and definitely not more deserving.

Why me?

"What is it, Lucia? Your face is so expressive, I can see the turmoil and questions written all over it."

"It's just all so overwhelming. I suppose I should be grateful that Elohim chose me for such an honor, but I can't help questioning why. I feel like I barely know who I am. And I want to be worthy of this, but I can't help but feel like I need more courage, more confidence, more everything, to be honest." I stare at my hands, afraid to see the disappointment in Elias's eyes. Even in this short time, I've come to respect and care for the older man like I would a father.

"Lucia, look at me," he says firmly.

I glance up and find his expression serious but warm. "You are human and emotions are part of that. Do not be ashamed; this is all part of your journey. First, we prideful humans often think that to be chosen by Elohim means we are some great and glorious thing. But in reality, Elohim is in the business of love and redemption, which almost always means He chooses those who are most desperately in need of both.

"Think of it this way: you don't set a lamp out to shine in a bright room; it's not necessary and will probably not be noticed. A lamp is truly powerful when it shines in the darkness. The beauty and power of Elohim's love and redemption is at its peak in situations of seemingly impossible odds. I believe He chose and created his Cores from abandoned orphans in desperate situations for this reason.

To show His glory and to show you that your worth lies not in your circumstances, but in something much deeper and more profound.

"You are His child and creation, His purpose for you is powerful, and your worth is immeasurable, not because you are a Core, but because you are loved and chosen by Him. Just in the short time I've gotten to spend with you, I see a quiet strength and depth of heart in you that mirrors Elohim. Your strength is not in loud and obvious things, but in the secret and stealthy places that leave you often underestimated and passed over by our enemies. Have no doubt, Lucia, Elohim chose you for a reason, for only you could connect with the Horseman you are meant to and protect him from being leashed by hell. A protection he himself could not muster with all the strength in the world."

CHAPTER 23

Elias's words stay with me long after he leaves me in that library chair with a father-like kiss on the top of my head. A headache is growing behind my eyes; I needed to turn my brain off and get some fresh air. I head out into the sunlight. Wandering a path through beautiful, dense trees, the sun creates a kaleidoscope of light that trickles down through the canopy. A sense of calm washes over me.

Up ahead, voices, grunts, and the clash of metal pull me from my reverie and have me slowing my pace. I must have stumbled upon the training arena. I approach a spot where I can easily see into the open area without disturbing anyone. A tremor works its way through my body as I see who's on the field.

Cai squares off with Nic. Both men are shirtless and sweating, and both hold long swords. Cai's hair is slicked back against his head, while Nic's hangs forward into his eyes, all wild and unkempt, much like the inner spirit of the man himself. I watch as they spar, the grace and strength with which they move almost like a dance. They are both beautiful, but Nic is like a beacon in the dark to me. Neither seems to get the upper hand over the other.

My desperate eyes soak up Nic after not seeing him for so long. I should move on, but I can't get my legs to respond. After a while, Nic and Cai stop. I swear Cai looks right to where I am hidden by the shrubs, but there is no way he can see me. Unless inhuman eyesight is another of the Horsemen's skills. I wouldn't be surprised at this point.

I watch as Cai bows his head, a mark between his shoulder blades glowing. In a flash of golden-red light, Ginger appears before him. He looks to Nic, gesturing with his hand, and a sense of foreboding fills me. I watch as Nic turns, his back to me. I'm struck by his seal again. The same one I traced with my finger, but now I notice that it is almost identical to Cai's seal, apart from one minor difference. In the center of the black horseshoe is a golden key.

My stomach sinks and my eyes widen as he bows his head. In a flash of brilliant bright white light, Adira appears before him.

It's as if all the oxygen has been sucked out of my lungs. A shocked gasp flies from my lips before I can suppress it. I stagger away from my hiding place, stumbling back as if dealt a physical blow. Nic's eyes find mine in less than an instant. Everything I thought has been thrown off-kilter, and yet my stupid, traitorous body still responds to him.

As if the time apart only intensified my feelings, heat pulses across my skin. Not the warmth of safety, but the flash of a spark, threatening to ignite an out-of-control flame. I tremble, my nails digging into my palms.

Everything is suddenly crystal clear. I know without a doubt that Nic is no stablehand; he is a Horseman. And not just any Horseman; he is my Horseman. That's why I dreamed of Adira. And it's how I know without a doubt that I am a Core; I feel it deep inside me with this connection.

But the worst revelation of all is that it doesn't matter if I am a Core and Nic is my Horseman. It's clear to me now he doesn't want this. He doesn't want me.

As though I'm underwater, everything muffled and dimmed, I stand frozen. I watch as Cai places his hand on Nic's shoulder, saying something in his ear. And then, with a pat on his back, he mounts Ginger and rides off. Nic's head is down as he runs a hand through his hair, clearly weighing his choices, maybe debating whether or not to run.

My shock gives way to righteous indignation. I am done with the distance. I practically stomp out of the covering of the trees toward him. One way or another, we are going to have it out and get to the bottom of this.

Stopping in front of him, I stare, my hands folded across my chest to keep them from fidgeting or even worse, shaking.

"It's time for answers," I demand. "No more lies and no more excuses."

He looks up, surprised by my tone. But I don't care. I am not the girl the Amilign tried to groom me to be. Elias's words flow through me now, and I know he is right. I am not weak.

"You're right. We can no longer avoid this conversation."

"I wasn't the one avoiding anything; quite the opposite, in fact. And because of that, I'll ask the questions. You can answer and fill in anything I'm forgetting."

He nods solemnly in response. Adira walks forward through the grass toward me. Her soft nose nuzzles my hair while she nickers at me. My heart rate calms a bit as I reach up to pet her jaw.

"She senses you're upset; she doesn't like it."

Adira turns her head to Nic and snorts at him.

"And clearly she's not pleased with you," I say, secretly pleased she's on my side.

"Yeah, well, she can get in line," he mutters.

"So you're a Horseman," I state as I rub Adira's soft coat, letting the motion soothe the frenzy that is my mind right now.

"I am the White Horseman of Conquest."

"Your seal, it's different from Cai's," I state.

He freezes at my words. "What do you mean?"

"There's a golden key in the center now. I saw your tattoo or seal or whatever when we first met, and that gold key is definitely new."

Surprise is written all over his face. He visibly swallows. "My seal has changed." He isn't really speaking to me, just quietly saying the words as though he is afraid to give them breath and make it all too real.

"What does that mean?" I ask, even though deep down, I know. Cai said as much in the woods when he told me about their seals. Still, I suppose I need to hear Nic say it.

"You." His eyes are downcast, fixing on an unknown point on the ground.

"What do you mean me?" I demand, annoyed with his short, vague answers.

He brings his eyes to mine. "It changed because of you. I don't know when, but I know it's because of you. It's gold, yes?" He steps closer to me.

I nod, words failing me at the awestruck reverence in his tone. His hand reaches out and a knuckle brushes my cheekbone. "Gold like your eyes?"

I barely breathe. I don't need to answer. He's probably

known for a while now, just like I did, deep down I suppose. He stares at me, waiting for a response.

I take a deep breath and turn away from him. I can't look at him as I say what I am about to say. "I am your Core."

It's only seconds, but it feels like hours until he answers.

"You are," he says softly.

I'm a storm of emotions. All the times we were drawn to each other, just for him to push me away. I thought his reasoning was because I'm meant to be with another, when the truth of it is much harsher.

I turn back to face him. "Did you lie all this time because you don't want a Core? You don't want me?" I hate the insecurity and vulnerability in my voice.

The harsh lines of his face soften at my words. "It's not about what I want. And I didn't really lie, I just avoided answering your questions." Something like grief colors his tone. I resist the urge to comment on that.

"A lie by omission is still a lie. I mean, I thought you were a stable hand, for crying out loud."

"Well, I do work with horses, so it's not a far-off assumption."

"And the trip out here...Adira didn't 'find' us, she was with you the whole time. There were so many opportunities for you to just tell me. And what do you mean, it's not about what you want? I don't get it. Why didn't you tell me who you were when you first met me?"

"I didn't know what you had been through, and Elias warned me to be careful with you. My conquering nature can have me coming on too strong in situations. I thought it would be overwhelming if you knew that I was there for you and who I was. And we didn't know if you would welcome that kind of news."

"I am not weak, Nic, I can handle the truth. I lived through far more challenging situations than hearing the truth from you. Which I asked for repeatedly, in case you forgot."

He goes to step toward me but then stops. "I know, Lu, I think you're incredibly strong. I guess part of me was trying to protect you, but another larger and more selfish part of me was trying to avoid this conversation altogether."

"You still didn't answer my question. What do you mean, it's not about what you want? I mean, you are my Horseman and I'm your Core. It's why I dreamed of Adira. And it's why there's this intensity when we are together. You're even marked by the truth, for crying out loud."

"Yes," he says, his eyes suddenly flashing black as his fists clench at his sides. "It's definitely not Cai." He practically spits this out, his chest rising sharply at the declaration.

How can he admit I'm his Core, reject me, and then get possessive and jealous about my friendship with Cai all in the same breath?

"I seriously don't get you," I blurt. "You are giving me whiplash with the range of your emotions and responses. You clearly don't want anything to do with me, but then you go all gorilla man on me regarding anything to do with Cai."

"You're wrong," he says, yearning in his tone. "I want you more than I've wanted anything in my long life, but I can't have you. That's why I stay away. It's too much of a risk." He sighs.

My breath hitches at his words.

"I wanted to spare you from this, because you've already dealt with enough in your life—this is my problem to worry about. But I know you won't let this go." He sighs again, running a hand through his hair. "There is a part of the prophecy that is vague regarding the weakening of the Horsemen."

"Yeah, I've been studying the prophecy with Elias. You are referring to the part that says, '*The seal of the Horsemen will be forever altered, in outward appearance as well as in the depth of each Horseman's being. For once you are made weak, only then can you truly be made strong.*' But I don't see anything overly alarming in that. It does say you will be made strong, right?"

"Well, one of the scholars believed that the *being made weak* portion means that we will lose our immortality and—"

"Wait, you guys are immortal?" I interrupt as memories start clicking into place. "Oh my gosh, that's why you didn't want me to see your back after the rock slide. You were hurt worse than you were letting on, weren't you? Cai said you were hard to kill but he didn't say immortal!"

"Yes, but I knew it would heal quickly, so it was no concern. And we aren't exactly immortal per se, but we have regeneration capabilities and let's just say are difficult to kill, not that we've fully tested it. But therein lies the biggest problem. We are created to fight for this world, and we can't do that if we are easily killed. I can't risk losing that. I can't be made weak, just to end up with some sort of inner strength of spirit or something that won't help me defeat what's to come."

"What does Elias say?"

"Let's just say he disagrees."

"Cai doesn't seem to share your concerns. He told me he sees the connection as an honor."

"Yeah, well, Cai is a bit of a dreamer, even if he is the Horseman of War." He rolls his eyes.

"But what about the whole 'leashed by hell' thing? I mean, that sounds like a huge risk you are taking."

"But that's the thing, it's not for me. I am a conqueror in my nature, so if there's anything I can do, it's conquer this beast that seeks to control me. It's what I was created for. Even more so than my brothers, it has to be me who remains as I am."

"I..."

"What?" He sends me a quick glance when I don't continue.

"It's just that it seems like you are letting fear of the unknown control your decision-making. And from what I've seen of you, it doesn't seem like you are having the best of luck conquering this. I'm guessing that's what the black eyes signify?"

"That's where you're wrong. The key is just keeping distance between us. When I am near you is when it's a battle. But I haven't let it win." He pauses. "It has gotten the better of me a few times, but it's only when my emotions are running high."

As if on a reel, my mind recalls memories of his black eyes after the passionate kiss in the woods, when he said cruel and hurtful words to me that were so out of character for him. And then, during the party, when he appeared like a wild animal after seeing Cai and I dancing together. His eyes shifted between jet black and the usual blue as he tried to regain himself.

I weigh his words. "What about what's between us? I know you feel the power of this connection. It's all-consuming, at least for me."

He sighs, his shoulders sagging. "I know, it is for me as well. But I think it will decrease as we stay apart over time, or at least I hope. And I remember what you told me on the journey here, Lu. I know you want your own life, and to make your own choices. This is the best decision for all of us. It will give you that freedom. And if my brothers find and accept their Cores, at least I will still retain my power and be able to protect them and all of us. I know the pain of denying this bond is an inconvenience, but we just need to give it time."

Adira moves between Nic and me as if she's trying to shield me from the heartbreak of his words. He can't see the tear that slips down my cheek, quickly absorbed by the hair on Adira's neck. It hurts that he sees what's between us as merely an inconvenience. That he can so easily push it aside.

And he can't see that the real choice I want the freedom to make is to choose him, to choose us, to choose love. But I know he bears the weight of the prophecy and he's afraid. It's hard to conquer what you can't see coming. But how can it be so easy for him to stay away from me?

Still, I will give him what he wants, because I know what it means to have no choice.

"Lu?"

A thousand retorts rise to the tip of my tongue, but I silence them all. "Okay," I say softly, as I cling to Adira to ground me.

"Let me see your face," he says.

"Why? You're not supposed to care, Nic, remember? If we do this your way, then you must stop with the back and forth. Drawing me close and then pushing me away. It's torturing me."

"Baim Lyy, Adira," Nic says, as if he's trying to conquer even this situation.

But Adira snorts and paws the ground in irritation. I rub her neck, giving her a gentle kiss. "It's okay, go to him. And thank you for everything." Another traitorous tear slips down my face as Adira disappears before my eyes.

"She's never resisted me before. I didn't even know she could." Surprise on his face, Nic takes me in, tracking the trail left behind by the tear. He begins to lean forward, but pulls himself back. His fists clenching and unclenching at his side, a muscle tics in his jaw.

I have to get out of here before I completely fall apart. I quickly turn to leave. The longer I stay, the harder it will be to leave him.

"Goodbye, Nic." And I don't look back as I let the tears fall, praying they can wash away the pain, too.

CHAPTER 24

LUCIA

I run to my room, hoping to reach a place of solitude before I'm seen; where I can fall apart without an audience. Instead, I run into Laz, quite literally. I grab him before he falls.

"I...I'm sorry Laz, I wasn't paying attention."

"Oh, it's okay, I..." he stops as he sees my face. He may be young, but he's not oblivious. "What's wrong, Lucia?"

I sigh. I don't really want to get into it, and I'd rather be alone, but he looks at me with such genuine care and concern in those dark, soulful eyes of his that my resistance fades away. He's about half a head shorter than me, his limbs all long and gangly, like a newborn giraffe.

"So much, Laz, I don't even know where to start."

He reaches out and grabs my hand. "Come with me."

He leads me through The Refuge to a small ladder hidden in the back of what seems to be a utility closet. He starts climbing toward a hatch at the ceiling. When he gets to the top, he turns to look at me; a boyish grin makes his eyes glimmer. He gestures with his hand for me to follow.

"Trust me, this is worth it."

Despite my reservations, his look of adventure and joy brightens everything, and I follow him up the ladder. "I'm going to open the hatch, so keep your eyes looking down. It gets covered in dirt by the wind, so stuff tends to fall in when it slides open, but it provides good camouflage from the outside."

He pushes a large button and the hatch slides away; dirt trickles down on top of us. Laz gets the brunt of it, being right at the door. The sun streams through, lighting up the dark room, and I can smell the fresh air beckoning as Laz climbs out of the hole into the light.

He reaches down a helping hand for me as my head clears the hole. As I straighten, my breath freezes in my lungs at the majestic view surrounding me. We are at the top of the cliff. Snow-capped peaks in the distance stand in stark contrast to the sapphire blue of the open sky. Interspersed between clusters of dense forest are fields of tall, golden grass stretching out for miles, moving in steady waves with the wind. The movement is a calming balm to my soul.

It's the golden hour, when the sun begins its descent and lights everything up in the hue of what I imagine Heaven to be like. It creates in me an awe and reverence at the beauty before me.

Laz gently takes my hand and leads me to a large rock, smooth and perfect for perching on.

"This is my favorite place here," he says softly. The black fringe of his hair blows across his light brown skin. "It makes me feel close to Elohim, like I'm sitting on a canvas of His making."

I glance at him as he looks out across the wide expanse; he seems so much older than he is. Still technically a child, but prematurely aged by his life experiences. I relate to him in that. My experiences often make me feel much older as well. The only difference is that my life started out in the light before entering the darkness; his started out in darkness before being brought into the light.

"How old are you, Laz?"

"I'm twelve, what about you?"

"Nineteen, though I often feel older."

"Yeah, me too. Everyone treats me like a child, though, since I'm the youngest here."

"You're special, Laz. They love you and want what's best for you. Even if their protection can sometimes be a bit misguided." My words resonate inside me, reminding me of Nic.

We sit in silence for a while, Laz doesn't push me, which is another sign of his maturity. He just lets me just soak up the peace of this place, cradled in the hands of Elohim. How I wish I could know what He wants from me in this situation. He has this grand purpose for me, but how I am to fulfill it in the face of such hurt and rejection is a mystery. Especially when I know what it's like to be forced into something.

"Do you ever wish we could know everything about Elohim? See Him, talk directly to Him? That there was less mystery and unknown?"

He looks at me, contemplative, before returning his stare to the horizon. "I think it's human to want that. We always crave more knowledge. But Elohim is who He is because His ways and knowing are so far above what we can understand. And I think that a Creator that you could know all about wouldn't be worthy of knowing at all."

The golden sunlight shines on him, making him appear like an angel. And at this moment, when I need a friend, need encouragement, I suppose that's exactly what he is to me. Expressing wisdom far beyond his years. I tilt my head to the side, resting it on his shoulder as he sits a bit higher on the boulder with his knees pulled up to his chest, his arms wrapped around them. We stay like that as the sun starts to drop below the peak, casting everything in a dimmer light. Dusk is settling into darkness as we return to The Refuge, back to reality.

Laz heads to the dining hall; I think he spends most of his time in there. At his age, he's a bottomless pit of hunger. He waves goodbye to me at the door.

"See you later, Lulu."

I smile at the familiarity of the nickname, the same one Ansel gave me. I wave at him and head to the library, in search of something to occupy my thoughts tonight instead of letting them drift toward heartache. As I walk through the shelves, scanning for a title or book that draws my eye, I hear voices in one of the reading alcoves. I glance through the shelves and see it's Cai and Nic, their expressions serious. It looks like Cai is giving Nic a tongue-lashing. Irritation flits across Nic's face. I move to the end of the aisle to try to hear what they are saying, hunkering down near the bottom shelves to hide.

"You're being a proud and ignorant idiot!"

"Your opinion isn't wanted or needed, Cai."

"I don't know how after over a hundred years of living on earth, you can't see how much is changing in the time you've known Lucia. You're making the wrong call out of fear, brother. I mean, geez, even your seal has changed! It's like your body is recognizing what you can't get through your thick skull."

One hundred years! They've been here for one hundred years even though they only look to be in their 20s! I sit dumbfounded as I shamelessly continue to listen.

"It's not just about the prophecy or my concerns. I know that's what I've told Lu, but it's more than that. She's never had a choice in anything, Cai, even my bringing her here. She deserves a choice. She deserves freedom. At the very least, I can give her that. I don't want her to resent anything. She's had enough stolen from her."

"Have you even tried to ask her what she wants, or did you just pull on your big conqueror boss man pants and tell her what's best?"

Well, Cai definitely has his number. I can't see Nic's face from this angle, but he doesn't respond right away. It's clear Cai's words carry weight, and he understands Nic's typical way of operating.

"Do you have any idea what she's been through, how tough she is? Did you know that one of those depraved monks beat her with a rod so badly, he broke it over her back when she was just twelve? And then there's the Den that's filled with hallucinogenic smoke; they threw her in there whenever they wanted to make her pliant. After all of that, don't you think she's strong enough to handle anything you could throw at her? I damn sure bet at the very least, she knows what she wants."

Cai is breathing heavily by the time he finishes, frustration clear in his voice. My heart warms at his defense of me. It's a weird sensation to be so *seen* by someone, when I am so used to being invisible.

Nic pauses for a while. When he finally speaks, he sounds somber, as if he is tired from the constant fight that is his life.

"Look, my mind is made up. She's too young to be forced into this decision, to be shackled to an overbearing conqueror like me. And I just can't risk what the prophecy hints at. It's really the best option. I am strong enough, no matter what you and Elias think, to keep the leashing at bay. I just need space from her." He says this in an emotionless tone, his barriers back up.

"You just got home, Nicanor. You can not just leave again. Especially with how precarious things are, we need to be able to help you. I'm your brother. Let me help you."

Nic sighs, rubbing a hand through his hair. "I just don't see how that's possible with her here."

His words are another knife in my heart. I know what I have to do. I finally found a safe place that feels like home, but now I need to leave. This was Nic's home before I ever came along, and I know he needs The Refuge more than I do. I can only hope that Elias will understand—I'll need his help if I am to get to where I need to go. And that Laz will forgive me for disappearing without saying goodbye.

The warm halls of The Refuge suddenly feel dimmer as I head to Elias's office. Before I even get a chance to knock, a voice from within says, "Come in."

I open the door, entering the space that so firmly says 'Elias' to me after my short time here. It's dark wood, beige walls, a worn-in couch, and an aged burgundy rug. A set of double doors in the corner must connect to his private bedroom. The space is small and cozy, with floor-to-ceiling windows that offer a glimpse into the training area and outer ruins.

"How'd you know I was there?"

"I just had a feeling," he says, coming around his desk and gesturing to the small couch. "Come, tell me what's on your mind."

"I am so grateful to you, Elias, for all you've taught me and how you've welcomed me in the weeks I've been here. But—"

"You're leaving," he interrupts.

My eyes widen in surprise. "I...I can't stay, no matter how I might want to. I would like to go back to the farm where I lived with Aunt Sid. You said she goes there on occasion. I want to see if I can get in touch with her."

He closes his eyes and sighs. "Yes, I too believe the next stage of your journey will take you away from us again, but it's vague. I can't see whether it's supposed to be now or later. I don't have a direction for you, Lucia, and that concerns me. I must say that it feels too soon."

"There's no choice, Elias, I must go." I plead.

"If you are sure, I will help you with directions and everything you need. The farm is only a day's journey from here on horseback. When would you like to leave?"

"Tonight. I wish to leave as soon as possible."

"Okay, then there's no time to waste. We will eat first, and then I will help you with everything."

"I have to say, I'm surprised by your willingness to let me go. I expected to have to argue and persuade you," I say, curious and a bit confused.

"You are not a prisoner here, or ever again Lucia. Neither I, nor anyone here, will ever seek to control you. We trust Elohim to guide you and all of us, if we will let Him. I sense in my spirit that there is a big next step for you, and somehow for Nicanor, too, even if it's unsettling to me to not have more clarity on this. And my heart wants to reject it and fight it. Truth is, I am not ready to let you go again so soon. I've barely gotten you back. But if there is one thing Elohim has shown me over the years, it's that sometimes we have to come to the end of ourselves to finally see the truth and surrender to the path before us."

CHAPTER 25

As I lay in the bed of my childhood, the blankets stirring so many memories and emotions, I wish Aunt Sid was here. Unfortunately, it looks like she hasn't been here for some time. No lingering scent of yeast and cinnamon wafts the air from something delicious in the oven; no freshly pulled flowers from the garden perfume the cozy space. Instead, the musty, stale air and thick covering of dust stands in stark contrast to my memories here. It desperately needs a good airing out.

But I got here late afternoon yesterday with the help of Elias's directions and almost immediately crashed. Not only physically exhausted, but emotionally as well. Overcome, not just by being back in this place of all my favorite memories, but because my mind constantly drifts to The Refuge and everything I left behind. To Nic. Distance has only made the hurt more acute. More than just a small part of me wishes I'd stayed.

Feeling more than a bit filthy after all that riding, I think a bath would be heavenly. I resign myself to heating the water the old-fashioned way on the stove. It makes me miss The Refuge even more.

I stay in the bath until long after my skin has wrinkled and the water has cooled, hoping it will cleanse more than just the dirt from me. Deciding to dress comfy today, I put on a pair of sweatpants that remind me of Nic, and a soft, bright blue T-shirt. I head out of the bathroom, towel drying my hair, and freeze at the sound of a distant yell. I pause, straining to hear if it's just a figment of my imagination.

But there it is: a distinctive "Help!" Part of me registers that it could be a trap, but I know what it is to be in a desperate place, and I know I can't possibly ignore the cry. Grabbing my knife, I leave the cabin and quietly sneak through the trees. I can see a figure in the distance. Small and frail in stature, with sandy brown hair cropped close to the skull. As I watch the figure's movements, I suddenly recognize the familiar hunch of the shoulders.

"Dee!" I yell, coming out from behind the trees. She turns to me and I'm shocked to hear her voice for the first time.

"Lucia!"

I run to her and pull her into a hug. She clings to me, whimpering. I want to ask her about her voice, but when I pull back to look at her, that question disappears on the wind as my eyes struggle to take in the horror before them. Deep purple bruises mar her face and neck.

I grab her cheeks gently in my hand and lift her face to mine. "What happened to you, Dee?" My voice is barely a whisper.

But Dee remains silent, a defeated soul standing before me. I put my arms around her shoulders. "Come, let's get you into a warm bath and get you fed."

I guide her to the small sofa in Aunt Sid's main room and put a blanket around her while I heat up fresh water for the bath. I head to the bathroom to get her a fresh towel and make sure she has everything she needs in an easy place for her to grab.

"Okay, it's going to take a few minutes to get the water ready, and then you should be good to go," I head back toward the kitchen stove, freezing at the sight of two familiar figures standing just inside the front door.

Tavarious and Cain.

My mind frantically searches for the how in this scenario. Then I notice Dee slowly stand and shed the blanket from her shoulders. She makes her way to where Tavarious and Cain stand, and the confidence in her stride gives me pause. She stands in front of them and turns to face me. "I'm sorry, Lucia, but they offered me something I couldn't resist if I would help them bring you in. I knew this place held a special spot in your heart, so I figured you would return here at some point. I was prepared to have to lure you away from your Horseman, but luckily you came here alone, making this all too easy."

Without waiting for a response from me, she turns and heads out the front door, the sureness in her steps alien for the girl I knew. Her betrayal cuts deep.

Knowing grins form on the faces of Tavarious and Cain. My bag with the knife Nic gave me is across the room. My heart sinks as I realize the direness of my situation, but there is no way they will take me without a fight this time.

"You might as well save us all some trouble and come with us willingly," Cain sneers. "We won't be fooled by your pretense any longer, and you won't be able to take me out so easily this time. Legion waits outside in the helicopter."

My heart sinks further at that detail; the last time I saw Legion was when he brought me to the ashram as a ten-year-old. I was not to see him again until I became Bolster Sage. If what Elias told me is to be believed and he's an upper-level demon, then I need to get out of here. The reality of how much they must want me to go to all the trouble of having Legion come here sinks in, threatening to drown me in despair. But I steel myself against the thought; I won't go willingly this time. I am not the girl they think they know any longer.

They take one step forward, and I bolt for my bag. Cain grabs me around the waist as I throw my elbow back as hard as I can, clocking him right in the side of his head. We both crumble to the floor. On my hands and knees, I scramble to the bag. Right as I reach it, Tavarious lands a kick to my stomach. The pain steals my breath and I instinctively curl into a ball. He draws closer, still not fully grasping that I am not some vulnerable, weak woman, because he is oblivious to how he's left himself open. I kick out my leg at an angle and get him right in the family jewels. He moans and curls in on himself as he topples over.

But there's no time to enjoy the satisfaction of seeing him whimpering on the ground; Cain is up and lumbering toward me. I grab the light off the nightstand and chuck it at his big head. It hurts my heart to destroy anything in the home of my childhood, but now is not the time for senti-mentality.

"What's with you and lamps?" Cain bellows. On my feet again, knife in hand, I turn to face Cain, while Tavarious tries to compose himself and get up off the floor. They still stand between me and the door.

Cain lunges for me, easily knocking my knife aside as he grabs my wrist and punches me in the stomach. I groan and double over as he pins my arms to my side, holding me in place, facing Tavarious. Tavarious walks toward me, radiating fury, as he brings his hand back and slaps me across the face, rattling my teeth. The burning sting on my face mixed with my blurred vision makes me want to cry, but by sheer willpower, I hold the tears in.

I struggle against Cain's arms as he drags me out the front door, kicking over a kitchen chair. I hear the dreaded sound of helicopter blades approaching. My struggling increases in fervor. I'm desperate to get loose so I can run.

"I hope you get loose Lu-Chee-Ah, so that I have an excuse to chase you down, tackle you to the ground, and feel your body pressed up against mine." Tavarious offers me a creepy grin. "I think you like the fight. I am happy to accommodate you when we get back to the ashram. And I am not the only one, I think."

Cain laughs into my ear. My skin crawls at the feel of his hot breath. Before I know it, I am standing before Legion. I don't know how it's possible, but he seems more imposing now than when I was a kid. Maybe because I know now what he really is. You wouldn't be able to guess his true nature just looking at him. With his long, golden blonde hair, chiseled physique, and fair skin, upon first glance, he looks like the angels from old Renaissance paintings.

Looking closer, though, you can see there's almost a grey pallor to his skin and an air of darkness that's unmistakably other and wrong. Even his smile feels backward, like the Cheshire Cat from the old story of Wonderland. He reminds me of a black snake I found in the garden once. Mesmerizing to look at, but a coiled danger urging me to keep my distance.

"Lucia, we have missed you," Legion purrs. "Not a very

good student, to run away from those who have cared for you for so long and raised you up to a position of such high esteem and honor. But no matter, it won't be happening again. Things are going to be quite different for you this time."

I watch, almost as if it's happening in slow motion, as his hand comes toward me. He places it where my shoulder meets my neck. I feel his fingers grip hard, and before I even have a chance to open my mouth, everything goes dark.

CHAPTER 26

NICANOR

After two restless nights of sleep, unable to keep Lucia's beautiful, broken-hearted face from a constant rotation in my dreams, I head to the training arena to burn off some energy and calm the jittery feeling in my blood. I don't know why I thought today's training would be any different than yesterday's, and after four hours, it's clear the outcome is the same.

I suppose I am just delaying the inevitable. I need to leave The Refuge, despite my desire to stay, and this restlessness must be a sign that it's time to go. With a sad sort of acceptance, I head back to my room to pack some things and then decide to visit the dining hall for one last meal. It's just after the lunch rush, so I should be able to grab a quick bite and then find Elias to let him know of my plans. The sooner I can get away, the sooner I can feel back in control, and the better it will be for everyone.

I head into the dining hall and immediately notice a somberness cloaking the room like a dense fog. Even the mood of the kitchen seems off as I grab a plate from Seb, Isa robotically going through the motions in the background, both siblings avoiding eye contact with me. Their usual effervescent nature is uncharacteristically dim. I see Elias sitting with Laz and Cai at a booth in front of one of the windows. Seeing it as providence, I head to their table. Laz is seated next to Cai, looking down at his plate; he's just pushing his food around, not really eating. Very un-Laz-like behavior. Cai sits with his arms crossed as he stares out the window. Elias looks like he's trying to talk with them. He goes silent when I approach.

A sense of dread fills me. "What is it?"

"Sit down, Nicanor," Elias says softly, as he scoots over to make room for me on his bench.

Reluctantly, I take a seat. Something tells me I need to be seated for what I am about to hear. "Tell me."

"Well..."

"She's gone!" Laz yells. "He just let her leave, by herself! I could've gone with her! At least then she wouldn't be alone out there." He shoves back from the table and leaves in a huff of fury, the likes of which I've not yet seen from the boy.

"I'll go talk to him," Cai mutters, getting up and leaving.

My stomach drops like a stone, my blood running cold at the revelation. "Is it true?" I ask, my voice low.

"She wanted to leave, and I'll not ever keep her prisoner. It was her choice, and I made sure she was well-outfitted."

"Why didn't you tell anyone? Someone needs to be with her! She can't be alone out there; she almost died twice on the journey here with me. I could've—"

"You could've what, Nic? You made your decision,

remember? You have no concern for her. Otherwise, we wouldn't be in this situation."

"Do not tell me what I feel, Elias! I am trying to protect her! Protect everyone!" I bellow as I stand, unable to sit any longer. My chest heaves in frustration. The dining hall falls so silent you could hear a pin drop.

"From what?" Elias continues. "From her purpose, from a life of the richest and most perfect love Elohim could ever gift from His very being? She is a Core, Nicanor! And if my assumptions are correct, she is the Core Trust. Ironic, isn't it, that she's Trust and that's the one thing you can't seem to work out how to do on your own? You are acting out of fear, and only out of fear. Even to the point of denying the conqueror nature ingrained in you. Fear is not from Elohim, you know that. It's only a sign that you are slipping closer and closer to the leashing."

I breathe heavily, my fists clenching and unclenching at my sides. And I know if I were in front of a mirror, my eyes would be flickering between blue and inky black. I can feel it in my chest, like a fearsome, wild animal, placed in a too-small cage for far too long, the pressing of the bars giving it a feral desperation. My will is the only thing keeping the bars from breaking, and I finally realize that one day soon, it will not be enough. And she's not even here to be the reason that I can't control it. To be the reason I've felt restless and out of sorts.

I look into Elias's eyes, and I know he sees it, too. He comes to stand next to me, putting a hand on my shoulder, grounding me.

"Son, she's your light and your anchor. She's the only thing keeping you from being lost to us forever. And if you really want to protect everyone, having her by your side is the only way that is going to happen."

Icy fear drenches my skin as I think about her out there alone. My heart cracks at all the memories of her face as I repeatedly pushed her away, denying her. The real question is how she will ever learn to trust me after all of this.

"When did she leave and where was she going?"

"She went to Sidora's farm. She left a few nights ago, after dinner, so she's probably only been there two days. I sent her on one of the bomb-proof horses—slower but less likely to spook on her. She also has plenty of food and even a weapon."

"I'm going to get her," I say, turning to leave.

Elias grabs my arm, stopping me. "Do not go to her if you are just going to continue to deny the truth. She may be the Core Trust, but that doesn't mean that you don't need to be trustworthy and earn her trust too. Trust is woven through your bond, on both sides. She needs you as much as you need her Nic. You are her counterpart, and you are only at your strongest when you're together."

A weight that has been bearing down on me these past weeks disintegrates as I make up my mind. The fog that's been clouding my thinking has disappeared, and suddenly the path is laid out clearly before me.

"I see that now." I heave a sigh at my obstinance. "I am done fighting against it." I pat his hand on my arm. "Thank you, Elias, for putting up with my stubbornness and never giving up on me."

"And I never will. Now go be who you were created to be and bring our girl back." He winks.

I turn from the hall and head out of The Refuge. As I reach the training yard, I barely slow my pace as I speak the words, "Lavo Veshuv."

Adira appears before me, pawing the ground and prancing restlessly. She already knows what's coming and she's clearly ready to go. She shoves me with her nose, eager to get moving.

"I know, I know, you were right this whole time. Took me long enough, huh?" I swing myself up onto her back. "What do you think, Adira? Let's see how fast we can get to her."

LUCIA

I slowly open my eyes. My lids feel heavy, as if weighted. I'm in a prison cell, completely surrounded by impenetrable stone walls, except for a barred door. There's not even a single window in this musty, damp space. As I slowly sit up, I realize I must be underneath the ashram, somewhere I wasn't allowed to go during my time here.

But Ansel knew. She snuck her way down here and tried to warn me, though I didn't or couldn't listen at the time. My head pounds at the recollection that Legion must have knocked me out somehow to get me here. I wonder how much time has passed. It's impossible to tell if it's day or night.

A key rattles on the other side of the door, and the hinges groan terribly as the door swings open to allow a small but familiar figure inside. Rage burns like a white-hot inferno inside me, replacing the grief. Dee leans against the now-closed door. Her bruises look the same, so not a lot of time has passed while I was unconscious. But I see the dark circles under her big eyes, and the weariness that she wears like a heavy cloak, and I wonder if I can get the keys from her and escape. I am bigger and stronger than her.

"I know what you're thinking, and it won't work," Dee speaks with a strong voice that's at odds with her frail appearance. "I have been given true power for the small sacrifice of these minor injuries, and as you've noticed, I have a voice now, too. I am stronger and more powerful now than I have ever been."

"Funny, how your supposed power came at the betrayal of a friend and the loss of your humanity. Seems to me like you gave up the ability to see in order to speak, Dee."

"I go by Delilah now. And how could you think we were ever friends? I tolerated your constant invasion of my space and endless prattle because I didn't have a voice, and I had no backbone to tell you otherwise. But every time you came down to that kitchen, you put me at risk. You with your cushy, elevated position. Who do you think would be punished for your visits? It definitely wouldn't be their precious Bolster Sage."

Her words are like a thousand miniature knives, making tiny cuts all over me. Could I really have been so blind? Was I so desperate for a friend that I was seeing things that weren't really there? Embarrassment and shame fills me.

"You have no idea, Lucia. I have been blessed to be a vessel for one with true power. Never again will I be insignificant, something to be used and discarded. I spent my childhood locked up in a cellar by the people who were supposed to love and care for me. I was expected to be quiet and pretend I didn't exist, unless I was cleaning or making meals for them. If I displeased them, which happened often when alcohol flowed freely, then I was their punching bag.

If you were ever a friend to me, you would be happy for me."

My stomach sinks at her declaration. Not just at what she's suffered, but from what Elias explained about vessels, she is demonically possessed now. She's as good as gone.

"You were never insignificant, can't you see that? It doesn't matter how you were made to feel in this hellhole or by unworthy people, that never equaled truth. And my heart breaks for you, Dee, because you had a shot at real freedom and a chance to heal from the things that tormented you if you would have just come with me. Instead, you let them convince you of your worthlessness and you submitted to the very darkness that left you scarred to begin with. Now you are more a slave than you were before."

"You know nothing!" Spittle flies from her lips as her face twists in rage. "I can speak now. I am a vessel of power, I demand respect wherever I go, and I have a valuable purpose among the Amilign. But I am done wasting my time explaining to the likes of you, who ran from your gift. I came because I felt I owed you an explanation, though it's clear you are too blind to see. But don't worry. Soon your eyes will be opened, and you will serve your true purpose."

She leaves, slamming the door behind her. As her footsteps fade, the grief of her choice threatens to close up my throat and I struggle to dam up the tears that beg release. Will my trust always be misplaced?

I take deep, ragged breaths, trying to calm myself. But as I look around the windowless dungeon, the panic begins to rise anew. I can't be back here again. And it's clear there will be no escaping this time. No one from The Refuge will even know where to look for me. Which means there will be no avoiding the path the monks set for me. A wild sense of panic thins each breath I take. Icy fear drenches my skin as a muffled sob tears from my lips.

Of course, that's when the monks choose to show up. At least some small mercy I am afforded and neither is Cain or Tavarious. One carries some fabric in his arms, his bald head reflecting what little light there is from the single overhead bulb, but I can tell he's older. The other has his hood pulled so low, I can't see much of his face, other than the smirk on his mouth at the sight of my tears. He's large and imposing, well over six feet tall. He has to duck to enter the space and he stands in front of the doorway. I will the tears to stop at the sight of his enjoyment of my misery.

"I am Drystan," says the hooded figure, and fear fills me at the familiar name, until now only spoken in hushed tones. "You will be dressed for your ceremony. I will tolerate nothing from you. Tavarious and Cain are puppies compared to me. This will be the only warning you receive. I take great pleasure in breaking pretty things."

His sinister smile appears again. Pure evil radiates from him, and my fear turns to terror. I say nothing in response. I just want to get this over with.

"Disrobe," Drystan says beneath his hood.

"But...su...surely you can't mean...with no privacy? I thought as Bolster Sage—"

So quickly I don't even see it coming, his hand lashes out, slapping me across the face. The same aching spot that Tavarious struck, now throbbing with renewed vigor. My head jerks to the side and my vision blurs as I crumble to the cold stone floor, trying and failing to suck in deep breaths to clear the pain.

"I'll stop you right there. After your great escape, there are no rules regarding you. This means, if you ask another question or delay this any further, I am at my leisure to decide if I want to see what it will take to break you." A malicious chuckle fills the room. "Besides, turns out you are not such a special snowflake after all. We found one of your sisters and will have her soon. She was right under our nose, too, even staying with us awhile."

I pale at his words. He clearly means another Core, of which there are only four. If the Amilign end up with two, that does not bode well for the prophecy. But I can't think about that now.

"Now, get off the floor and disrobe."

Trying to control my trembling, I stand on shaky legs. I turn my back on the two monks. I begin to undress, leaving my undergarments in place, praying they will not take those from me as well. The other monk approaches with the fabric. It's a diaphanous white and silver material that will leave little to the imagination. I can't fathom how it's considered a dress. He stands behind me and I feel the cool slide of metal along my skin, along with the telltale snip of scissors. My undergarments fall to the floor; a startled gasp escapes from me as I fling my arms over my body in a pathetic attempt to cover myself.

I fight the quivering of my lips at being treated as less than human by these men. As merely a piece of property or chattel. But then again, they aren't really men, are they? And the thought that it isn't me against man, but me against demon makes me feel less vulnerable and more like the warrior I am beginning to believe Elohim created me to be. At that thought, Elohim's peace fills me and I know I am not alone.

So I capture my thoughts and emotions, making them obedient to my will, and let the cool mask of determination and indifference slide into place as I stare ahead, my gaze focused on a spot on the wall. Gnarled, speckled hands move around my body, sliding the material into place. To suppress the rising nausea, I keep myself focused on conversations with Nic, my memory of his charming grin and the butterflies it always left in its wake, the nights by the fire that had me snuggling into him, seeking warmth and shelter. I let the memories carry me far away from this place.

Before I know it, I am pulled from my memories and turned to face the mirror that's been brought in. The material twists up my back, winding its way around my neck like a noose before coming over my shoulders, down across my breasts, and coming to meet below my belly button. It falls almost to the floor between my legs, the same way it falls in the back, barely covering my backside. A thick, black silk sash is tied low around my hips to hold the material in place. Other than the area of my hips covered by the black sash, my sides are completely exposed, from under my arms all the way to my ankles. My chest peeks through the barely-there material leaving nothing to the imagination.

I've never felt more exposed in all my life. I ignore the hungry look of the old monk who dressed me as he ties my hair up on top of my head, removing any last covering it might have offered. My gaze is focused on my own eyes in the mirror, the gold of them glowing more intensely. I urge my mirrored self to be strong and unfeeling. I am a Core created by Elohim Shomri, and He is my Protector. I will not be shaken.

Of course, the moment I think that to myself, Drystan steps forward with what appears to be a glass jar of shimmery gold powder. He has a paintbrush in one hand that he quickly chucks aside. He dips his fingers into the jar as that sadistic, knowing grin appears. I dread what's coming, but keep my face impassive; it's my only weapon at this moment. Clammy cold fingers begin to move across the exposed surfaces of my body, applying the gold powder. It takes everything in me to swallow the bile that rises at the unwanted touch of his hand.

I keep trying to will my thoughts to Nic, but then Drystan's meaty palm reaches under the fabric to grab at my bare backside while he stands in front of me. My gaze breaks from the mirror and I can finally see under his hood, into the icy white of his gaze. His eyes are inhuman, and bear no coloring other than the pinprick of a black center; his face around his eyes and forehead is scarred, as though it's been burned. His predatory gaze fixes on me. I want to shrink from his grasp, but I know that will only cause me further abuse, so I force myself to remain still, my gaze shifting back to the mirror.

Leaning forward, his stale, fetid breath blows across my cheek as he whispers, "Keep pretending, my pet. I know you are not unaffected, and it pleases me so to see you trying and failing to hide it." My stomach roils as he slides his hand across my skin one final time. He stands behind me, pulling my arms back behind me and tying them in place with more black silk. The action causes my semi-covered chest to stick out even further. He starts walking me out of the cell and my stomach sinks, the trembling taking hold anew despite how much I resist it. He steers me down hallways until I recognize the path ahead. A new sense of dread takes hold of me. I know where he's taking me.

"I look forward to my turn with you, when I will get to see that mask fall from your face and listen to the glorious sounds of your screams," he says from behind me. He pulls my arms back and down, causing my back to bend, my head landing against his chest as my tied arms force my body to contort. With his other hand, he opens the door to the room of my nightmares. A plume of dense, grey smoke floats out.

A loud, sadistic laugh comes from him, as though he just shared a delightful secret.

"Alas, you will first spend a week in the Den of Consciousness; we don't want you fighting us every step of the way. Nothing better than a soft and pliant body. And we have waited so very long for you to ripen like the sweetest fruit." At those parting words, I feel his slimy tongue lick its way up the side of my neck to my ear, leaving a trail of repulsion in its wake.

"Oh, and happy belated nineteenth birthday, Lucia," he says mockingly as he shoves me into the dark, cloying smoke. His parting words are a final nail in the coffin as the door closes and locks me in this place that will strip me of my identity and purpose. Hopelessness threatens to drown me. I flatten myself on the ground, desperate to delay the inevitable for as long as possible by keeping the risen smoke far from my face, even though I know there's no escaping it.

I let the tears silently fall as I think of all the things that could've been. I cling to the pieces of myself as my mind slowly becomes hazy, and I start to feel them blink out of existence like dying stars. And ever so slowly, the canvas gets wiped clean as my world goes dark again.

CHAPTER 28

NICANOR

It's times like now that I'm grateful for the power of being a Horseman. Jumping long distances on the back of Adira is a useful tool that's come in handy before, but never have I appreciated how amazing it is until now, when I am desperate to get to Lu. The only caveat is that I must have been to a place before. I imagine it's part of why we got here over a hundred years ago, so that we could familiarize ourselves with this world and learn its ways and people well. So we would have an understanding of things when the time came for us to ride.

Thanking Elohim that I'd been to the small farmstead over thirty years ago, I bring Adira to an open plain before urging her to a full gallop. Drawing on the power within me, I envision the small field leading up to the white picket fence surrounding the place. Adira's strides eat up the ground, and in a flash of light, I am instantly transported to that exact spot. I slow Adira, bringing her to a halt right at the gate that swings open, the force of the wind repeatedly slamming it into the fence. I glance up the path, noticing the front door also swings open. Dread surges through my veins.

Quickly dismounting, I run to the door. My stomach sinks as I take in the shattered lamp and knocked-over chair. There was clearly a struggle, and knowing how much Lucia loves this place only heightens the anger now flowing through my blood.

I don't step foot in the small house. The Amilign clearly have some kind of sensor that triggered, signaling them when someone was here. The last thing I want to do is alert them to my presence. I turn and head back to Adira. Once astride her, I notice how the grass of the field in one area is flattened and spread outward in a circle. The telltale mark of the helicopter the Amilign love to use. Probably the same one they used to retrieve her with all those years ago.

I reach out to my brothers through our mind link, another useful skill Horsemen have.

"The Amilign have taken my Core. I believe they are back at the mountain ashram. I am heading there now to retrieve her. Please let Elias know."

"Do you need help?" Zion's voice sounds in my head.

"Actually, yes. I need someone to create a diversion to draw them out. Something that might keep them occupied for a bit."

"No problem, I got that covered," Cai's voice rings out.

"Our prayers go with you, my brother," Azmaveth chimes in offering his solidarity.

"Nic, you need to know something," Cai says. I feel Azmaveth and Zion's presence fade to give us privacy. *"When Lucia told us about her time at the ashram, she mentioned a place they used to control her. It was not pretty. It was a room designed to wipe a person of their free will, with hallucinogenic drugs that were pumped into it. She*

spoke as though it was what terrified her more than anything. They called it the Den of Consciousness or something. I just thought you should know. She said if she misbehaved in any way, they put her in there. You might want to start your search there."

"Thanks for the tip," I send back to him as my blood boils further. His presence still lingers in my mind, hesitating. *"What is it, Cai?"*

"Elias wasn't sure I should tell you this. He said it could do no good, but that was before. With Lucia taken, I feel like it's information you should know. If our roles were reversed, I would want to know. But I am warning you, Nic, it's not information you are going to want to hear. I need you to prepare yourself."

A stillness settles over me at his words, a sinking sensation filling my stomach, *"Go on."*

"A few days before you and Lucia arrived, Elias got word from one of his inside sources. It was regarding the original plans the Amilign had for Lucia with their bogus role of Bolster Sage. The real goal was to turn her into a, uh...gah, this is harder than I thought, uh... breeding chattel, really. To bring in a new species bred from the full demonic Amilign. They believed with her being a Core, they could hijack the heavenly power in Lucia and it would strengthen and empower any demon children born. Give them an advantage."

I fight to control myself, clenching and unclenching my hands at the thought of the plans they had for her, still have, and what they might be doing to her now. This beast within my chest is getting harder and harder to contain, trying to claw its way free with a feral-like desperation. I fear that the state in which I find Lucia might be what finally pushes me over the edge.

"I'm sorry Nic, but I have faith you have everything you need in Elohim. You'll get her back in time."

Cai's words give me the resolve I need to steady myself. I turn to Adira. No words are needed—she knows my thoughts and heart. She's at a full gallop in just a few seconds, while I envision the cabin I built just on the other side of the mountain to the ashram. I choose a field that is a mile out from my cabin because I imagine they will have that place watched, too.

Adira makes fast work of the steep terrain and tight trails, taking us up the ridge. No normal horse could make this journey. Before I know it, we are on the other side of the ridge, scoping out the ashram from behind a cover of trees and bushes. I see the side door that Lu mentioned escaping from. At the same time, I notice a large group of the Amilign head to the chopper pad in the open space to the south of the ashram's front gates. A smile lights my face. Cai must be creating quite the mess, given the speed with which they are moving.

Sending up a prayer to Elohim Shomri, our Protector, I call Adira to me before I leave the clearing and head to the side door in the fading daylight.

CHAPTER 29

NICANOR

The hallways are quiet once I get inside. Not sure where I am or how to find Lu, I close my eyes and attempt to calm my breathing. It doesn't take long until I feel an urging to let my instinct guide me, and I know it's Elohim's leading. I imagine Lucia's beautifully expressive face, captivating golden eyes, and silky dark hair. I let the love that I've been suppressing pour out of the dark recesses I tried to bury it to. It takes no time for it to flow through my veins like flood-water. I start walking in the direction that I am being drawn.

I wind through hallways before coming to a corner, pausing at the voices I hear ahead. I peek around the corner and see three monks standing in front of a door.

"So how long has she been in there?"

"Almost two days now."

"Do you think she'll be affected enough, yet? I mean, all the higher-ups just left. I bet we could take turns having some fun with her. No one would ever know."

"I wish they didn't put her in there. I think it's more fun when there is still some fight in them."

"Oh man, did you see what she was wearing? All that soft, flawless skin exposed. Like delicacies on a platter."

Listening was a bad idea. My body shakes with the force of my anger. My vision changes, sharpening, and I know without a doubt that my eyes are black. I walk around the corner, not trying to sneak up on them. I am itching for a fight and I want them to see their destruction coming.

They turn toward me. It's barely the blink of an eye and I'm on them, no time for them to even think. I smash two heads together while kicking the third one in the stomach, sending him flying down the hall. He groans but stands quickly and pulls a blade from underneath his robe. He come at me like a crazed man, all flailing limbs, which I easily dodge. I shoot forward, grasping the arm with the weapon. I twist hard until I hear a snap and his howl of pain. I pick him up and throw him into the wall. With a sickening crunch his body cracks the marble, and he lands in a motionless heap.

I'm barely breathing hard; this new power flowing through my veins seems to make me faster and stronger. It's effortless. I break the door lock with my hand and am greeted by a massive cloud of grey smoke. How could anyone spend hours in here, let alone days? And Cai had said this place was her nightmare. My jaw clenches, and unfettered fury burns through me.

As the smoke begins to clear, I take a deep, shuddering breath at the sight before me. She is curled in a ball on the rug. Thin, sheer material wraps around her, barely covering her skin, her hair twisted high atop her head. She is awake but unaware; her hands incessantly pick at pieces of the rug. My anger simmers below the surface.

"Lu, it's me. I've come to take you home."

She doesn't react. Doesn't register my words at all. I kneel down in front of her face, but her eyes don't move from the obsessive ministrations of her fingers. I gently extend my hand to cradle her cheek, turning her face to me. Her eyes are dull, unfocused. The large, dark bruise on her beautiful face resurrects my murderous desires, and it takes every last bit of my control to quell the shaking. I lay her head down, move to her back, and slide my hands under her knees and around her shoulders. I stand, lifting her in my arms. Like I once did when we first met, not so long ago.

The action brings her close to my chest and shows in detail what the monks were talking about. She is clearly dressed for male appetites. This fabric does little in the way of covering her, and with the shimmery gold powder covering her skin, it is clear she is going to be presented as some sort of dessert. With the state she is in right now, she wouldn't fight them. Underneath the gold powder, I see more dark bruises, remnants of the fight she must have put up when they took her.

A strange lump forms in my throat at what she's been put through, all because of my stubbornness. She wouldn't have left if I hadn't pushed her away. This is on me. How will she ever want anything to do with me? How can I ever earn her trust after what she's suffered because of me? When it's my job to keep her safe.

The urge to burn this place to the ground, destroying everything in it and turning it into nothing but ash is riding me hard. The only thing anchoring me is the feel of Lucia in my arms. Getting her home and to safety is my top priority.

I can feel pressure in the seal on my back, and I know Adira is feeling all my emotions, wanting to be released. Weaving through the labyrinth of hallways, I let Elohim guide my steps. Things start to look familiar, and we are almost to that little side door when the fiery pain of a blade slices through my back. I whirl to see a monk with a sword grinning at me with malice. Grasping Lucia tightly to me, I kick out my leg, knocking the blade from his hand. Gently placing Lucia on the ground away from the monk, I turn to deal with him.

His blade back in his hands again, he trembles as I stand to my full height. His gaze fixes on my face. My eyes must be black again. The smirk vanishes from his face now. Wanting to make fast work of this, I walk forward, grabbing the blade in his hand, welcoming the bite of pain as it slices into my skin. Then, I slam my head into his head like a battering ram. He drops like a stone.

I sweep Lu up into my arms and head for the door. It's night, so it's easy to make our way to cover. Once in the thicket, I go to call Adira forth, but nothing happens. Then it dawns on me; the blade must have sliced through my seal. I will be unable to tap into that power and call her to me until it heals. And seeing as it hit bone, it will be a while. I need to get Lucia to safety until then.

Taking off with her in my arms, I head north, higher up the peak. It's tougher terrain and the air is thinner, but it will give me the advantage if anyone comes after us. It's the most unexpected path for me to take, and it should be easy to find a cavern that's out of the elements.

After hours of hiking at a steep incline, I finally find an adequate spot. I'm amazed I haven't grown fatigued yet. I've always been stronger than most, but this is something new. I feel as if I could run for days right now. I can't wait to talk with Elias about this newfound power.

I look around me. There's nowhere to set her down that won't scratch her up or worse, especially since she's barely covered. She'll be much colder if I put her on the ground, too. And if I'm being honest with myself, I am not ready to let her go. I don't think I'll ever be able to again. So I sit in the small cavern, out of the wind, leaning against the stone wall. I shift Lucia in my arms so that I can take off my shirt and provide her with some more cover.

With Lucia on my lap, I slip my shirt over her head, pulling her arms through the sleeves one at a time. She's swimming in it, but at least it provides her some cover. Not just from the cold—this way she won't wake up feeling exposed. My arms cradle around her, her head resting on my shoulder. I can't help but stroke the soft skin of her neck. She sighs and brings a hand up to rest over my heart as she has before, and I am completely undone. I cherish the small touch, knowing that all too soon, she'll despise the sight of me.

The quiet continues for some time. The gentle sound of her deep breathing is a soothing companion as the darkness slowly starts to give way to the rising sun. Questions whirl in my mind, of how long it will take for the effects of the smoke to wear off, and if there will be any lasting damage.

Suddenly, Lucia starts to move against me. It must be a nightmare. My hands grasp her cheeks as her head falls back. A breathy moan escapes her full lips. Her body starts undulating even more, her hand fisting my shirt as she pulls herself upright, ripping off the shirt I put on her. She brings her knees to either side of my hips, straddling me. I look into her eyes, but they are glassed over, almost unseeing. I freeze, horrified by the realization that this must be one of the side effects of the smoke—some kind of aphrodisiac.

My body wars with rage at what they had planned for her, and the overwhelming sensations of her body rubbing against my bare chest. Her hands slide up my shoulders and around my neck, her soft fingers threading through the hair at the nape of my neck. The sensations and feel of her are a special kind of torture, especially knowing that she's not really here with me in this moment. Add this to the list of things I'll never be able to atone for. My heart breaks at the injustice of it all. It's rare I am in a situation that leaves me this confused as to how to handle it.

I grip her hips to stop her movements. She uses the distraction of my occupied hands to pull my face down to hers and press her lips to mine. Her soft, lush lips taste mine as she moans into my mouth. A shudder runs through me as I try to pull away, but she's wrapped around me like a python. I gently turn my face from hers, resting my cheek against her cheek as I try to move us away from the wall so I can stand and get some distance between us before the heat in my blood becomes an inferno. But the action pushes my upper body further into hers, and she wraps her legs around my waist, laying back across my outstretched legs, all that gorgeous, sun-kissed skin on display.

I freeze. In the 100 years since I have been here, this is by far the most difficult and punishing position I've ever experienced. I tilt my head back against the rough stone wall and breathe deep, trying to get my heart rate and erratic breathing under control. But the smell of her is consuming each breath I take. Her movements and breathy moans make it near impossible to focus. This has to stop before it goes too far. I grab her wrist, pull her up to my chest, and wrap an arm around her waist. With a big push, I bring us both to standing. I place her on her feet, making sure she's steady before I tuck tail and flee to the back of the cavern like a coward fighting an unconquerable beast.

In the darkness of the cave, stalactites hang from the ceiling, slowly dripping water. I stand directly under them, the ice-cold drops attempting to cool the raging inferno of my body. I'm trembling, my heart pounding like a drum. I stand there for some time. I rub my hair, trying to clear my thoughts. Then I hear a soft sob from the mouth of the cave. Like I was doused in icy water, the sound of her grief flips a switch and the flames die instantly.

I approach her carefully, trying not to startle her. She sits in my way-too-big-for-her T-shirt, her knees pulled into her chest with her arms wrapped around them, and she shakes. I sit next to her, just to let her know she's not alone. Tears roll down her face, and it's as if cold, sharp fingers have pried apart my rib cage to rip my still-beating heart from my chest.

"I am so sorry, Lu. This is all on me. I pushed you away. I wasn't here to protect you. I know I can't make it right, but I promise to get you to safety." I am at a loss of what to say or do. This feeling of helplessness is so alien to me. It's driving me to insanity.

"Thank you for coming for me," she says, her hoarse voice barely above a whisper. "I know it's a sacrifice for you. I'm not in the clear yet; the smoke still has a strong haze over me. As I recall from last time, I will drift in and out of reality for a while yet. I imagine it will be a few days before I start to feel normal. Then I'll be out of your hair again."

Each time I think there's no way my heart could break further, it somehow manages to force another crack. I hesitantly touch her cheek, fearing her rejection, and turn her face to mine. She doesn't make eye contact with me, and the action is agonizing. "I know you don't believe me, and I don't blame you, but I am not leaving your side. I vow on my life to care for you and bring you safely home. It is no sacrifice. It is the greatest honor of my long life. But let's not talk about this now. Just rest and heal some more. We can talk later."

She lies on her side in the sunlight that streams through the opening, curling up on the dirt and rocks. I lift her head and place it on my lap, gently stroking her hair back from her face. I say a prayer to Elohim, to make her whole again and give me what I need to love her the way she deserves, with the power of His love.

CHAPTER 30

LUCIA

Waking is like pulling myself out of thick mud. Each time gets a little easier, but I long for the day when it will no longer feel like this. My eyes start to focus, and I realize I am once again cradled in Nic's arms. A gentle, swaying motion tells me we currently ride Adira. I sit with my legs draped to one side, while his arms hold me to his chest, my head against his shoulder. I don't want to move. His comforting warmth seeps into me, his scent surrounding me, sharpening and overwhelming my senses. The gentle rocking of Adira's steps is a peaceful lull, and I wish I could stay like this forever.

"Don't move," Nic says. "Just let me hold you a bit longer. We're going to stop up ahead."

I should distance myself; it'll make it easier when he leaves me again. But after everything I just went through, I crave the soothing comfort he offers. Thoughts of him anchored me back in that desolate hellhole. Maybe it makes me weak, or maybe I just know what I want? For once, I am not going to worry about the consequences. I turn my face further into him, breathing in his scent of mint and rain. He kisses the top of my head.

All too soon, we come to a stop in a clearing. I sit up in his lap, looking around, wondering where we are. Nic still has an arm around my waist. I am unused to feeling so awkward and uncomfortable around him. I don't want to look into his eyes, afraid of what I'll see there. More doubt. More apprehension. It doesn't help that I'm still just wearing a T-shirt over the gauzy material, gold dusting my arms and legs.

And at that thought, all the memories come rushing to the forefront of my mind, making me want to gag anew. I need to get this off. I need to get clean.

I scoot forward off his lap in an effort to get down.

"Let me help you."

But I am desperate to get away from him; I can't have him touch me. My skin is poisoned. I need to get it all off. The urgency overwhelms me. Not waiting for his help, I slide forward, pushing off Adira, dropping onto my bare feet.

"Lucia, wait."

Ignoring his plea, I flee. Toward what, I don't know. My pace is rushed and frenzied. The need to get away is a driving force. I have to wash off the disease of everything. I feel like an overstretched rubber band about to snap. Part of me registers that I'm not thinking straight, but the anguish pressing down on me is like a living and breathing thing. I hear flowing water up ahead and veer in that direction. I take off Nic's T-shirt and start tearing at the silver fabric. It's like a noose tied around my neck, winding around my body like chains, and I can't see well enough to get it off. It's like I am trapped all over again.

I fall to my knees, a rippling wave of despair spearing through me as I frantically tear at the fabric, struggling to calm my erratic breathing and pounding heart. I sense Nic before I see him. I feel him pull the fabric from my back and hear the shearing sound of it being cut. His fingers at my neck unwind the fabric from my throat. I should care that I am fully exposed to him, and not just physically, but in the ravaged state of my mind and heart.

But there's no room for caring. I continue tearing the fabric off, leaving it like shimmering pools around me until the only thing left is the gold powder coating my bare skin. I stand and walk to the creek ahead, not stopping as I head directly into the icy cold depths. The shock of it steals the breath from my lungs. It's shallow, only coming to my thighs. I drop to my knees in the water and start vigorously rubbing at my skin with the cold water, desperately trying to get the powder off that clings to my skin like glue. I grab a rock from the creekbed and start scrapping.

Nic is on me before I can do much damage, grabbing my wrists and plucking the rock from my grip. He doesn't say anything as he dunks a bar of soap in the creek and starts lathering a small piece of fabric. I sit there, shivering, the pain of the cold a welcome distraction from the turmoil in my mind, as he starts lathering up my back. Slowly, and ever so carefully, he goes down each of my arms, all the way to the tips of my fingers. Then he starts lathering up my hair. His strong hands rubbing my scalp soothes the erratic pace of my heartbeat.

All too soon, his hands leave my hair. "I'm going to give you the soap and cloth so you can clean the rest of your body. I'll be sitting on that rock over by the bank, with my back to you if you need me." And with that, he reaches from around my back, grasping my wrist and placing the items in my hand. After he leaves, I tip my head back in the creek, letting the flowing water rinse the soap from my hair. I stay like that for a few minutes, breathing with the movement of the water flowing all around me. All sound is muffled, like I am set apart from the world, protected.

After a few minutes, I sit up, wrapping the soap in the cloth. I renew my efforts, scrubbing my legs and upper body. This time, the gold dust comes away, leaving my skin clean and red from my vigorous efforts. But no longer gold. If only I could clean my mind of the memories in the same way.

I walk out of the creek and head to Nic, who sits on a rock with his back to me. He doesn't turn at my approach, but holds out another one of his T-shirts and a pair of sweatpants. My heart squeezes as I think of the first time we met, when I wore something similar. The grey sweatpants almost fall off my hips every time I move. I roll the waistband a few times until they sit snugly on my hip bone. Then I ball up the extra material of the T-shirt and knot it at the back. It's a small thing, making the borrowed clothes fit me, but the action gives me some small semblance of control and helps to clear away the cobwebs of my mind. Dressed, I climb up on the rock to sit next to Nic. Before I can even contemplate what I am doing, the words start flowing out of me. Like my mind is trying to purge itself of what happened.

"They took me from Aunt Sid's place. But I fought them. I wouldn't go willingly this time. I made it to my bag with the knife you gave me when Tavarious kicked me in the stomach. I still managed to get him in the balls, though. But then Cain grabbed me from behind, pinning my arms. But I still fought to get loose, even when Tavarious hit me in the face. I was so scared to go back; I knew things would be worse and there would be no getting away on my own this time."

Nic is unmoving beside me; I wonder if he's even breathing. I can't look at him. I just need to get it all out, so I keep going.

"Legion did something to me that knocked me out. I woke up in a dark, damp, stone cell with no windows. I assume it's what was beneath the ashram—I was never allowed down there before. I met Drystan for the first time down there." I despise the shaking of my voice at the memory of the evil that radiated from him. He felt more demon than man. I push on.

"He told me he likes to break beautiful things. He scares me more than any monk I've met so far. He made me get undressed in front of him. It was him and another monk who dressed me in the material. But Drystan rubbed the gold powder all over my body himself. Even to the point of discarding the paintbrush and using his bare hand." I visibly shudder at the memory. I have to pause and breathe through the nausea.

A vibration in the air draws me from my thoughts. I glance towards Nic to see he's shaking, at such an intensity as to create a change in the atmosphere around him. His jaw is clenched so tight, I'm surprised he has not cracked teeth. An obsidian hue consumes the whole of each eye. Remembering what he said about the leashing, I fear my story has pushed him over the edge.

"Nic," I gasp. "Your eyes."

He turns to me, and I fear he's no longer himself until he reaches out a hand and cups my cheek. "There's a power that flows through me right now, like lightning in my veins. I first felt it at the ashram when I came to get you. It doesn't feel like it did before with the leashing, like I am fighting some beast. Instead, this feels like something was poured into me, like a gift. My senses are sharpened, my strength and speed increased. It feels like raw power."

"Are you okay?"

"Yeah, but this seems to happen now when the need to conquer rises within me. Like it did when I fought off the monks blocking the door you were behind. And I think now, because I want to burn the world to the ground for what was done to you. But there's no enemy to conquer right now," he says roughly. "Please, keep going. I think I need to hear this as much as you need to tell me. We can figure out what's going on with me later."

I nod at him, looking back to the creek. "Drystan was painstakingly slow and thorough with his efforts, reveling in my discomfort and vulnerability. I've never struggled not to be sick so much in all my life. He is scarred from the tops of his cheeks up to his forehead, wearing a hood low to hide it. His eyes are terrifying and inhuman; solid white, except for a black pinprick in the center. I sensed nothing good in him. I'm not even sure there's any man left in him."

"After that, he said they were going to put me in the Den of Consciousness for a week. He walked me there and shoved me in. And I guess that was it. Until bits and pieces of memories of you." I glance up at him. "Do you know how long I was in there?"

He clears his throat and takes a deep breath. "I overheard the monks saying around two days, before I incapacitated them and got you out. It's been four days since then."

I take deep breaths, trying to clear the lingering fog. "Okay," I murmur. I'm not sure what to say from here. Before I can overthink things, Nic hops off the rock, getting on his knees before me.

"Wh...what are you doing?" I say, startled.

"Lucia, I don't know where to begin to make amends with you. I've pushed you away at every turn, denying Elohim's gift to us both. Letting my fear, doubt, and arrogance reign supreme. My actions have put you in danger and led to your debasement and suffering. In ancient cultures, when a wrong was done to another, self-imposed punishment was given as a sign of penance and atonement." Contrition laces his tone.

Still on his knees, he removes his shirt. My blood runs cold as he pulls a huge blade from a sheath around his leg. He angles the blade against the beautiful, unmarred skin of his chest, and blood wells as he presses it down. I realize what he's about to do.

I scramble off the rock, falling to my knees in front of him, my hand over his. "No, Nic, I don't want this."

"It's only right, Lu. Justice for the injustice my actions caused you, and you know I will heal."

"Nic, when are you going to get it? The love of Elohim is gentle and kind, patient and good. It does not seek its own selfish ways, and it does not keep a record of wrongs. That is the love He gave us. I see it so clearly now after everything. The thought of seeing someone I love suffer is the very last thing that will heal what's hurting within me."

He drops the blade into the grass beside him, grabbing my hand. "You love me?" he asks, in a low tone filled with awe.

How is he so oblivious? "How can you not see it? It's why I left The Refuge. I overheard you and Cai talking in the library, and you were going to leave. He was adamant that you stay because you were fighting the leashing. The Refuge was your home, and I knew you needed to be there, so I left before you could tell me otherwise. And I did that because even if you wouldn't accept what was between us, my soul recognizes its partner in yours. I love you Nicanor Cascus, White Horseman of Conquest. I will always seek to do what's best for you."

A look of shock and wonder fills his face. "I don't know how you can after everything. It's an absolute miracle, and yet has me at such a loss. The conqueror in me demands justice for what was done to you, but it was because of my fear and stupidity. I don't know what to do and it's killing me. How does one conquer when the enemy is my own failings? I am undeserving of you." His face falls, and I'm shocked at the tear that rolls down his cheek. What it must take for him to be so open and vulnerable with me. My mighty conqueror.

I reach out, cupping his warm, wet cheek. He places his hand over mine, closing his eyes and sighing. I take in the strong line of his jaw, the stubble on his cheek, and the dark hair that hangs forward across his brow. I reach my other hand up and run it through the soft locks. His piercing blue eyes open, locking on mine.

"I am so sorry. For ever resisting this. You are awe-inspiring. It is the greatest honor of my life that Elohim chose me to be yours. I don't deserve your trust, but I want you to know that I will spend my life working to earn it and be worthy of you. I love you, Lu, with all that I am. And not because of some prophecy, but because you're you. You are important to me because of who you are, not what you are."

His words are like a balm to my battered heart. I close my eyes as they wash over me, tears running down my face now. I had almost given up hope that he would ever submit to the bond. I can't get words past the knot in my throat. I feel his arms come around me, pulling me forward onto his lap. My legs straddle his. One arm wraps around my waist, and his other hand comes up to cup my jaw and cheek, wiping away the tears. Our foreheads touch.

"You," he whispers softly, kissing my closed eyes and the tip of my nose, "are like a wildflower growing in the desert. You are this fiercely strong, resilient, and exquisite creation. You said once you didn't think you were prophecy material. I've lived for over a hundred years, and I can tell you right now, there is no one better chosen for such a time and significant purpose." Such raw trust fills his eyes. His faith in me anchors me in a sea of my insecurity. I'm no longer a boat unmoored, tossed about by the waves of my doubt.

Before I know what I am doing, my lips are on his. I slant my head as my fingers curl through his hair. With a sigh, he deepens the kiss. He kisses me with a depth that leaves me feeling light as a feather, like I could float away at any moment. The kiss softens again and slows. Both of us catching our breath.

"As much as I want to stay here in this moment with you, I need to get you back to The Refuge."

"Wait, I almost forgot," I say pulling back to look at him. "Drystan was bragging about finding another Core. They were on their way to get her, and he said she's been right under their nose. I think it's my friend Ansel. Something in my spirit just tells me it's her. She came with the Feminea Potentia to stay at ashram, and we both felt a connection, even before we talked. But she knows nothing about all of this. And she's a fighter. Our best hope of bringing her in lies with me."

CHAPTER 31

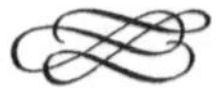

NICANOR

The thought of taking Lucia anywhere other than to the safety of The Refuge almost turns my eyes black as the conqueror fights for dominance. She's been through so much, and I just want her safe. But I trust her, too, and if she thinks this is the best way, then we will try. I owe her that much.

"Okay, let me check with Cai and see if he has a tip on where the FP might be."

Her face lights up at my trust in her and I know it was the right call.

"Wait, how can you check with Cai?"

"Another cool trick us Horsemen have. We can communicate with each other in our minds if we deeply focus. It can be hard in certain settings and over long distances. Give me a sec and I'll see if I can get him."

I close my eyes, focusing on Cai only.

"Cai?"

It takes a few seconds, but then I hear, "*Nic, good to hear from you, man. How's our girl?*"

"*She'll be okay, I'll make sure of it. But your tip made a world of difference. I was able to get in and out pretty quickly.*"

"*So she was in that place she hates then?*"

"*Yes, and how I will ever move past the guilt and shame of knowing it's my fault, I've no idea.*"

"*You can't do that to yourself. There's no life down that path. We make the best decisions we can with the information we have. We will make mistakes, for sure, but that's where the growth happens most of the time. You got her out of there. Just keep your eyes looking forward.*"

"*Thank you, my brother. I'm actually reaching out for a different reason. Do you have any information on the location of the FP?*"

"*Yes, actually. They seem to have split into two groups. There's one heading toward The Wastes, in the direction of the swamplands. I am just about to head in that direction and scope it out. The main group is near the foothills of The Range—that's probably closest to you. Be careful, Nic.*"

"*You too.*"

I open my eyes and find Lucia focused on me. The bright sun shines on her tanned face, lighting her eyes to a gold so radiant, it steals the air from my lungs. There's information I need to share with her, but in moments like this, my thoughts scatter at the sight of her, everything else falling away.

Now that I've stopped fighting it, the words of my heart are only of her. It's as though the very blood in my veins answers to hers. She has this way of looking at me that's all-encompassing, filled with so much promise and devotion. I realize how grey my world was before her. I've lived so long, and yet it's like I am seeing the sun and feeling its warmth for the first time. I feel reborn when I look in her eyes.

"Nic?"

Shaking my head to clear my thoughts, I say, "Um, yeah, so we're close to a large grouping of FP." I pause, trying to figure out how to say this. "I have a theory that I might be able to distance jump with you because you are my Core."

"That teleporting thing?"

"Well, yeah. Another Horseman perk. We can jump to places we've been before when riding our mounts."

"And you think I can come with you?" She says, her skin flushed with excitement.

"Well, I am definitely not going without you," I say, a wry grin tugging at my lips. "Are you up for trying?"

"Yes, absolutely!" she says like a kid on Christmas morning. Her excitement is contagious and it fills my heart with stupid male pride to know I am responsible. That I could bring her fun, excitement, and adventure. Cai's words came back to me and I realize he was right. I will strive to focus on the now and the future. There are so many things Lucia has yet to experience because of her isolated life, so I will focus on giving her a life filled with everything she should have never had to live without. I will make it my mission to make her life so full of love and goodness that it overpowers all the bad.

"Okay, I will try to place us in the general vicinity, but Cai was kind of vague on the details. This could be dangerous, so please stay close, and if I say run, do not hesitate."

"Yes sir," she says with a mocking grin and a little military-style salute.

With an air of seriousness, I approach her, cupping her face in both my hands, my gaze intent on her golden eyes. "I mean it, Lu. I am fighting so hard not to throw you over my shoulder like a barbarian and hightail it to The Refuge where I know you'll be safe. I want you to know I will never lock you up or keep you from being who Elohim called you to be, but if we're going to do this, I need to know you will do what I say."

"Nic," she says with a breathless whisper as her hands reach up to my jaw, her delicate fingertips brushing through my hair. I close my eyes with a sigh and lean into her hand, soaking up the feel of her skin and the wonderment of how she calms me with just a touch. "When are you going to see we are strongest together? I know it's terrifying to think of us in harm's way, but we have to trust. Elohim created us to be a partnership, and we are at our strongest and most powerful when we are united. Asking me to run if you are in danger is like asking me to cut out my heart. I would never do it. Would you be able to if our roles were reversed?"

And as much as I am loath to admit it, I know she's right. There's no way I'd leave her in any circumstance. But the thought of something happening to her, again, has me paralyzed with fear. Before I can try to take my thoughts captive, I am shaking again, and I know when I open my eyes, they will be black once more. Logically speaking, fear is how I got us into this situation to begin with, but despite all the power I have in me right now, the one thing I don't know if I can muster on my own is the ability to trust. At that thought, I realize why Elohim made her my Core. So she can be my trust when I can't muster it myself.

I open my eyes, locking onto Lu's like a lifeline. Lu's arms go around my neck; she pulls herself closer to me, and then her lips are on mine. A soft, barely-there caress and then a whisper; "Let it go."

I scoop her into my arms, her legs coming around my

waist. She wraps herself around me like a security blanket; my nose buries into her neck breathing in her soothing scent. My shaking stops and my heartbeat slows. She pulls back in my arms to look at my face. "You're back," she says with a wink.

I touch my forehead to hers. "Thanks to you."

Her eyes shine with hope and determination. "Let's do this," she grins.

"You're the boss," I say. Hefting her over my shoulder, caveman-style, I carry her to the open field, her laughter floating on the wind like a song. I slow my pace, close my eyes, and call Adira forth. I lift Lu from my shoulder, sit her atop Adira, and hop up behind her.

"Hang on, we need to pick up some speed."

I bring Adira to a run, say a quick prayer to Elohim for Lu's safety, and close my eyes, thinking of the field near the abandoned warehouse in the foothills where the FP like to train.

Here goes nothing.

Popping out right in the center of the field, we quickly dismount and Adira vanishes back into my seal with a thought. Thankfully, the grass is tall, so we hunker down. We can see the whole warehouse from here, but no one seems to be outside. Something feels off about this whole situation.

"What does your friend look like?" I whisper.

"She's easy to spot. Fiery red hair and bright green eyes. She's tall, or at least taller than me, and slender, but athletic."

"Okay, I'm going to go in for a closer look. Stay here until I get back."

"We should stick together, Nic," she says with a tone of warning.

"We will...we are," I say, weighing her words. "I will only be a few minutes, and then we can plan our next move from here."

She nods, though it's obvious the decision does not sit well with her. Giving her a quick kiss on the forehead and telling her to stay low and hidden, I head off toward the warehouse.

Carefully sneaking around the outside from a distance to confirm there are no guards, I find a fairly hidden corner of the warehouse where the terrain starts to incline and rocky crags offer some good cover for an approach. From one of the boulders, I peer in one of the windows, using my enhanced eyesight, and there's no movement or lights on. It's clear the place is locked up and shut down. No vehicles are parked inside or out either, and I know the FP operates all-terrain vehicles.

I make my way back to Lu. From my vantage point, I can see small stirrings in various areas of the grassy field where I left her. There are many similar movements, but all with the same goal: they're sweeping toward the center of the field where Lucia is hidden. I think I just found the FP.

Trying to draw their attention, I barrel toward the field pulling a short sword from my back. Four of the nearest figures halt and stand up in the field to face me. But behind them, there are still plenty of circles heading toward Lu. The berserker power floods my veins at the danger heading her way, my eyes darkening as my senses sharpen.

Time to make fast work of this.

With dizzying speed, I bat away an arrow aimed at my chest. Then before my opponent has a chance to react, I pivot in place and deflect the downward arc of another blade. Sweeping out with a leg, I knock the one with the blade back, pulling a small blade from my thigh sheath to throw at the one with the arrows, impaling her in the eye. Like a maelstrom, I tear through the remaining three. I start moving toward Lu again. If I can get to her, then I can protect her.

A whip cracks from behind me, going around my neck, stopping me dead in my tracks. But like an oak rooted in the ground, I am unyielding in my position. Two more come at me from either side. I use the blade to slash through the whip. I move at a pace so explosive, I barely register my actions before only dust stirs and all movement of life near me ceases. It is innate within me, as easy as breathing.

The hair on the back of my neck stands on end, and I turn to the center of the field, only a few feet away now. But I'm still too late. Lucia stands perfectly still in the middle of the field. The shining glare of a blade at her neck. My breath seizes in my lungs. I can barely see the arm that's holding a blade to her throat.

A feminine face appears from over her shoulder. "Stop there, Horseman. That's close enough."

At her words, over a dozen of the Feminea Potentia warriors stand out of the tall grass. None of them are redheads. With the power flooding my veins, I know I can defeat the warriors before me, but not before they hurt Lucia. I am effectively unarmed with her in their grasp. And they know it. If only I had listened to her and hadn't left her. We were safer together, and now she's in danger again because of me.

"What do you want?"

"The real question is what do you want, Horseman?

You can fight us and we can kill your Core here, or you can surrender and she will remain unharmed and returned safely to the monks."

For just a moment, I see the flash of dread that flits through Lucia's eyes, but like it never happened, she steels herself for what's ahead. Her eyes lock on mine as if her soul is speaking directly to me, I know she's giving me her trust.

"I will surrender."

"Smart move, Horseman. Put your hands behind your back."

I do as she says and feel someone approach from behind, wrapping something around my wrists to hold them in place.

"There, much better," she says, sending me a mocking grin. She nods to the warrior to her left. As if in slow motion, I watch her pull a crossbow from behind her back. She winks at me as she fires the bolt directly into my chest. When it hits it feels like my heart explodes in my chest. The action throws me back against the ground. I stare up at the blue sky, distantly hearing Lucia's screams. I try to focus on ignoring the pain and getting to her. I manage to get to one knee, but the pain is incapacitating and I can't seem to get any air in my lungs.

The woman who held the blade to Lucia's throat walks into view, Lucia struggling against her. Blood drips down her throat from pulling against the knife. The FP woman removes the knife and shoves Lucia to the ground in front of me.

"Here she is, unharmed. We keep our word, Horseman. Enjoy your last few minutes together," She says with a saccharine smile. "And don't think about running, girl. The

Amilign will be here in no time to collect you, and you'll only make it worse for yourself if you run."

I vaguely sense a sudden, bright white light with searing heat. A fierce, agonizing yell rends the air. Screams of dread and panic burst forth and quickly fade into nothing. The white light dies, and only blissful silence and lingering warmth are left. Out of that warmth, I see Lucia's face appear. Her hair drifts around her, as if swept up in a gentle wind of her own making. Her vivid golden eyes are ablaze as they peer into mine and bid me stay. It's a command I want nothing more than to obey, but as I begin to drift toward the in-between, I know it's a command no amount of conquering will be able to enforce.

CHAPTER 32

LUCIA

There's no space inside me to wonder at how I just decimated an entire field of Feminea Potentia. A pain like none I've ever felt floods my veins and consumes every part of me. My heart seizes in my chest and all the fight goes out of me, leaving me cold and empty. I drop to my knees by Nic, his hands holding the arrow in his chest as if he's trying to dam up the blood inside.

"Y...you m...must run," he stutters out. The blue in his eyes is fading. I can distantly hear the distinct whir of a helicopter.

"No!" I yell through a ragged, broken sob. "I am never leaving you and you are not leaving me! There has to be something we can do. Tell me what to do?"

He touches a bloodied hand to my face. "I w...wouldn't change it, you know. Saying y...yes to you. It's the only time I was ever really alive."

His ashen face is sheened with sweat; his hand shakes as it drops to the ground. This cannot be happening. I will not allow it. He is a Horseman and I am his Core; we were to be this momentous force together. We are designed to be stronger together. And that's when it strikes me... *together*. I don't know what to do, but I trust Elohim Shomri, our Protector, to show me the path. This is not the end for us.

I hated the idea of hurting him, but I sense the arrow needs to be removed.

"I need to get the arrow out, Nic, okay? On three?"

But he only mumbles incoherently. I pray to Elohim, count to three, and pull. His body shudders and he groans as more of his lifeblood pours from the wound.

I cover his chest with my hands, attempting to staunch the flow, and desperately trying not to panic. My thoughts are in upheaval, seeing Nic's blue-tinged lips, his blood pushing out between my fingers. I give into the urging of my heart and I lean forward, pressing my lips to his. My tears try in vain to cleanse away what's happening.

I will him to stay with me. I think of the bright crystal blue of his eyes; the creases on his face when he laughs that deep, soulful rumble; his soft, dark hair when the wind blows through it; the stubble of his jaw under my hand; the feel of his strong muscles. My hands begin to warm as I cover his chest, but I don't let go. I let my love for him fill me up, and imagine it pouring out of me through my hands and through my kiss.

It seems like forever, but I won't let go. Then I feel his hand come up through the curtain of my hair, grabbing the back of my neck and holding me to him. He's clinging to me as much as I am clinging to him. The kiss that was once mine quickly becomes his as he takes over. The urgent way he claims my lips cuts off all thought. Behind my closed lids, a bright light strains through. Nic's kiss slows and moves to my cheeks, my nose, and my eyes before he whispers, "Open your eyes."

As I do, I notice a cocoon of light—golden, living flame surrounds us, but it doesn't burn. Instead, it is warm and soothing. Nic grasps my wrist and holds my hand up between us, and that's when I realize *I* am the source of the golden flame. I try to jump off of him, but he doesn't let go of my wrist.

"You're not hurting me, Lu. In fact, you've healed me." Reverence colors his tone.

My head jerks back to his face. My eyes immediately go to his chest. The tattered, blood-soaked hole in his shirt exposes unmarred pink skin. I stretch out my hand to touch him, but I am still covered in flame. Instinctively, I jerk back, but Nic gently reaches through the flames, unafraid, grabbing my fingers and pushing them against his exposed chest. I gasp. I suppose I expected his clothes to go up in flames.

"What's happening to me?" I say looking down at my arms awash in flame.

"The gift of Heaven from the prophecy," he says, awed. "We must have activated it when we mutually accepted the bond. You have the gift of Heavenly Fire."

I should be more focused on the fact that I am covered in Heavenly Fire, but as I look at him, really look, he becomes the only thing that matters. "You're really healed," I whisper, stunned by the surrealness of it.

He sits up as if to substantiate my words.

I throw my arms around his neck, trembling. "I couldn't lose you. I just prayed and kept thinking about you whole and healed and how I couldn't be in this world without you. I trusted Elohim to guide me and He did."

He rubs my back in soothing patterns. The flames

around us die down and eventually go out. I pull back from him, clasping his jaw between both my hands, my gaze intent on his. "You are mine, Nicanor Cascus, White Horseman of Conquest, and I am yours. You will go nowhere that I will not follow. You hear me? Together, we are one creation. Always."

He shudders at my words, his bright eyes luminous. He brings his forehead to mine as he whispers, "Your eyes are like the molten core of the sun itself right now. My very own sun looking back at me." He smiles.

The hair on the back of my neck stands up as a voice that haunts my nightmares oozes across the grass like an oil spill. "Have we interrupted something?"

We both jump to our feet, standing side-by-side to face whatever lies in front of us. And my stupid heart skips a beat at the fact that Nic stands by me, as my partner, instead of pushing me behind him like a guardian. I've spent so much of my life feeling useless and insignificant. The gravity of that action and what it must take for him to do it is not lost on me.

Drystan stands in front of us. Behind him are what I can only assume are the Silent. Rumors whispered on the wind no longer.

Four of them, dressed in robes of black that they shed like snake skins, revealing head-to-toe black uniforms that hug their forms but allow for movement. They remind me of ninjas from the storybooks I read as a child, even down to the blades strapped across their backs. Only these men are monstrous in size, like they were grown and altered in a lab, not actually of this world. They move into place beside Drystan, dwarfing his over 6-foot frame.

The aggression rolling off them tells me all I needed to know about their purpose: they were bred for annihilation.

"The FP said you'd be dead," he says, pointing at Nic.

I practically snarl at him.

"Ooh, looks like someone grew a backbone. Think you're brave now that you're next to your boy toy and not cowering naked in front of me, huh?"

Like that of a blast zone, a shockwave radiates outward from Nic, causing even Drystan to take a step back. The air around Nic vibrates as if on edge. I look up at him and see his eyes blackened with the power that floods his veins, but he looks at me and winks, as if to ease my mind and show me he is still in control.

"I'd honestly like to see you sic your boyfriend on the Silent," Drystan says to me, "so we can make sure he's dead for real this time."

"Well, I hate to disappoint you," Nic drawls with a mocking grin. "But she doesn't need me to fight her battles. I'll fight by her side anytime she wants, but she can take out the trash all by herself."

My heart swells at his trust and faith in me.

"The declawed kitten grew claws after all, huh?" Drystan sneers. "You know, I was against keeping you as one of us from the very beginning. I didn't understand all the bother with pretending. Educating you, giving you a comfortable place to live, and leading you to believe you held a high place of honor. It would have been better to throw you in a dungeon, raising you to know you were nothing. That way when we finally pulled you out and presented you with your purpose, you would've been eager to do our bidding."

My breathing thins and my hands shake. Any sound fades to the background over the hammering of my pulse. Nic puts a hand on my lower back, steadying me. Reminding me I'm not alone, I'm not that girl anymore.

"But alas, I was overruled. Something about needing you at your optimum physical and mental health in order to be a strong vessel for offspring. I guess dungeon life isn't very conducive to that. Though, I still believe my methods would have avoided the current predicament. But no matter. I hope you enjoyed your taste of freedom. Soon you'll be serving out the purpose you were made for."

Even at this distance, I can see the dark gleam of eagerness in his eyes. Drystan gestures with his head and the Silent began their advance.

I look out across the field at the unholy otherness of the creatures. They move in a way that drives home that they're clearly not of this world. A liquid stealth marks them despite their jerky movements. As if too much power has been poured into them, and their shells are struggling to house it. The closer they get, I can see their skin has a grey pallor, as if it's been leached of warmth and life. Their eyes, a bright, unearthly red, stand in sharp contrast to the rest of them. Tiny black veins, like the roots of a plant, branch outward from their eye sockets. The one closest to me smiles or growls, exposing rows of razor-sharp pointed teeth.

I have never seen the like of them, even in the worst of my nightmares. Fear is a living and breathing beast inside me, threatening to paralyze me.

As much as I wanted to be a warrior, I'm not Ansel. I don't have battlefield experience or years of training. Yes, I have this newfound power that totally demolished the Feminea Potentia, but that was a fluke. I have no idea how to use it, or if I even will be able to again. Maybe it was a one-and-done thing that came out of my desperation to save Nic. My weakness and ineptitude threatens to swallow me whole.

Then I feel Nic lean in and kiss my forehead. As he

pulls away, I look into his eyes and see only love and acceptance shining back at me.

"You saved me once today. Now let me return the favor." He pulls the short sword from his back and charges the four monstrous and hulking figures that make my fierce warrior Horseman look like a child.

He reaches the one that showed his teeth first and holds his own. Slicing, ducking, and blocking with ease, his movements are a choreographed dance. When a second Silent joins the fight, Nic's moves increase in speed as he taps into the berserker power within him. He is a fierce and beautiful sight to behold, but as I watch, the two Silent headed toward me start to veer to Nic. I just know that four will be too many for him. They mean to take Nic out of the picture first, and then take me captive. And Nic will die if I'm not around to heal him.

A roar erupts from Nic, turning my blood to ice. A blade slipped past his defenses, slicing across his abdomen. I cry out, reaching toward him as I take a step in his direction. But thinking him close to defeat, the other two Silent turn back toward me again, blocking my path to Nic. Rage simmers in me. In that moment, truth pierces through the haze of my thoughts and I know that the fear and the lies telling me I am worthless are only desperate attempts from the darkness that wants to keep me bound.

But no more. I am a Core, a creation of Elohim's love, and I am filled with His pure light. Darkness has no weapon against me.

I glance at Nic as his eyes meet mine. One of the Silent he fought is down, but Nic is panting, one arm limply holding his sword while the other hand presses against his abdomen. He is weakening.

I allow my protective rage to boil over. I take slow,

measured steps forward as I hold onto the truth of who I am; the power of Elohim's love is an eddy within me. The flame begins to pour out of the center of my chest, licking down to my limbs and the tips of my hair, causing it to lift and dance around my head. Undiluted power tingles over my skin, supercharging me into something other. I am the flame and I can choose what to burn or leave untouched by my will alone. I focus on scorching the ground beneath my steps as I walk, leaving destruction in my wake.

The Silent advancing on me pause, hesitation in their demon eyes as they look at each other, the first crack in their shield of confidence. Drystan gestures to the two closest to me and they separate to come at me from the sides, pulling swords from their backs. They move like snakes as they head toward me.

My eyes meet Nic's as he watches through my flames, a look of pure awe on his pained face. The Silent who was closing in on him for a deathblow has now lost all interest in him as he moves to protect Drystan.

It's almost cute that those two Silent thought I'd let them get close to me. Acting purely on instinct, I lift my hands at them and smile as I imagine the power collecting in my hands. I will it to shoot out like a blast, summoning the Heavenly Fire to vaporize them. One of them dives out of the way of the blast, but he is not untouched; his body is now a smoking, moaning mess on the ground. The other Silent has disappeared. A patch of scorched earth is all that is left of where he once stood.

I look at Drystan and tilt my head in question. Fear, plain as day, coats his expression. Like the disgusting rat he is, he scurries back to the helicopter. The other Silent grabs the injured one and they flee in Drystan's trail, like beetles whose rock has been upended. I watch, lit up like a torch, while they retreat.

As soon as the helicopter moves over the horizon, I make my way to Nic, placing my hands over the hand that holds his stomach wound closed. I close my eyes and focus again on my love for this man in front of me. I picture him whole and healed once more, and let that love and desire swell and grow, bursting forth from my chest. Suddenly, I feel his hand comb through my hair, gripping my head as his lips crash into mine. His hands slide around my waist, pulling me to him. He kisses me with such a fervent hunger, I would have gone up in flame if I wasn't already burning. As it is, I feel as though at any moment, I am going to drift away on the wind as nothing but cinders and ash. He sweeps me into his arms, untouched by and unafraid of my flames, then slows his assault on my lips, softening to a worshipful caress.

He pulls back from the kiss, holding me up with his arms around my waist as my feet dangle above the ground. "You are such a badass," he says with a serious tone, but a twinkle in his now blue eyes. I tip my head back and laugh, letting the joy pour out of me.

I douse my flames and Nic makes a mock pouty face that has me laughing all over again.

"Let's go home." He lowers me to the ground. Smoothing the hair behind my ear, his gaze is a caress across my face. "Elias needs to see this." He grins. "And then we can figure out what to do about Ansel."

CHAPTER 33

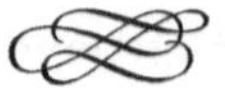

Distance jumping with Nic and Adira is a bit disorienting and all I can deduce is that we arrived in an open field. Immediately, the harsh sounds of weapons clashing and men yelling assault my ears. On instinct, I drop from Adira's back, summoning my fire as I land. In a matter of moments, everything is as still as the ashram during meditation. Weapons are lowered and looks of wonder and disbelief light up all the faces.

That's when I notice we are in the training field outside The Refuge. It's just some of the Prophets and a huge, shirtless man with a short, faux mohawk going through training. A little embarrassed by my overreaction, I withdraw the flames.

"Uh, sorry for the interruption."

I look up at Nic to see a big grin on his face.

"You couldn't give me a heads up?" I ask him. "Like, 'Hey Lu, we're going to the training field and people might be in the middle of it, so don't get startled.'"

"Uh, definitely not! This was way better." He smirks as he hops off Adira's back, stroking her neck before sending her off to graze. "And as I said before, you're a badass. I'll never get tired of people being blown away by you, literally." He winks as he grabs my hand, his words warming me. "Come with me. I want you to meet another of my brothers."

We walk toward the mountain of a man, arms folded across his tawny chest. He is pointing at one of the other Prophets with a sword, barking commands at him, I assume correcting his stance.

"Hey Z," Nic says, "I want you to meet someone."

He turns toward us, his face expressionless. His head is almost shaved, other than a short, cropped mohawk and some day-old stubble around his jaw. The golden brown color of his skin makes him look like he was birthed from the sun. He appears rough, like a jagged piece of granite just torn from a mountain. His dark brown eyes are like deep pools to the darkest parts of him, and something in me senses pain in him. Like an unwanted companion that can't be eradicated. But he isn't closed off. He stands there, strong and intimidating, almost daring me to take his measure. A rippling wave of hesitancy goes through me.

"Knock it off Z, you're going to freak her out. Geez, you're freaking me out."

Z softens just a touch, barely perceptible. He reaches his hand out to shake mine. "I'm Zion."

I shake his hand, surprised to find it warm and his touch gentle. "Nice to meet you, Zion, I'm Lucia."

"Z here is the Black Horseman of Justice." Nic slaps him on the back, and then addresses Z. "And you probably guessed this, but Lu is my Core."

"Interesting party trick you got there, Lucia." Zion's

eyebrow lifts, the most expression I've seen on the reserved man yet.

I smile, as my cheeks flush. "Yeah, sorry about that. Nic didn't warn me, and well, I've been on edge these past few days."

A shadow flits across Nic's gaze for just a moment, but Zion notices. He grabs Nic by the shoulder, quickly turning all business.

"What happened, Nicanor?"

As Nic fills in Z on the events of the past few days, sparing some of the more intimate details for my sake, I feel something sniff my hair. I turn to see Adira.

"I haven't gotten to thank you yet, girl" I stroke her soft muzzle. "For helping get me out of there, and for taking care of my guy while I was gone." She whinnies and lowers her head. I press my forehead against hers, wrapping my arms around her big head, under her jaw. Our connection smoothes away the sharpest remnants of my ordeal. I release her, giving her one last rub and turning back to see Nic and Z staring at me.

"What?"

A soft smile lights Nic's face, radiating adoration. But it is the intense look of longing and awe on Zion's face that almost makes me take a step back. Nic pats Z's shoulder, with a promise to catch up later, and heads over to me, taking my hand. I follow him to The Refuge's entrance.

"Z hasn't met his Core yet," Nic explains, "despite an exhaustive search for her for years. The longing you see on his face isn't for you, but for what we have. Watching your bond with Adira hits him in the heart. It's why he may seem a bit moody." He pauses, as if he wants to say more, but isn't sure how to proceed. With a sigh, he presses forward.

"You see, about two years ago, Z felt a searing pain in his

leg that lasted for days. It faded, but it left him with a phantom numbness in that leg ever since. We figure that it's in some way tied to his Core, like maybe the intensity of emotion she was feeling allowed her to form some sort of connection across space, despite the two of them never having met."

I glance back at Zion, seeing the tension in his shoulders, the seal between his shoulder blades incomplete, and my heart breaks for him. "So are you saying that something horrible might have happened to her, and through the pain, she was able to connect to Zion?"

"That's what the scholars believe. And it makes sense with what he experienced. Poor Z, I can't imagine what it's like. Knowing his Core is out there, somewhere hurting. That he can feel her pain, but he can't get to her. That's the worst kind of torture. It's why he is the way he is. Elias fears that it will be what finally leashes him."

"We can't let that happen, Nic. We've got to do something."

He stops walking at the seriousness in my tone. Turning to me, he brings a hand up to my face and rubs a knuckle down my cheek. It seems impossible for him to resist touching me, like it is his subconscious way of reminding himself I am here and I am his.

"We will, Lu. You are the first key to this whole puzzle. We're going to go talk with Elias, and hopefully, with what we've learned and experienced, we'll be able to discover more about the other Cores."

Walking into The Refuge is like coming home, despite my having only lived here for a few weeks previously. And that feeling of coming home is new and wholly unexpected. I can feel my eyes water as I fight the lump of emotion in my throat. Nic squeezes my hand. It's uncanny the way we sense each other now that the bond is fully connected. We are naturally drawn together, both of us wanting to be touching in some way when we are near, whether it's our hands, or even just the brush of our arms connecting. And then that keen awareness, not just of each other's presence, but our emotions as well. His soul is the twin to my own, and they will forever be reaching toward each other. He is part of me now.

We make a beeline for Elias's office. In typical Elias fashion, he opens the door to us while Nic stands there with his fist in the air, prepared to knock.

Before we can even get any words out, Elias yanks me into a crushing embrace. I'm surprised to feel the older man trembling, emotion pouring out of him in waves.

"Oh my child," his voice cracks. "I prayed nonstop for you. After I heard that you were taken from the farmhouse, I prayed to Elohim Shomri for your protection. I struggled with fear for your safety."

He pulls back, his hands on my shoulders, to meet my gaze. "How are you? Truly?"

I glance up at Nic, flashes of what we went through going through my mind. It was definitely a trial, the likes of which I have never experienced. But what was intended to destroy me, Elohim faithfully used to strengthen me instead, to strengthen both Nic and me. And seeing the end result now—Nic by my side, our bond solidified, my heavenly gift activated, an unshakeable trust between us, and my inner strength, gifted by Elohim Himself, reaching its full potential—I can honestly say it was worth it.

Nic smiles at me, as if he can read my thoughts, leaning

in to kiss my head. With a smile at Elias, I say, "I've never been better."

Elias smiles a smile that lights up the room and yanks me back into his arms. His relief is palpable. Then, turning to Nic, he puts a hand on his arm. "I always knew you had it in you, son. I am proud of you."

Nic leans in to hug the man who is so much to so many. When he pulls back, both men have unshed tears shining in their eyes.

"Come, we have much to discuss."

Elias pulls up a chair while Nic and I move to the couch, sitting together. Nic spreads one arm across the back of the couch, encircling my shoulders while I move into him, tucking my knees up across his legs.

"Interesting," Elias says contemplatively.

"What?" we ask in unison.

He smiles at us. "The way you both move. It's so cohesive, almost like a dance. It seems as though it's simply intrinsic for you to be in contact constantly. I wonder, do you even realize you're doing it?"

I look up at Nic, our eyes connecting. His brighten as he gazes back at me. An invisible tether between us seems to pull taut. The air thickens and all sound fades away as I stare into his innermost being, captivated by the entanglement of our souls.

"Good grief," Elias's words break through the daze. "And to think I thought what was between you both was intense before. Tell me everything, start at the beginning."

Feeling a bit burned out after being a human torch several times over, I let Nic do the talking. He begins with his arrival at the farmhouse and his discovery that I'd been taken against my will. When he describes Dee's betrayal, he squeezes me tighter. He relates the events leading up to my rescue, including his thoughts and fears regarding what might have happened to me. Then he shares how and where he found me, and what happened afterward.

Heaving a loud sigh, Elias leans back against his chair. "So many things make sense now."

"What do you mean?" I ask.

"Well for one, the berserker power in Nic that you speak of, that has to be the part of the prophecy that says he will be forever altered in the depth of his being. It says that once you are made weak, only then can you truly be made strong," Elias's lips purse and his brows pinch in thought. "You were made mortal when you surrendered to the bond, and by doing so, you were altered in your physical state with the power of the berserker, which gives you a strength and speed that far exceeds what you had before. And even though you are no longer immortal, you and Lucia have the power to protect each other, as well as heal each other. So in a way, you were made weak, but now together, you are stronger than ever."

"Wow," Nic reflects. "I was such a prideful idiot."

"No, Nicanor, you are a conqueror. It's not in your nature to surrender to anything, especially if it will make you weak. It was always going to be a battle for you, and in different ways, it will be for your brothers as well."

But I feel the heaviness of regret in the air around Nic. So I do the only thing I can think to let him know that I don't hold anything against him. While he's distracted, I rest my hand over his heart as I lean up and press a kiss to his cheek, and then whisper in his ear, "I love you, Nicanor Cascus, just as you are. I have no regrets."

Before I can pull away, he pulls his arm tight around me, pressing me to him as his nose finds the sensitive spot of my neck just below my ear. He breathes me in deeply, as if calming or reassuring himself.

"I am so sorry about Dee, Lucia," Elias says. "I would take much of what she says with a grain of salt. She's a vessel now. I'm sure the pure Dee saw you as a friend. But demons only sow hatred and discontent." Elias sighs as if his world-weary soul is deeply affected by the news of another lost to darkness.

"Also, you should know that Cai left us just yesterday. We'd been monitoring the movements of the FP for a while, because our intel suggested corruption within. Well, about four days ago, there was movement. One group broke away and headed in the direction of The Wastes. It was when that group broke away that Cai started behaving jittery and restless. There was an urgency in him, and when one of the Prophets suggested he wait until we have further information before pursuing the group, his eyes flashed black.

"As the Horseman of War, Cai believes he's being pushed in pursuit to prevent the evil in the FP from spreading. He's on a mission to destroy them, especially after he learned they were working with the Amilign and might have played a part in what went down with you, Lucia. After hearing your theory about your friend Ansel, I can't help but wonder if the pull he's feeling is for an entirely different reason."

I stand abruptly as the information soaks in.

"You think Ansel is his Core? And he's on his way to kill her!" I turn to Nic as I remember his special Horseman connection. "Can you reach out to him, warn him?"

Before he gets a chance to try, Elias makes a halting gesture with his hand. "Don't bother, Zion has already attempted to do so twice. He is unreachable for some reason. And we can no longer locate that group of FP, because they are in the dead zone of The Wastes. Which might be what is interfering with the Horsemen's mental connection as well. There's something unnatural and unholy about that area."

As my mind gets ready to run away with itself, Elias reaches out and grabs my hand. "Trust, my sweet girl. That is the Core you represent, after all. We must trust that Elohim will guide them both, just as He did you and Nicanor."

My heart steadies at the reminder, but a flicker of worry remains. "She doesn't know about Elohim and His ways. She was raised by the FP. She knows nothing of the prophecy."

"Worry not, Lucia. She may not know Elohim, but you can sure bet that He knows her. He has a plan. And if Cai is her Horseman, well, it is in Elohim's perfect design that someone as faithful and reverent as Cai be the one to guide her. Remember, Lucia, Elohim doesn't call the qualified; He qualifies those who are called."

I know he's right, but I also know Ansel. She's a firecracker with an act first, ask questions later mentality. And Cai is the Horseman of War, for crying out loud. I only hope and pray they don't kill each other before they get the chance to learn who they are to one another.

CHAPTER 34

Elias hopes to see my heavenly gift in person, but I can't hide how exhausted I am, so he sends us away to rest with the reassurance that he can wait until I am recovered. As we head back to our rooms, a sinking feeling hits my gut. I don't want to leave Nic. I haven't left him since he got me out of the ashram. I need his nearness like I need oxygen.

But I can't say that to him; this is still new to both of us. I don't want him to feel trapped by some needy girl. But what if he feels the same? Should I say something or ask? Ugh. What previously felt as natural as breathing now has me second-guessing all my actions and words.

He comes to a stop in front of my door. I fidget with my shirt, still wearing the one he gave me to wear. I don't look at him as I grab the door. I feel so unsure all of a sudden. Where is the powerful fire-wielding girl who faced down an Amilign monk and four of The Silent?

Nic grabs my arm and turns me to face him. His opposite hand coming up to my face, he smooths my hair behind my ear and cups my cheek.

"Don't," he commands.

A shiver runs down my spine at the firmness in his voice.

"Don't shut me out. I can feel the turmoil and confusion in you. We are one, remember? Trust me with all the parts of you. Please." his voice breaks, his tone rough. I look up at his almost glowing eyes and the love and acceptance in them undoes me.

"I don't want to leave you," I confess. "And not just because I went through something traumatic and I need you to keep the nightmares at bay, but I don't want to be apart from you. It feels alien and wrong to have you drop me off at my door. But I don't want you to feel pressured or trapped. I know this is all new and—"

"Stop," he blurts out. "What do you feel from me right now?"

"Umm, I—"

"Close your eyes, Lu," he interrupts softly, placing my hand over his heart. The heart that was pierced by an arrow just a few hours before. "Let go of any fears about all the unknowns and focus on me. What do you sense?"

Taking a deep breath, my eyes close and I let his scent fill my senses. I feel his warm chest beneath my skin; the steady, soothing beat of his heart. The warmth of love, the sharp edge of need, and the softness of peace surrounds my senses, with a small flicker of concern.

"I feel peace and love from you, and a bit of concern," I whisper.

"There's something else I am feeling."

"Need?" I dare to ask. My eyes are still closed, but I feel

him step closer, his hand sliding around my waist, pulling me to his chest. His forehead rests against mine.

"What do I need, Lu?" he asks in a low, gravelly voice.

"Me?" I ask breathlessly.

"Only ever you." His chest rises sharply. "Though I am afraid of scaring you away with the intensity of my feelings. But since when has fear served either of us? Let's make a promise—no more does fear get a say in our life. Deal?"

"Deal," I agree. "So what now?"

"What do you mean?"

"Well, do we need some kind of ceremony or ritual before we can be official? Like something that recognizes us as bonded?"

His eyes dance with amusement. "We were bonded and activated in the eyes of Elohim when we acknowledged our love and you healed me. We can't get much more official than that. As far as the world and the heavens go, we are one, now and forever. You are Lucia Cascus, Core to Nicanor Cascus, White Horseman of Conquest."

My heart swells at his words, a tear of joy rolling down my cheek. "You promise?"

At my words, he places me on my feet. He opens the door to my room, confidently striding in before pulling me with him and closing the door with a kick. He walks me to the light of the window, grabbing both my hands in his as he drops down to one knee in front of me.

"Lucia Cascus, Core of my heart, twin soul of my soul, the flame of my life. I vow to be yours until the end of all time, spanning the vast distances of the universe and heavens. We are one spirit and one creation together. No matter the circumstances of this life or the next, I will love you with all that I am and will ever become until I am nothing but memory and ash, and even then, my love will endure on without me."

Tears roll down my cheeks in steady streams as I drop to my knees in front of him, bringing his hands to my heart.

"Nicanor Cascus, conqueror of my heart, twin soul of my soul, the kindling of my flame. The vast grey nothingness that was my life has been reborn in vibrant, living color because of you. You, my love, are my greatest gift from Elohim, my sweetest dream brought to life, and my most enduring and steadfast anchor. All that I am is yours. I will love you for all time, in this life and the next."

A tear tracking down his cheek, Nic stands, slowly pulling me up with him. As we gaze at each other, something charges the air—a mixture of love, need, and desire. My toes would have curled in my shoes, if I'd been wearing any, at the look on his face and the way his eyes devour me.

Boldly, my gaze dips lower, caressing the strength of his chest, and down the flat plane of his stomach. I feel so out of my depth in this. I know nothing of what I'm heading toward, but I know how I feel, and what I want. It's him, only ever him. I covet the warmth of his touch. His lips. His breath. I don't want to live without the feel and taste of him. He makes me feel alive and seen. Like the glue that holds me to this world, assuring me I am not here for no reason.

And suddenly I know, with absolute certainty, that there is one more way we need to connect to forever lock in the bond. Our souls demand this connection. I also know, without a shadow of a doubt, that Nic will never say anything to sway me toward that decision. That he will exist with me, as we are now, for however long I want or need. He will suppress the conqueror in him eternally, if it means giving me that choice. Always my safety and security.

Summoning the confident fire wielder within me, I

reach out and take Nic's hand in mine. I pull him over to the bed and push him to a sit on the edge. I lift my hand to his strong jaw; his eyes drift shut with a sigh. I smooth my fingers up the line of his jaw and through the soft, wind-tussled dark hair that brushes across his cheekbones. He holds still, eyes closed, soaking in my touch as I explore him. I kiss his cheeks, eyes, nose, chin, jaw, the lobe of his ear, and his neck before he finally holds me at arm's distance, trembling. His eyes flash black.

"I need a minute, Lu, maybe a shower to cool down." His chest rises sharply as he rakes a hand through his hair.

"What if I don't want you to cool down?" My words are soft and steady.

His head jerks up, eyes locking on mine. He looks as though he is being pulled in two directions. I sense the turmoil in him, which instantly triggers my own insecurities. But before I have a chance to say anything, he stands, enveloping me in his arms as his lips devour my own. A low curl of heat intensifies in my stomach as he tilts his head, deepening the kiss. He leaves my lips, kissing his way across my jaw and down my neck. Everywhere his hands touch me, sparks dance across my skin. He brings his lips to my ears, his breathing heavy.

"I want all of you, every part. You have no idea how much I ache to connect with you this way. But I'll not have anything between us, and in the rush of everything, I haven't gotten a chance to tell you about something that happened in the cave."

He quickly pulls me to sit on the bed next to him. His obvious nervousness sends a ripple of wariness through me.

"What is it, Nic?"

"When you were coming out of the haze of the Den, there was a night when you were overcome." He pauses, clearly trying to proceed cautiously. "You climbed onto my lap and I swear I thought you were only seeking comfort, but then you started moving against me and it was clear that the drugs had some sort of aphrodisiac effect on you. To say it was intense would be putting it mildly. I felt like I would go up in flame at any moment. What I need for you to know is that I didn't know how to remove myself from you gently and maintain control. I am ashamed to say that when I finally did get free, I pretty much ran and hid like a coward, instead of staying with you. Leaving you to deal with it on your own."

He looks genuinely downcast and ashamed. Like I would look on him poorly for his actions. In reality, I am really struggling not to laugh at the predicament I put him in. I put a hand to my mouth to stifle a giggle.

His head jerks to me and he balks. "How can you laugh?!"

"Oh, Nic," I say through my laughter. "You are such an incredibly honorable man. You thought I would be disappointed in you for what? Leaving your post at my side?"

He nods solemnly.

"Do you not see how you took the temptation out of the equation by removing yourself? You protected me from myself, and sounds like you protected yourself from me, too." A grin tugs at my lips.

"You're really not let down?"

"Absolutely not. In fact, I think you did what most men wouldn't have had the strength and decency to do."

Having had enough of words, I decide to show him. I stand, moving in front of him, and climb onto his lap, straddling him with my knees on either side of his hips. I curl myself around him, bringing my lips to his neck and breathing in his delectable scent.

"Oh man," he mutters, his voice husky. "I am definitely having flashback dreams again, aren't I?" His hands caress up my back.

I giggle against his neck as I kiss my way from his collarbone up to his ear. He shudders, and before I realize it, he grips my thighs and flips me onto my back, lying between my legs.

"Are you sure?" he asks. "There's no rush."

I stroke the hair hanging forward over his brow, smoothing it away from those piercing blue eyes that drink me in.

"Most of my life, I never got to choose things for myself. For a while, I thought I wouldn't even have my own life. Well, for once I am choosing what I want. I've never been more sure of anything in my life. I want all of you, Nicanor. No more keeping me waiting." I grin.

He chuckles as his eyes heat. "Yes, ma'am." And he spends the rest of the night showing me what it means to be loved by him, connecting our souls in a way that will never be undone. Truly making us one creation.

<h1 style="text-align:center">EPILOGUE</h1>

And now these three remain—
faith, hope, and love.
But the greatest of these is love.
1 Corinthians 13:13

NICANOR

For the first time in over a hundred years, my soul is at rest. Connected, tranquil, infinitely blessed. I hold Lucia across my chest, her dark hair sweeping across her bare shoulders and across my stomach. I stroke the soft, satin-like skin of her arm and a contented sigh escapes her lips. It has to be almost lunch by now, but I am perfectly happy to lie with her like this forever, basking in the afterglow of our souls uniting and our love being made complete.

A rap at the door draws me from my reverie. I am loath to move, but I gently slide out from under Lucia and throw on sweatpants on my way to the door. I crack the door to Elias's grim face.

"I'm sorry to disturb you. You deserve uninterrupted

260

solitude and peace after your ordeal, but I'm afraid this can't wait."

I step out into the hall so as not to wake Lucia. "What is it, Elias?"

"Well, it seems that seeing you and Lucia together has only worsened Z's ability to fight the leashing. I'm afraid that we'll be forced to resort to our emergency plan if we don't find his Core soon."

I stare at Elias, dumbfounded. He can't be serious. I could never let that happen to my brother.

"I see the look on your face, Nicanor, and you have to know that I would never resort to such extremes if it weren't necessary. But he injured a few of the Prophets in training this morning, and when I got to the arena his eyes were fully black. It took far too long for me to help him refocus and regain control." His voice cracks; a sure sign that this is killing him. Elias thinks of us as his sons.

"What can I do?"

"Well, some of the scholars have a theory that Lucia might be able to have a calming effect on any Horseman due to her nature as a Core."

My stomach sinks at his words. She's been through so much already, and I've almost lost her so many times. I am not ready to put her in another dangerous situation so soon.

"I care for Lucia like a daughter, and I would never ask this of her if it weren't the last resort."

Of course, he's right. I know this in my head, but my heart isn't as easily swayed. I nod grimly at him. "I'll talk with her. But if she does this, I have to be close by."

Elias nods at me. "Z is in my office, so we'll wait for you there."

I pause. "Is he ok?"

Elias looks into my eyes with a seriousness I rarely see.

"No, Nicanor, no he is not." I notice the heaviness in his shoulders. "We will not let him fall, Elias," I say with all the conviction and hope I can muster.

To my dismay, as I head back into the room, Lucia is already up and dressed and throwing her long, gorgeous hair into a ponytail. Her eyes connect with mine through the mirror and she freezes, seeing the expression on my face.

Turning slowly, she says, "What is it?"

I hate to bring more hardness to her life, but she is not some soft flower, and I have to remind myself of the quiet strength in her. I will not place her in a glass case up on a shelf when she is meant for greatness.

"Z is not good. Elias thinks it has something to do with seeing us together, our bond complete, that has put more strain on his ability to fight the leashing. He's already been fighting a lot longer than most of us because of the situation with the possible injury to his Core. I hate to ask anything of you after everything you've been through, and if I'm being honest, I don't want you to do this. But it's the only choice to help save Z right now."

She wraps her arms around my waist, her head fitting perfectly under my chin. I kiss the top of her head.

"Tell me," she says.

"Elias is asking you to spend some time with Z, because some of the scholars believe that you will be able to calm him and help him fight the leashing using your nature as a Core."

"Of course, I will help any way I can," she says, as I knew she would. She tilts her head back to look up at me, her arms still around my waist.

"Trust, remember? That's what we do. I trust you, and you trust me."

I tilt my forehead down to hers, breathing in her scent. "You're right, and I do. Just promise me one thing. If he gets out of control, you'll fry his ass with a little heavenly fire."

She tips her head back and laughs, and it warms me deep in my chest. She's like the sun, bringing light and warmth to everything she touches. And it's that realization that calms my fears. Of course she can do this; she will bring that light and warmth to my brother, who is struggling not to be consumed by darkness.

"Let's do this," she says with a wink.

As we reach Elias's office, the door is ajar so we just push it open. Z is on the couch, his head in his hands, and Elias kneels on the floor in front of him. I am immediately struck by the severity of the situation as Z looks up at me and I see tear tracks on his cheeks. The agony on his face threatens to break me.

Before I can say anything, Lucia is across the room. She says nothing as she sits on the couch next to Z. Despite the intimidating appearance he projects, she's focused only on his pain and her mission. She reaches for one of his big hands and gently lays her head on his shoulder, then she starts humming a soft tune, her eyes closed. The tension begins to dissipate. Like a new star in a dusky sky, a soft glow begins to surround her. Z leans back against the couch and Lucia follows, her head never leaving his shoulder. She traces some sort of pattern on the back of Z's hand as she continues to hum and glow.

I am awestruck as I watch a look of serene peace replace the tension on Z's face. I am afraid to move, like I am witness to a transcendent miracle of Elohim Himself. This is the living power of Ruach, the very breath and spirit of the Creator. And just as suddenly, the light fades and the miracle is finished. A quiet reverence fills the room and I notice Elias, sitting on his heels, hands in his lap, tears on his face. Lucia sets Z's hand in his lap, leans over and whispers in his ear, and with a last pat on his shoulder, she rises to her feet, grabs my hand, and leads me from the room, gently closing the door behind her.

I follow her as she leads us back to her room. She pushes me to sit on the bed, and then curls up on the other side, pulling me down so she can lie on my shoulder.

"How'd you know what to do?" I ask.

"I can't really explain it. It felt like I was being guided. I sensed the darkness in him pushing against his defenses. He needed more light. So I just trusted Elohim to provide what was needed, and He did."

"What were you humming?"

"It was a tune that my Aunt Sid used to hum when I was a child and had nightmares."

"Did you know you were glowing?"

She shakes her head no, her expression surprised. "Really? Was I on fire again?"

"No, this was different. It was like you were a star or something. It was this beautiful, ethereal glow."

"Wow," she replies wistfully.

I reach a hand up to stroke the hair back from her face. "It's no surprise. I always knew you were the sun and the stars in my sky. Now it's true for others too."

She nuzzles into my neck, leaving a sweet kiss in her wake that squeezes my heart. I have one more question before I can let her rest. Something tells me that being a conduit of Elohim's power has taken it out of her.

"One more thing?"

"Mmmhmm," she replies sleepily.

"What did you whisper in his ear?"

"I just told him that he would not fight the dark alone.

That I would loan him the light until my sister was home and in his arms." She paused. "And then I felt the urge to tell him to persevere."

I lie there long after she is asleep in my arms, thinking of what happened with Z and what a precious gift Lucia is, not just to me, but to the world. No doubt, we have many battles coming our way. I sense a darkness stirring and preparing to strike. But with Lucia by my side, I am ready, now more than ever, to take my place as the White Horseman of Conquest, and usher in the reign of Heaven on earth. I know what it is to trust now, I've been given the gift of trust in Lucia.

"Thank you, Elohim," I murmur, "and please help guide my brothers and their Cores home."

MORDECAI

Our sources tracked the location of the small contingent of FP, and Ginger and I left to catch them before they got to The Wastes, where my abilities would be rendered useless. Something about that place blocks the Horsemen's ability to mind link with each other and makes us incapable of distance jumping. Ginger and I distance jumped to the FP's last projected location, and then the hunt was on.

They may have slipped my grasp once, but it won't happen again. After I extract information out of this group and dispatch them if need be, I can head to the compound and finish the job, giving us one less enemy to contend with.

As I head into the sands of The Wastes, I slow Ginger down. The Wastes are unpredictable and alien with a general *otherness* to them. It's as though the footprint of darkness has irreparably altered the natural environment. Located directly to the west of The Range, a vast mountain range surrounded by forests that seem to abruptly end at an unspoken demarcation line, The Wastes are in direct contrast to their eastern neighbor. A history of bombings, destruction, and death, paired with unnatural storms and weather, give the area an eerie feel that makes the hair on the back of my neck stand at attention.

This place is devoid of any rhythm or purpose. In essence, it's chaos. Even most motorized vehicles fail to work here. Most people aren't even sure what lies on the other side of The Wastes, if anything does. A place where men and women fear to dwell, The Wastes is a well-earned moniker.

As the land starts to undulate, forming hills, the shifting sands beneath Ginger's feet make it difficult for her to progress. I dismount. "Baim Lyy," I say softly, and Ginger disappears in a flash of red, once again a part of me.

I stand there, the wind blowing erratically around me, and my heart begins to pound. I close my eyes and trust Elohim to give me direction. It's only a moment before I begin to move forward in the direction I feel pulled. The farther I trek, the more my restlessness increases until I am practically vibrating with tension. This is an unusual response for my body, but it must be a sign that I am close to a formidable enemy.

I see a partially dilapidated brick structure in the distance and pull the short sword from my back. I tilt my head side to side, working any kinks out of my neck. The armor of my true identity slides into place like a well-worn leather jacket. My senses sharpen, my breath steadies, and everything around me stills.

The Horsemen of War has arrived.

BONUS SCENE

Did you love The Flame of the White Horseman but wish
for a bit more?

You'll receive a free extended bonus scene when you
subscribe to my newsletter at www.jesskchavez.com.

ACKNOWLEDGMENTS

First and foremost, I want to give thanks to my Heavenly Father, without whom this story would never have been brought to life. Although this is a fiction fantasy tale, the threads of the love of Elohim woven throughout are completely inspired by my experiences with Jesus. His overwhelming and relentless love is what inspired and guided me through this writing journey. I wouldn't be who I am today without Him.

To my incredible husband Josh, who encouraged me and pushed me to write, thank you for believing in me. You are my greatest support, my safe place, my home—I know what real love is because God gave me you.

To my incredible kids, thank you for cheering me on with excitement and support, it's the greatest honor of my life being your mom. To my mom and sister, thank you for being my biggest, most loyally devoted fans, and my very first readers.

And to my incredible, book-loving crew of beta readers; Stephanie, Christine, Molly, Becca, and Jessalyn; your excitement, feedback, keen eyes, and encouragement were absolutely vital to me and helped to keep me sane when I couldn't read one more word.

To my amazing editor, J.J. Fischer, you are a true gem. Thank you for helping me grow as a writer and offering feedback in a way that only ever empowered me. I am so grateful the Lord led me to you.

And most of all, to you, my reader. I am so grateful to you for choosing my book and for even reading this far. You make writing a true blessing and a huge source of joy. If books are one of the great gifts in life, then you, dear reader, are the force that brings them to life.

ABOUT THE AUTHOR

Jess K. Chavez is an emerging author of the fantasy/romantasy genre. She has a B.A. in Journalism and a voracious love of reading. She's a wife to her best friend and high school sweetheart, a mom to three amazing and inspiring humans, a fur mom to two goldendoodles, and a lover and follower of Jesus. She lives with her crew in sunny Colorado, nestled in the landscape of the Rocky Mountains.

Sign up for her newsletter to stay up-to-date on new releases in the Tales of the Four Horsemen series, promotions, and all the exciting happenings:

www.jesskchavez.com

Follow her on social media here: